than either the crust or the filler. Stan and Jessie looked down at Jessie's plate, where only a couple of crumbs remained.

"Did anyone know about the recipes? Was he close to unveiling them?" Stan asked.

"He was close. He didn't talk about it much. I'm not even sure what type of pastry. I guessed it had something to do with chocolate. They don't call him Monsieur Chocolate for nothing. That man is a *genius* with chocolate in any form." Her eyes took on a dreamy look, and Stan noticed she'd fallen back to speaking in the present tense. "He didn't want to jinx himself by saying too much. These recipes are like, the Holy Grail for these guys, you know? If it gets into the wrong hands your career is over. But over the past few weeks especially, he was jazzed. He told me this recipe would change the pastry landscape. I think he was going to do some test groups before a mass rollout, but it was definitely happening soon."

Stan and Jessie looked at each other. Stan knew they were thinking the same thing: Was this recipe enough to kill for?

Books by Liz Mugavero

KNEADING TO DIE

A BISCUIT, A CASKET

THE ICING ON THE CORPSE

MURDER MOST FINICKY

Published by Kensington Publishing Corporation

Murder Most Finicky

Liz Mugavero

KENSINGTON PUBLISHING CORP.
http://www.kensingtonbooks.com

KENSINGTON BOOKS are published by

Kensington Publishing Corp.
119 West 40th Street
New York, NY 10018

All Kensington Titles, Imprints, and Distributed Lines are available at special quantity discounts for bulk purchases for sales promotions, premiums, fund-raising, and educational or institutional use. Special book excerpts or customized printings can also be created to fit specific needs. For details, write or phone the office of the Kensington special sales manager: Kensington Publishing Corp., 119 West 40th Street, New York, NY 10018, attn: Special Sales Department, Phone: 1-800-221-2647.

Kensington and the K logo Reg. U.S. Pat & TM Off.

ISBN-13: 978-1-4967-0017-9
ISBN-10: 1-4967-0017-1
First Kensington Mass Market Edition: January 2016

eISBN-13: 978-1-4967-0018-6
eISBN-10: 1-4967-0018-X
First Kensington Electronic Edition: January 2016

10 9 8 7 6 5 4 3 2 1

Printed in the United States of America

For Kim, my favorite foodie, always. xo

Chapter 1

*Cooking is like love. It should be entered into
with abandon or not at all.*
—Harriet van Horne

"Ouch. The blindfold's too tight." Stan Connor
reached up to adjust the scarf digging into her eyes and
wondered why on earth she'd agreed to this. Of course,
she hadn't realized blindfolds would be involved when
she accepted the invitation to a weekend retreat for
Sheldon Allyn's "star chefs."

"I'll fix it, Ms. Connor. How's this? Better?" Her
would-be captor loosened the tie and gave the scarf a
satisfied tug. He had politely introduced himself as
Joaquin Leroy, assistant to Sheldon Allyn, before blind-
folding her. Joaquin had green fingernails, candy-apple
red hair, and smelled like he'd bathed in Drakkar Noir.

Stan wiggled her nose and opened and closed her
eyes behind the purple silk a few times to adjust the
material. At least it felt supersoft. "All good," she said,
flashing a thumbs-up. Since the last time she'd been
blindfolded she'd been pinning the tail on the donkey
at her sixth birthday party, she wasn't exactly sure how it
should feel. But it wasn't terrible.

"Excellent!" Joaquin said, clapping his hands.

"And you can call me Stan," she said. "Ms. Connor is too formal."

"That's such a trendy name," Joaquin said. "I adore it. Is it real?"

"It's short for Kristan," she explained. "Does Nutty need to be blindfolded, too?" Stan's Maine coon cat sat at her feet. She could feel his tail swishing with his displeasure at this event. For one, he was in a harness and leash. Nutty didn't do harnesses; he found them demeaning. And he hadn't had any snacks since early this morning. Completely out of routine, and Nutty swore by his routine.

Joaquin laughed. "I think the cat can keep a secret. We're going to get into the truck now. You'll be in the back near all the sweet-smelling ingredients. Think of it as your limousine for the day. Isn't that fun?"

Stan had seen "the truck" and wasn't sure how much fun it would be. The bright yellow boxy structure with neon green trim and pink lettering spelling out EVERY SWEET THING ON WHEELS did not look like a "travel-in-style" vehicle. Those mobile pastry trucks didn't even look like they had anywhere to sit in the back. Hopefully they weren't going far. Maybe she'd get a cupcake for her troubles. She directed her brightest smile in the direction she thought Joaquin stood. "Fabulous!"

It wouldn't do to show a lack of enthusiasm. As Sheldon's assistant, Joaquin would report back on everyone's reaction to this exercise. And Sheldon—more commonly known as Mr. Pastry to his foodie fans—expected enthusiasm from his people. Especially at a weekend retreat for his star chefs, no matter how eccentric the arranged mode of arrival. Like a blindfolded jaunt in the back of a pastry truck to an undisclosed location.

The cryptic invitations Stan and Nutty each received promised a fabulous weekend of food and fun that would've been political suicide to ignore, given her still-in-its-infancy partnership with Sheldon for a pet patisserie in her Frog Ledge, Connecticut, hometown.

So this morning she'd kissed her pub owner boyfriend, Jake McGee, good-bye, loaded Nutty into the car, and driven from Frog Ledge to downtown Newport, Rhode Island. The address on the invitation took her to the downtown parking lot, where Sheldon had arranged for her to leave her car. The ocean air beckoned on this beautiful August day. If the bus—well, pastry truck—didn't leave soon she might have to wander over to the beach and dip her toes in.

But Joaquin was moving things along. "I'll help you into the truck now. Let me take your bag." He took it from her hand and grasped her arm, leading her up the metal ramp used to load supplies. Nutty stopped moving. Stan tugged. Nutty resisted.

"Come on, Nutter," she urged. "We're going for another ride."

Nutty meowed.

Joaquin laughed. "Stubborn fella, eh? I'll get him." Joaquin clanged back down the ramp, then rejoined Stan a few seconds later. "All set. You can sit right here." He guided her to what felt like a bench seat. Once she sat, he deposited Nutty in her lap. "Right next to Mr. McLeod. And we're off! Next stop, well, it's a surprise."

She heard his footsteps moving away, then a thud as he jumped to the ground. The back door to the pastry truck slammed shut behind him. "Why'd you do that, Nutty?" She stroked his fur. "I promise we'll have fun."

He meowed at her again, an agitated cry. She hoped he wasn't sick.

Joaquin climbed into the driver's seat up front a minute later and started the engine. She lifted her blindfold just a smidge to see the guy in the truck with her.

"Don't do that, honey!" Joaquin's singsong voice sounded over some sort of tinny speaker system. "I can see you!"

Okay, that was creepy. "Sorry!" she called. "You think he can hear us, too?" Stan whispered to her companion. She'd gotten a quick glimpse before Joaquin caught her. Young, tanned, and blond, he'd certainly be handsome behind the gaudy, glittery, green silk scarf tied around his eyes.

"I have no idea," he said.

They both paused, waiting to hear if Joaquin would answer them like the voice of God from above. He didn't. As the truck maneuvered out of the parking lot and turned left Stan felt herself lurch off balance, almost landing in her companion's lap.

"Sorry," she said, bracing herself on the slim bench. Thank goodness Joaquin hadn't tied her hands, too. "I'm Stan Connor, by the way. Seeing as we weren't properly introduced."

A pause. Typical reaction to her nickname. She'd shortened Kristan to Stan as a teenager, mainly because it annoyed her mother. It had stuck. She'd later found it worked to her advantage in corporate America. It threw people off nicely. Another reason to keep it.

When her companion spoke again she thought his voice sounded a little odd. "You're the pet chef. Cool."

He recognized her name? She immediately felt stupid, since she didn't know any of the other chefs. Certainly not this guy. "And what do you cook? What's your first name, by the way?" she asked.

"Sorry. I'm Kyle. I'm a vegan chef."

"Nice to meet you," Stan said.

"Likewise. So what do you think would happen if we both revolted and took the stupid blindfolds off? I think I have glitter in my eyes."

Stan laughed. "I'm jealous my scarf doesn't have glitter. I bet we'd get dragged to Sheldon's office and get detention or something. I don't want to cause trouble. Especially since it's my first rodeo with him and his crew."

"I guess." Kyle sighed. "I hope this isn't some cockamamy idea that's going to get us all thrown in jail or something."

Stan's eyes widened behind her blindfold. "Has that happened before?"

"Not that I know of, but with Sheldon, all bets are off." Kyle grabbed for something to hold on to as the truck took another sharp turn, this time to the right. "Really, someone should teach his entourage how to drive."

"You don't sound thrilled to be here," Stan said as Nutty attempted to wiggle away from her. He leaned over and rubbed against Kyle.

"What the heck is that?" he exclaimed.

"That's Nutty, my cat," Stan said. "He's very friendly."

Kyle laughed. "I wasn't expecting a handful of fur. To answer your question—no, I'm not a fan of surprises. A 'delectable weekend in glorious Newport, Rhode Island, celebrating the most exquisite talent in the food industry today,' like the invitation said, is one thing. Having to get there blindfolded is another. But he loves games."

"How long have you worked with Sheldon?" Stan asked. She still didn't know what to expect from her new—what was he, anyway? Business partner? Colleague? She'd done her research, watched his guest appearances on The Food Channel, and visited his shop in Providence, but hadn't spent much time with him yet.

And the brief time they'd spent together had been wrapped up in negotiations about the shop, which they hoped to open by the end of the year.

"Long enough to know he's crazy as a loon," Kyle said, and Stan could sense an edge to his humorous tone.

Stan'd gotten that vibe about Sheldon as well but had been willing to overlook it, hoping it was his attract-new-talent persona. Before she could probe more deeply the truck engaged in another hair-raising turn, then began climbing a hill. It lurched to another, more final stop, and she heard the sound of a parking brake scraping into place.

Kyle sighed again. "Get ready," he said. "Looks like we're here. And a word of advice? Expect the unexpected."

Chapter 2

The door at the back of the truck opened and the ramp hit the pavement. Joaquin clanged up the ramp and entered. "We're here, friends," he called in that same cheery voice. "Did everyone enjoy the ride?"

"Loved it," Kyle said in an overly exuberant tone.

"Definitely," Stan said when it appeared Joaquin waited for her answer also.

"Wonderful!" Joaquin said. "We're not quite ready to start yet, so I'm going to leave you here and keep you in suspense for a few moments longer. Just adding to the mystery!" He chuckled at his own joke. "Back in a few!"

He left again, closing the door behind him. Kyle groaned. "Is this guy for real?"

"Sounds like it," Stan said. She itched to slip her blindfold off and take a tiny peek at her surroundings, but figured Joaquin still had some camera trained on them.

"Where do you think we are, anyway?" Kyle said.

Stan considered. They hadn't been in the truck more than ten minutes. They had to be near the heart of Newport. Plus they'd stopped a bunch of times, probably for traffic lights or summer tourist jams. "We're probably over by the mansions," she said. "Or somewhere around the beaches."

"How do you know that?"

"I grew up around here," she said.

Another silence. "Narragansett?"

She cocked her head, even though she couldn't see him. "How did you know that?"

"I think Sheldon mentioned it," he said. "Listen, I wasn't trying to be a downer about the weekend. Are you excited?"

Odd, because she didn't remember telling Sheldon specifically where she'd grown up, just that it had been in Rhode Island. "I am. It's kind of fun, even the weirdness of this," she said. "I'm anxious to get started."

They lapsed into silence, which seemed loud given their lack of sight. Just when Stan started to see purple stars blinking in front of her eyes, Kyle spoke again.

"I'll bet my latest order of organic avocados that someone hasn't shown up yet, and that's what's holding up the works." He fell silent as footsteps sounded on the ramp outside.

"Let's go," Joaquin chirped. "Stan? Ladies first! Hold on to the kitty." He grabbed her elbow and tugged her to her feet.

She rose, steadying herself against the side of the truck. "Are you taking this thing off so I don't fall out of the truck on the way down?"

He laughed. "Alas, no. I'm here to help you, but the unveiling will only happen when everyone has arrived."

Kyle muttered something Stan couldn't quite make out. It was her turn to sigh.

"Okay," she said. "Let's get this over with. I have to warn you, I'm not coordinated even when I can see." Hugging Nutty to her, she took a few tentative steps toward the exit.

"You're doing fine. Coming up to the ramp. Watch the speed bump! You're doing great, aaand . . . you're down. Wait right here while I get Mr. McLeod." He went back into the truck.

"You don't need to hold my hand," she heard Kyle say, and smiled.

When Kyle had arrived safely on the ground, too, Joaquin herded them forward, his hand at the small of Stan's back. "We have some of our other friends here, and we're just waiting for one more. And the infamous Sheldon, of course. Sit tight, people. But do mingle." He squeezed Stan's arm and moved away.

Mingle. Funny, since they couldn't even see each other. Stan squinted, trying to see through the thin fabric of her blindfold, but Joaquin had created enough layers that she couldn't. She took a deep breath and sniffed the ocean air. A slight clue about where they were, although it wasn't a stretch to find ocean in Rhode Island.

It felt good to be home. She'd missed this smell and the bliss of a summer's afternoon on the sand. It had been a long time since she'd allowed herself an afternoon at the beach. When she'd worked in corporate America she'd never made the time. After her job elimination last year she'd spent the summer moving to Frog Ledge and getting used to her new town, which left no beach time either. So maybe this weekend with Sheldon and his crew was a sign. Maybe Jake could join her after this shindig and they could spend a few days at a B and B overlooking the ocean.

"I haven't heard Pierre's big mouth yet," a grating female voice said near Stan's ear, jolting her out of her thoughts. "He never showed up at our meeting place. He's the one holding up the works."

"Figures." A man's voice this time. "He's probably protesting something."

The woman snorted. "As usual. He can be such a turd. Poor Joaquin is running around like a maniac looking for him. He's got Sheldon's whole staff on it."

Pierre. She wondered if they were talking about Pierre LaPorte, one of the only other names she knew in food besides Sheldon. Another pastry guy. His bakery in New York had been linked to Sheldon—a tidbit she'd discovered when doing research last year—so it made sense. Pierre's creations, though geared to humans, looked exquisite. Maybe he could help her adapt a recipe like his puffed apple pastry for cats and dogs. Her earlier excitement returned. This weekend could be a huge opportunity.

Two more vehicles roared up the driveway. They didn't sound like mobile pastry trucks. More like fast cars. Doors slammed. Voices hummed through the summer afternoon air. Stan felt impatience stirring. *Let's get on with it, already.* She wanted to get this stupid blindfold off.

"Everyone! Wonderful news!" Joaquin called. "Sheldon is here! Please, let's gather."

Stan put Nutty on the ground and took a few tentative steps forward, arms outstretched in front of her. Someone jostled her, stepping on her foot.

"So sorry," the same man's voice said. "I can't see a bloody thing!"

"Which is kind of the point," another male voice said. "Genius."

Joaquin clapped his hands to get their attention. "Okay, everyone, presenting . . . Sheldon!"

"Don't you all look adorable!" Sheldon's unmistakeable silvery voice rang out. "Welcome to our weekend. Thank you for humoring me with my covert operations to get you here. We're missing Pierre—yes, the famous Pierre LaPorte—but I'm sure he'll be along soon."

"Probably throwing a temper tantrum because it wasn't a limo come to get him," the female voice murmured.

"So without further ado, I want to share our upcoming adventure." Sheldon paused for dramatic effect. "As you know, I've called you all here this weekend because you're chefs in some stage of working with me. What you may not know is that you're my top group of food artists. And so very special to me." He paused again, waiting, Stan thought, for some recognition. She clapped. The others followed suit. Nutty sat on her feet.

"Thank you, thank you. When you take your blindfolds off you'll see our haven for the weekend, where we'll create together, cook together, bond. This house is very special to me and I'm thrilled we'll all be sharing it. And then on Monday . . ." He trailed into silence for another bout of dramatic effect. "On Monday, we'll present a sit-down, five-course dinner to a group of investors at The Chanler at Cliff Walk."

Stan raised an eyebrow behind her blindfold. The Chanler was one of Newport's oldest mansions that had gone through many iterations to become what it was today—a luxury hotel with ocean views, guest chauffeurs, and pricey rooms. And a delightful restaurant, which Sheldon apparently had designs to hijack for the day. She wondered how he was pulling that off.

"I have brought you all together because you have a specialty that will be featured at the meal," Sheldon continued.

Stan heard *oohs* and *aaahs* from her fellow chefs. A couple of them clapped in earnest now. She frowned behind her blindfold. Unless her investors were going to eat gourmet pet food, she probably didn't belong here. But Sheldon must have anticipated her thought process.

"And my dear Stan. You look lovely in purple, by the way! I'm sure you're wondering what your role will be. Well, let me assure you I'm not losing my mind. You will provide the food for one of our investor's Siamese cats. A meal that will be equal in importance—maybe even more important—than the humans' meal, because this cat is very special. A three-time winner of the World Championship Cat Show! And your lovely feline, who accompanied you here this weekend, will be our taste tester. What do you think of that?"

A Siamese. Lord help her. They were only the pickiest breed of cats. "Wow," Stan managed. "That . . . sounds amazing."

"I knew you would think so. This is a phenomenal opportunity for all of us. First"—Stan could picture him jabbing a finger into the air to highlight his point—"the event will be a featured spread in *Foodie* magazine. The photographer will arrive Monday morning and follow us through the day. And two, it will allow me to expand our enterprise, if everyone signs on. And the best for last. One of our guests works for The Food Channel. And he's on the lookout for chefs like us. . . ." He paused for added effect. "For an *exclusive, regular* . . . series!"

This time, the *oohs, aahs,* and claps were more enthusiastic. Who wouldn't want to be on The Food Channel? Maybe this weekend wasn't so crazy after all, despite Sheldon's eccentricities.

"So are you ready to see your new home away from home?" he called. "Ladies and gentlemen, remove your blindfolds and join me at the Allyn Retreat for Top Chefs!"

Chapter 3

Stan tugged the silk from her eyes and blinked in the bright afternoon sunlight. Directly in front of her, Sheldon Allyn filled her vision. He stood on the hood of an honest-to-God, for-real pink Cadillac wearing aviator sunglasses and beaming at them. The sun glinted off his metallic pink suit, which matched the tips of his short, spiky white hair. A lime green shirt peeked out from under the suit jacket. Silver wing-tipped shoes completed the outfit. She always wanted to break into a disco number when she saw him. Which opened the door for "I Will Survive" to start a continuous loop through her brain, but found it fought for purchase against "Pink Cadillac."

Once she could tear her gaze from him and his finery, she assessed her surroundings. She stood at the top of a long, slightly inclined, circular driveway along with four other people doing the same blinking routine, as well as a small crowd around Sheldon. His staffers-turned-drivers. Joaquin; a young woman weighing about eighty pounds wearing a skintight leather tube dress; and a tall, slim, punk-slash-retro looking guy with bleached blond hair, earlobes stretched around giant rings, and headphones in his ears, the cords of which snaked down the front of his shirt and disappeared into the pocket of skintight jeans. He was the complete opposite of Joaquin, who was short and round and wore a yellow suit and a turquoise blue tie with his fire-engine red shoes.

Stan did get a better look at Kyle McLeod, her travel companion. She'd been right—handsome in a tanned, golden-boy way, with sparkling white teeth and just enough stubble to be fashionable. He wore his blond, sun-bleached hair cut short and carefully gelled. He caught her eye and smiled at her.

"Maybe that ride was worth it after all," he murmured. "The Food Channel. That would be a dream come true."

The Food Channel hadn't yet made it to Stan's bucket list, but she didn't say so. She already felt out of place with this crew and she hadn't officially met them yet. "Mmm," she said noncommittally, bending down to scoop Nutty into her arms. "Look at this place." She nodded at the house before them. The four-story structure looked like more than a simple weekend retreat. A combination of glass, steel, and stucco resulted in a futuristic feel. Skylights, balconies, and rooftop decks all vied for her attention when she wasn't drawn to the sculpture in the yard facing the circular driveway. The enormous piece of twisted steel towered above them, no doubt in the modern contemporary family. It would make quite a picture tonight against the dusky purple sky with yellows and oranges burning in the windows behind it, contrasting brilliantly with the blue gray of the ocean glimmering in the background.

Which got her excited all over again. She couldn't wait to sneak around back and stand in front of the sea, breathing in the energy of the water. She hoped her room faced the ocean.

Kyle gave a long, low whistle. "Now that's a house," he said. "Maybe when we sign our contracts we can buy something like this, too. Hi, cat. Nice to see you finally." He rubbed Nutty's head. Nutty pressed his face into Kyle's palm.

"Sheldon owns this place?" Stan asked.

Kyle nodded. "That'd be my guess. Not too far from his place in Providence."

Every Sweet Thing had been born in Providence. Sheldon had established himself as a true hero of sweets in the tiny state, and his fans ate it up when he showed up on the cover of some fancy foodie magazine or a prime-time cooking show.

"That's where I'm opening my second restaurant, too. Not far from Sheldon's place," Kyle said.

"Another vegan restaurant?" she asked.

"Yeah," Kyle said. "My restaurant in Boca Raton, Green Cuisine, is doing really well. Sheldon wanted me to bring one here."

It occurred to her that Kyle might be the other odd duck of the group. Sheldon's chefs didn't look like a vegan crowd. "That's fantastic," Stan said, setting the squirming Nutty on the ground. "We need more of those around here. And Providence is a great place for it. Very diverse."

Nutty howled, that plaintive Maine coon cry that signaled his unhappiness. The sound caught the attention of the only other woman in the group, who turned and hurried over. Short and round, her generous bosom spilled out of her glittery sky blue sundress. She screeched to a halt in front of Stan, teetering on silver stilettos, and beamed. Even with the shoes the woman wore, Stan towered over her. She found herself eye level with curly, layered hair teased nearly straight up off the woman's head and sprayed with some silver, glittery shellac.

Like her first glimpse of the house and the competing statue, Stan had trouble focusing between the dress's plunging neckline and the too-tall hair. She hadn't seen hair that high since some time in the late eighties. The silver color sparkled with a metallic sheen that matched the shoes perfectly.

"Stan Connor, the pet chef!" the woman boomed in that nasally voice Stan had heard earlier making comments about Pierre. She grabbed Stan's hand and pumped it enthusiastically, nearly yanking it off her arm. "And the cat! Oh my, I have been *waiting* to meet the cat. What is his name?"

"Nutty," Stan said.

Forgetting about Stan, the woman dropped to her knees and began cooing baby talk at Nutty, her tone high pitched and grating. Nutty pressed himself against Stan, as far away from the woman as he could get, ears flattened against his fluffy head. His look of disdain rivaled that of the late Joan Rivers encountering a particularly bad outfit on the red carpet.

Stan met Kyle's eyes over the woman's head. He rolled his.

"I'm sorry, I didn't catch your name," Stan said, raising her voice so the woman could hear over her own gibberish. Instead of salvaging the meeting, that made things worse. The woman immediately stopped insulting Nutty's intelligence. Slowly, she rose, eyes narrowed, hands going to her bulky hips.

"I beg your pardon," she said. Her tone had dropped a few degrees and the hint of an Italian accent emerged. "I didn't realize I needed to introduce myself. I'm

Maria Ferranto." She rolled the *r*'s in both names. "I am the owner of Cibo in New York and Rome. I am a *well-known* Italian chef."

"Oh," Stan said. She vaguely recognized the name of the restaurant. She'd probably visited it during her past life, wooing journalists at fancy New York eateries. "I'm so sorry, Maria. I should've known that. It's lovely to meet you. Nutty thinks so, too."

Maria's gaze raked over her, glaring for another moment before her face cleared. "Well, it's lovely to meet Nutty."

Before Stan could say anything else that got her in trouble, Sheldon commanded their attention again. "I'm so very sorry," he said. "Joaquin just reminded me—I must be getting old!" He tapped a finger to his temple. "We have packets for each of you with some pertinent information for the weekend—facts on The Chanler, a pamphlet on our investors, some meal suggestions. We'll hand those out once inside. And Joaquin reminded me that not all of you know each other. So I'd like to take a moment and introduce you."

"Since we apparently need introductions," Maria said in a snooty tone that now sounded more New Jersey than Italy.

"Let's start with our newest member. Stan? Please join me." He held out his hands as she scooped up Nutty and approached him. "And the lovely kitty. How delightful." He beamed at her, then turned her to face the group. She felt like a brand-new car on *Wheel of Fortune*, with Sheldon playing Vanna. "This is Stan Connor of Pawsitively Organic, a gourmet pet food business. She's been dabbling in many things. Treats, meals, catering, even a wedding! We're thrilled to announce her new shop—which will be headquartered in Frogtown, Connecticut—opening soon!"

"Frog Ledge," Stan corrected.

"Hmmm? Oh, yes, dear. We can open one there, too," he said absently. "And this delightful creature . . ." He took Nutty from her arms and held him up high in the air. Stan watched in horror as Nutty flattened his ears and hissed. "Is Nutty. He's the taste tester. Thank you, Stan." Returning the cat to her, he gave her a slight shove back toward the others.

"It's okay, Nutter," she whispered. "Next time you can bite him."

Sheldon went through the same spiel with the rest of them. Maria first, then a man named Leonardo Brandt, who could've been Elton John's distant cousin, with his tousled burnt auburn hair, jogging suit, and round, happy face. Brandt specialized in soups and bisques. Then Kyle, and finally a man in a white suit and bright pink shaved head named Marcin Houle, who apparently made melt-in-your-mouth fish dishes. Marcin didn't look pleased to be here. He stood slightly off to the side and didn't acknowledge Sheldon's introduction. Stan noticed that while Maria and Kyle were noted as having restaurants of their own, Leonardo and Marcin were not.

Sheldon rounded out the introductions by gathering his three "assistants" together. "You all know Joaquin, who organizes my entire life."

Joaquin beamed at them. "We're gonna have *fun* this weekend!"

"And of course Therese, who can do hair, makeup, massage, anything you need. Finally, Tyler, my public relations and social media expert. Group hug, assistants!"

The three huddled with Sheldon in an awkward hug. Stan felt an immediate kinship to Tyler. PR had been the center of her previous world. Although Tyler didn't really look friendly enough to do PR.

"Now that we're all friends, let's go inside!" Sheldon headed toward the front door, brandishing a key. The rest of them followed except Stan, who took a few stealth steps toward the back gate.

Kyle turned. "Coming?"

"In a minute. I'm going to peek around back and check out the water. Nutty wants to see it, too." She couldn't wait any longer. She had already imagined sneaking off to the beach to plot her pastries.

Kyle looked over his shoulder again, uncertain. Sheldon made a big show of unlocking the front door.

"I'll be fast. No one will even notice I'm gone. Cover for me," she said, letting Nutty down. He strained against his harness. She led him to the gate and unlatched it.

They stepped into a backyard straight out of a magazine. What looked like miles of grass in a lovely shade of green stretched out before them. It felt wrong to step on the well-manicured, plush lawn. There were no dead spots. It looked like someone had hand-clipped it blade by blade. A lovely raised patio spanned the length of the back of the house, with stone tiles and elegant furniture. A wooden fence with a gate gave the yard privacy. And over the fence she could see the blue of the ocean.

Nutty mewed again.

"I know, it's gorgeous," she said. "You could totally be an ocean cat, couldn't you?"

She started forward, glancing over to admire the patio. Real furniture, nicer than in her own living room, had been placed strategically under the umbrella, which was large enough to cover the whole patio, practically. She paused. Someone sat on one of the chairs, his or her back to Stan, slouched over as if napping. She could see the faint shadow against the white stones of the patio and moved over to look more closely.

"Hello?" she called. Nutty hissed.

No answer from the person sitting on the love-seat-sized chair. Maybe one of the house staffers? Poor guy or gal was probably trying to get some rest before the madness began. She should tiptoe past and leave him or her alone. But curiosity got the better of her and she circled around to the front of the chair.

"Hi. Sorry to bother you—" She stopped, a sick, greasy feeling rising up in her stomach along with the remnants of her last meal. She forced it back down, clenching her teeth together as her mind registered the horror of the sight before her.

The man slumped on the bench looked, based on her memory of a couple of YouTube videos, like Pierre LaPorte, the famous pastry chef who'd been late to the party. He had good reason. His throat had been cut. The wound gaped. Blood dried in the sunlight. His eyes stared open and unseeing into the Newport horizon.

Chapter 4

Stan had seen her share of dead bodies, but nothing compared to this one. The horror of it had her torn between paralysis and the urge to throw up. And she couldn't—shouldn't—do that on this beautiful grass. Or the crime scene.

Get it together. Get to the house. Call someone.

Whimpering, her skin clammy with a cold sweat, Stan gave the scene a wide berth. She dragged Nutty, who strained to get closer to the body, nose going furiously as he tried to sniff everything. She stepped carefully, trying to avoid the blood spattered on the beautiful white stone, the furniture, and Lord knew where else. Then she raced like a maniac the few steps to the French doors and turned the knob.

Locked.

Trying to hold back a scream, she pounded on them, then fumbled in her pocket for her cell phone. She yanked it out and somehow managed to dial 911 after three tries, and finally heard a voice on the other end.

"Nine-one-one. What is your emergency?" the female operator's voice droned.

Stan opened her mouth to speak and realized she had no idea where she was, since she'd arrived blind-folded. It probably wouldn't do to tell the operator that.

"Nine-one-one. What is your emergency?" the operator repeated in a stern voice.

"Someone . . . someone's dead. M-m-murdered. I'm in Newport, Rhode Island. Not sure of the address." She pounded on the door again. Where on earth were they all?

"Ma'am, can you stay on the phone with me while I determine where you are? Are you in danger?"

Crap. She hadn't thought of that. She spun around to take stock of her surroundings, as if expecting whoever had killed Pierre to lunge at her from one of the perfectly shaped shrubs next to the house. "I . . . don't think so. I have no idea. Oh, thank God," she muttered as Sheldon approached the door from inside. "One second, I'll get you the address."

He yanked the door open, frowning at her. "Really, my dear, I started the tour in front for a reas—" His words trailed off as he followed her pointing finger, stunned into silence.

"Sweet Mary, mother of God," he finally breathed, his face going from white to green. "What the . . . ?"

She thrust the phone at him. "Tell them the address."

He stared at the phone like he'd never seen one before.

"The address!" she hissed. "It's the police!"

Sheldon snapped to attention and took the phone while she picked up Nutty and slipped past him inside the house. Her stomach still lurched and the queasiness threatened to overwhelm her. She pulled out the first chair she saw and sat, dropping her head to her knees and sucking in air. *Don't faint. Don't faint.* This group seemed like the type who would never let her live it down. Hopefully they were all occupied touring the rest of the house and wouldn't come in here. She heard Sheldon's voice in the distance, talking to the operator.

"This is Sheldon Allyn. Four-one-three Sunset Avenue in Newport." He disconnected without waiting for further instructions, then shut the door. He yanked the heavy curtains over the glass, a shield against the hideous sight outside. His face had turned even whiter than his favorite powder, and his mouth sucked air like a fish searching for water. "I don't want the others to see. My God, Stan. Who . . . how?" Either he couldn't bring himself to say Pierre's name or he didn't realize it was him. Or he was asking who killed him—she wasn't sure.

"It's Pierre," she said. She knew it instinctively, though she'd never met him. And since he'd never arrived . . .

But he had arrived. Early, it seemed. Along with someone else—who had slit his throat. She shivered. The air-conditioning cranked, but that wasn't the reason. If this was such a top-secret mission, how had Pierre known where to go before the scheduled time? And even more disturbing, who had known he would be here early and slaughtered him?

Voices and laughter from the other room came closer and Marcin poked his head into the room. Nutty growled, long and low. Stan hadn't heard him do that ever, but it reinforced her fear.

"Sheldon, we're waiting for the rest of the tour," Marcin called. "Leo wants a drink and feels like he can't have one until he's properly *oohed* and *aahed* over the house." He paused and took a closer look at Stan. "Darling, what on earth is wrong? You look like you just lost your best friend." He eyed Nutty suspiciously. "Why is he making that dreadful noise?"

"Marcin, not now," Sheldon said, his voice strangled. "Please keep the others occupied."

"What's going on?" Marcin stepped into the room.

Sheldon jumped up, blocking him. "Please," he said. "Keep the others occupied. And out of this room."

Marcin picked up on the tone, Stan could see, because he didn't argue. He slipped away. A minute later, she heard him say to the others, "Let's go in here and find the booze, shall we?"

It sounded like everyone could get on board with that. The noise dimmed as they moved farther away.

"Sheldon," Stan said. "How did Pierre know to come here if it was a big secret?"

Sheldon stared at her, shaking his head. Stan could see the pulse jumping in his neck. "I have no clue. This is just . . . sickening. Sickening," he repeated. "Are you sure it's him? I need to see." He moved to the door.

"No! Don't go out there," she said. "I've already walked through the crime scene. You shouldn't do it, too."

He hesitated. Then the sirens sounded, from a distance but quickly coming closer. A minute later, the doorbell rang.

Sheldon went to answer it. He returned a minute later with two Newport cops. They zeroed in on Stan. "Did you place the nine-one-one call?" the younger of the two asked, without so much as a *hello* or *are you all right?*. He was heavyset and had clearly suffered from acne as a boy, given the scars on his face.

Stan nodded.

"Can you come with me, please?" the older cop said to her. He had a droopy mustache and had to keep hitching his uniform pants over his stomach.

Still clutching Nutty's leash, she followed the cop into another spacious sitting room. Living room or den? She couldn't tell. All of it belonged in a magazine spread. Her next insane thought: *At least they didn't kill him inside the house—it would've made such a terrible mess.*

The cop motioned for her to sit. She sank down on a red ottoman and pulled Nutty into her lap. "Wait here," he said, and left her there alone.

She had the fleeting but disturbing thought that she wasn't in Frog Ledge anymore.

Chapter 5

Stan waited alone for half an hour. More cops arrived. She heard a lot of activity outside the windows. Nutty finally settled into a big, furry circle on her lap, tail swishing as he kept an eye on his surroundings.

She wished they would hurry up and get this part over with. They were all probably gathered outside with the crime scene people looking at the body. The thought made her shiver. She wondered if they'd found the murder weapon. If she'd walked right past it somehow and not even noticed.

Why had she gone out back, anyway? She cursed herself for not following the group inside. Then maybe Sheldon would've had the honors of the gruesome discovery. She had no desire to sit through the endless questions the police were sure to ask. They'd be suspicious of her. They were always suspicious of people who found dead bodies.

Unfortunately, she knew this from experience. Since moving to Frog Ledge a year and a half ago, she'd stumbled upon more murder investigations than most people probably had in their lifetime. When it happened in Frog Ledge, she had to explain herself to

Jake's sister, the resident state trooper. But at least Jessie Pasquale knew by now that Stan wasn't some serial killer. Just unlucky. Her first meeting with Jessie over a dead body had been sub-par, so she didn't expect anything different with these detectives.

The first detective in the room, an African-American man, was tall enough that he might have to duck despite the cathedral ceilings. Thin and lean, a smattering of gray at the temples of his curly black hair hinted that he might have been older than her first impression. His female companion, by contrast, stood about five-five. Stocky build. A bit of muscle combined with some padding. Pin-straight brown hair pulled back in a ponytail accented her plain, unexceptional face. Both of them looked at her curiously. Probably wondering why she held a cat on a leash.

"I'm Detective Genske," the female said. "This is Detective Owens. What's your name?"

"Stan Connor."

She gave Stan a skeptical look. "As in Stanley?"

"As in Kristan."

"Odd nickname for Kristan," Detective Owens said, scratching his head.

Stan didn't comment. They had a dead guy in the backyard and they were asking about her nickname? He must know her mother.

Unlike her mother, though, Owens let it go. They both sat opposite her on the sofa, after wary glances at the modern, odd-shaped chairs. "Tell us what happened."

"I have no idea what happened. We just arrived for the weekend. I went out back to see the ocean, and found . . ." She trailed off. "Is it Pierre?"

They exchanged looks. "We can talk about the victim

in a bit," Genske said. "First we have some questions for you."

"Okay." She stroked Nutty's fur nervously. His tail swishing had kicked up a notch.

Genske eyed Nutty. "That your cat?"

"Yes."

"He friendly?"

"He is. His name is Nutty."

Genske stepped forward and held out a hand for Nutty to sniff, then pet his head. Nutty blinked at her.

"What else did you see out back?" Owens asked. "Anything look out of place?"

"I have no idea. I've never been here before."

"Oh yeah, this isn't your house," Genske said. "Whose is it?"

"Sheldon's, I guess. You'd have to ask him. It's either his or he's renting it."

"Tell us about this weekend," Genske said in a conversational tone, looking up from petting Nutty. "What's everyone doing here?"

Nutty didn't seem to like this line of questioning. He stared at the detective with open disdain. He looked like he might smack Genske with his big paw. Which could land them both in the clink.

"It's a chef's weekend. I'm a pastry chef." She decided to leave the pet part off. "We all work with Sheldon. We're preparing for a dinner event at The Chanler Monday night."

As if on cue, Sheldon appeared in the doorway, the young acne-pocked cop trying to hold him off.

"Are you harassing my chef?" he called. "This poor girl has already been through the mill, finding that grisly scene outside. Don't you think you should be catching the person who did this?"

"That's the idea," Owens said, turning to give Sheldon the once-over. He took in the metallic suit, the hair, the silver-lidded eyes and matching shoes, and one eyebrow went up. "And you are?"

Sheldon stopped and puffed his chest out. "Who am *I*? My dear boy, I am Sheldon Allyn. Don't you people eat dessert?"

Owens stared blankly at him. "Okay, Mr. Allyn," he said finally, and it was clear he didn't have a clue. "I'd ask that you wait out there, and we'll be with you momentarily."

Sheldon didn't look happy. "You don't need to talk to them without a lawyer, you know," he said to Stan, then turned and marched out. The cop trailing him gave his colleagues an apologetic look, then went after him.

Genske smiled for the first time. "You don't know Mr. Allyn?" she said to her colleague.

"I'm afraid I don't," Owens said. He didn't smile.

Genske looked at Stan and tipped her head at Owens with a mocking look. "He works out for fun. I eat for fun. Do you need a lawyer, Ms. Connor?"

Stan shook her head. "Why would I need a lawyer?"

Genske shrugged. "Just asking. So tell me about the work you do with Sheldon."

"He and I are negotiating a joint business venture. We're opening a pastry shop for pets in Connecticut."

Genske raised an eyebrow. "For pets?"

"Yes."

"What about the rest of them?" Owens jerked a thumb behind him. "Same deal?"

"I'm not really sure about the different relationships," Stan said. "You'll have to ask them. But they all do human food."

Owens made a note in his pad. "So the shop isn't open yet?"

Stan shook her head. "We found a suitable location and were finalizing price negotiations. I'm hoping to open by end of year."

"And will Allyn be involved in the day to day?"

"Nope. It's all me. He'll check in, I'm presuming, when it's time to review the profit and loss statement."

Owens shifted in his chair. "Walk me through the day. The rest of you all got here at the same time?"

"Yes," she said cautiously. She had no idea how to explain her trip here, blindfolded and in the back of the pastry truck.

"Was Pierre supposed to get here at the same time also?" he asked.

"I assume so," Stan said. "I wasn't involved in the planning."

"So who noticed he wasn't here?" Genske asked.

"There were some rumblings about someone being missing. I couldn't tell who, since we were all blindfolded."

"Blindfolded?" Owens and Genske said in unison.

Stan nodded. "Sheldon likes games. He organized an . . . experience for the chefs. He didn't want us to know where we were going. He thought it would be fun to send us all to a parking lot, blindfold us, and drive us here."

Owens and Genske exchanged glances that clearly said, *I knew it. These people are nuts.*

"This some kind of kinky foodie thing? Or is the chef stuff a cover?" Owens asked.

"Neither," Stan said through gritted teeth.

"Huh," Genske said in an *I don't believe you* tone. "He really blindfolded you?"

"Yes. Well, he didn't. His assistant did."

"And you let him." Dumb, her tone suggested.

Stan raised a shoulder in a shrug. "Yeah. Hey, Sheldon's kind of quirky. You never know with him." In hindsight, it could have ranked as Something Potentially Really Stupid, considering she didn't know either Kyle or Joaquin. But she didn't say that to the cops. It would confirm the "crazy" assessment.

Another glance passed between the two.

"So where did you go first? To get blindfolded?" Owens asked.

"To the parking lot downtown. Sheldon bought passes for us to park for the weekend. I left my car there and the mobile pastry truck came and picked up me and Kyle."

"The mobile pastry truck," Owens said.

"Yeah. Sheldon has a bakery in Providence and he went mobile last summer."

"What's the name of the shop?"

"Every Sweet Thing."

"Okay. So you were blindfolded and put in the back of a pastry truck. With Kyle. Kyle who?"

"McLeod. The blond guy. He's a vegan chef," Stan added.

"How did everyone else arrive?"

"I didn't see. Since I was blindfolded. Different cars, same drill."

"And someone didn't show."

"Right. Pierre LaPorte. He's another well-known pastry chef."

"Was anyone looking for him?"

"People speculated on his whereabouts."

"But no one thought to look around. Except you."

"I wasn't looking around for him. I wouldn't have

thought to look for him. No one would, since none of us . . . planned to be here. I wanted to see the ocean."

Owens and Genske exchanged glances. "Sheldon identified the body. It's Pierre LaPorte, like you thought," Genske said to Stan.

She nodded, swallowing against the lump in her throat. She hadn't even had a chance to talk pastry with Pierre. She wondered if he'd been as insufferable as the others suggested, then immediately pushed the thought away. Even if he was the world's biggest jerk, he didn't deserve to have his throat slit.

"That would leave me with one important question," Owens said slowly. "How is it that he showed up at this house if everyone was supposed to meet somewhere, get blindfolded, and arrive together? And presumably didn't know the location to which they were going?"

Stan didn't answer. She had the feeling a lot of people were going to ask that question.

Chapter 6

"Would you mind sticking around while we talk to the others?" Owens asked when it became clear Stan had nothing more to say.

She would. She wanted to pack up and head back to Frog Ledge and Jake. But it didn't seem like she had a choice. And she didn't have a car.

"Sure," she said unhappily.

"Great. We'll be back in a bit. Oh," Genske said as if suddenly remembering. "Can you give me your contact information, please? A cell phone number and address. And your full name."

Stan scribbled her info in the notebook Genske offered her, then handed it back.

"Thanks," Genske said.

The detectives left her sitting there, still holding Nutty. He'd finally stopped swishing his plumed tail, in favor of a nap. She figured any minute he'd start yelling for dinner. She didn't blame him. He hadn't even gotten any treats today.

She picked him up and moved to the pristine white couch, leaned her head back, and closed her eyes. She had a splitting headache and wanted to crawl into bed and sleep for the next week. She recognized the look they'd given her on the way out, that murder-suspect look. All because she'd wanted to see the ocean and had the misfortune of finding a dead body instead.

Tears swam into her eyes. She blinked them away. She'd been so hopeful coming here. After a rough year—transitioning to a new home, leaving behind her old corporate life, being dragged into three separate murder investigations, starting a new business, and trying to sort through her feelings for Jake—she'd finally thought she'd found the right path. The opportunity with Sheldon seemed like the icing on an already sweet cake. And now another dead body had fallen at her feet. A fresh set of tears filled her eyes and spilled over. She gave up trying to hold them back and let them fall. They dripped down onto Nutty's fur.

She needed to talk to Jake. He would be at the pub now, probably getting ready for the evening rush. He'd recently upgraded the McSwigg's menu, and the food orders were as robust as the beer these days. When she came in, he'd have a plate of her favorite, homemade French fries, waiting for her. He'd pour a glass of her favorite red wine—pinot noir—and top it off with that smile that made her all melty inside. Give her a quick kiss before he had to go pour drinks, scraping her cheek with that sexy stubble.

The last time Stan could remember feeling homesick she'd been twelve years old. Her mother had sent her to a ridiculously expensive dance camp for the summer. She hated dance and she missed her dad. She spent most nights crying into her pillow. Today, she felt that kind of homesick. And as much like a prisoner now at thirty-six as she'd been at twelve.

"Hey."

She looked up. Kyle stood in front of her. "Hey," she

said, forcing her voice back to normal. "They let you off the hook?"

Kyle shrugged. "They didn't arrest me. Although they did ask us to 'remain available.' And swore us to silence with threat of jail if we leaked this before they had a chance to notify Pierre's family." He rubbed his face with both hands. "This is crazy. Who would kill Pierre? And why here? *How?*"

"I don't know," Stan said. They were silent for a moment. "It didn't sound like some of the people here liked him very much," she said finally. "Was he really that unpopular?"

Kyle shrugged. "I didn't know him as well as the rest of them." He glanced over his shoulder to make sure no one had joined them. "He could be a jerk. I know that's bad to say about a dead guy." He looked up at the ceiling, a silent apology to heaven.

"So what now?" Stan asked.

"I have no idea," Kyle said. He watched her for a minute. "Are you okay? That couldn't have been a pleasant sight."

"I'm fine," Stan said. "Great. How are you?"

"About the same." He blew out a breath and sat in the chair across from her, a cushy red blob that looked like a cross between a beanbag and an oversized pillow. They sat in silence for a while. Stan closed her eyes, trying to discourage conversation, but she could feel her companion's eyes on her. Finally Sheldon came in.

"Folks?" He'd toned down his normally loud, animated voice to a low, even keel. "Can you join us in the kitchen?"

Stan gathered Nutty's leash around her wrist. They followed Sheldon and Kyle into the other room. The entire group had assembled. Detective Genske leaned against the counter. Owens was nowhere in sight. He'd probably gone to oversee the activity outside.

Maria Ferranto huddled on a bar stool. Joaquin had his arm around her. Therese clutched a glass of Scotch. She drank in big gulps, a deer-in-headlights look plastered across her face. Tyler, on the other hand, had a computer out on the table and typed furiously. Stan felt a pang of sympathy. The weekend had just gotten complicated for him. Life in public relations. Leonardo and Marcin stood together near the table, talking in low voices. They trailed off into silence when Sheldon, Stan, and Kyle entered the room.

Sheldon took his position at the front of the room and cleared his throat. He looked at Genske. She met his eyes, hers cool and coplike. "May I?" Sheldon asked her.

She shrugged. "Be my guest."

Sheldon's brows knitted together in consternation, but he turned to his people. "Team, as you know, we've had a horrible tragedy. The police are working very hard to find out what happened to our friend and colleague." His eyes watered and he dragged his wrist across his face, smearing silver eye shadow. "They've asked a couple of things from us. One, that we continue to make ourselves available during this ongoing investigation, and notify them immediately if any information about this crime comes to our attention."

Maybe they thought the murder had been a group effort, Stan thought. The sinking feeling in her stomach grew more pronounced.

"Two," Sheldon continued, "they would like permission to search the cars of anyone who has their vehicles here, as well as your cars in the lot downtown. I trust no one will have an issue with that, and if so, you'll hand over keys."

Everyone nodded and fished in pockets or bags.

"And three, they've asked that we vacate the house so they can peruse the entire, aah, crime scene without us getting in their way. To that end, I've made arrangements with a friend nearby to put us up for the weekend. I guarantee you'll find the accommodations just as pleasant."

Silence. Stan saw Leonardo's eyebrows shoot straight up as the others cast furtive, confused looks at each other. The same thought seemed to go through their minds: *We're still doing this weekend thing?*

"Sheldon," Leonardo said, clearly the bravest of them all. "Do you mean that we're still going on with our cooking show?"

Sheldon's expression could have curdled milk. "But of course, Leo," he said in a voice that suggested Leo was extremely stupid. "We have an *obligation*. Sheldon Allyn's team always keeps its word, no matter the circumstances. And this is how Pierre—God rest his soul—would've wanted it." He looked at each of them in turn to make sure they understood completely.

"Tyler is working on our media statement. And Joaquin is going to find us a replacement chef for Pierre's portion of the meal." He nodded, as if convincing himself. "We'll cook a meal that will make everyone proud. Pierre will smile down on us. We'll pull this off in Pierre's name!" He raised his fist in the air, a private battle cry. No one followed suit.

Stan got the distinct feeling his tenacity had more to do with a potential Food Channel contract than the memory of his dead pastry chef. She met Genske's eyes across the room. Judging from the detective's face, she had the same doubts. But that was the least of Stan's worries right now, considering she might be rooming with a killer this weekend.

Chapter 7

Genske stayed on them like a hawk until they'd vacated the house. Sheldon called for the limo Maria'd joked about earlier. No mobile pastry truck this time. They all piled in with their belongings. Stan worried about Nutty. He hadn't used a litter box since this morning and she prayed he wouldn't have an accident in the car. Since once again they had no idea where they were going, she didn't know how long it would take to get there. At least this time they weren't blindfolded.

She piled in with Maria, Leonardo, Marcin, and Kyle. Sheldon drove his pink Cadillac. Tyler and Therese got in another car that appeared to be Tyler's. Joaquin drove his own car, a royal blue Ford Fiesta.

No one spoke during the short trip. The car drove down Ocean Avenue and pulled into what looked like a private driveway. Stan recognized the resort on the hill ahead of them. The Newport Premier, another of Newport's finest hotels. It wasn't quite as pricey as The Chanler, where an "ocean villa" could run you $1,200 a night, but it was up there. She and her friends used to come here as teenagers for the afternoon tea served in the lobby after a day at the beach, pretending they were

celebrities. If Sheldon could afford to put them up here,
she wondered if he even needed a Food Channel contract. The place resembled a mini castle, with circular
rooms and decks that jutted out over the ocean. Stan
had never stayed here, but presumed it cost a small fortune for one night. And for nine people—she couldn't
even do the math. Maria sniffed when she saw the
resort. Stan figured she had some villa in Italy that
made this look like a shack. Next to her Kyle stiffened
and muttered something that sounded like, *You've got to
be kidding me.*

"I hope they have the right accommodations for our
guest of honor," Maria said, reaching across the seat to
rub Nutty's head. Nutty head-butted her hand, then
Stan's.

He wanted his dinner. She rummaged through her
bag for her packet of emergency treats and fed him one.
He gobbled it up and waited expectantly for another.
She fed him two more while the limo parked in the circular driveway meant for unloading. Maria had a good
point, though. She needed a litter box for Nutty, stat.
She hadn't brought any of his normal traveling paraphernalia because his invitation had been specific—
Nutty would have everything he needed, especially
delicious food. But with this change of plans, who
knew?

The doorman opened the limo door and offered his
hand. "Thanks," Stan said, shifting Nutty under her
arm. He kicked at her, scratching her arm with his back
claws. The doorman pretended not to notice. Like when
a kid has a temper tantrum in a store and people avert
their eyes from the embarrassed parent.

Kyle lingered in the car. "You coming?" Stan asked.

"I'll be right there."

She shrugged and followed the doorman. "Right this

way, miss," he said. "We have someone coming to collect your bags. If you could just step into the lobby."

They all went through the revolving door. Sheldon joined them a minute later with Kyle on his heels. "Let's gather," he called. "We'll have room assignments momentarily."

Stan tried to hide her impatience. She wanted to feed Nutty, take a shower, and crawl into bed. Away from these people, preferably.

A woman swept down the grand staircase in the middle of the lobby. She could have walked out of the pages of *Newport Life* magazine, with her perfect hair, perfect outfit, and perfect smile, in the perfect setting. Everyone in their group fell silent as she approached.

"Good evening," she purred in a voice best suited for a phone sex hotline. "I'm Lucy Keyes. I'll be your host tonight. We're delighted to have such a talented group of chefs gracing our halls."

Stan knew she'd never looked that perfect even straight out of the shower with clothes fresh from the cleaners. Despite the seven o'clock hour, no wrinkle dared in7fringe upon Lucy's expensive gray suit—Chanel, undoubtedly. Her gleaming chestnut hair, long and layered and glossy, looked like she'd just left a professional stylist's on Fifth Avenue. Her pink-studded Louboutins helped give the impression that she towered over all of them, though without them Stan estimated she would be around Maria's height. Sheldon rushed over and kissed both her cheeks and spoke softly to her. Lucy nodded a few times, then turned her attention to the rest of them. Stan noticed her gaze linger on Kyle McLeod just a tad longer than everyone else. He seemed to look everywhere but at her.

"We've reserved three suites for you tonight," she said. "My sincere apologies that I couldn't have a suite open for each of you, but we're quite full this weekend due to the Jazz Festival."

Jazz Festival weekend. Stan'd almost forgotten, it had been so long. She wished Jake could meet her here and they could sneak off to enjoy it.

"I think you'll find the suites quite roomy in any event," Lucy continued. "I have the three ladies—and our star feline—together." She winked at Stan. "And I'll leave you boys to decide how to divide yourselves in threes. Jackson will show you to your rooms. I'll take the ladies." A small man in a bellhop uniform magically appeared at her side.

"Gentlemen, if you could follow me," Jackson intoned in a pinched voice that made Stan want to blow her nose. Everyone but Kyle McLeod immediately fell in line, Sheldon herding them from the end position like a corgi herding a flock of sheep. Kyle stepped over to Lucy Keyes. He bent his head close to hers and said something. She shook her head, then turned so Stan couldn't hear. A minute later, Kyle rejoined the group and they headed off.

Lucy watched them go, then said, "Follow me, ladies." She led them to an elevator and hit the Up button.

Therese and Maria took off after her. Nutty dug his heels in and refused to move, so Stan had to bend down and scoop him up again. He'd clearly had enough of this weekend of stardom. He meowed his displeasure loudly enough that Lucy turned around, amused, as the elevator operator held the Door Open button.

"Is our star kitty unhappy?" she asked.

"He's had a rough day," Stan said, ducking into the elevator. The door slid shut behind her.

"I bet. Fifth floor, please," she said to the man, and he pressed the button.

The ride took about two seconds. Lucy led them off

the elevator and down a marble hall, her heels *click, click, clicking*. Stan felt frumpy and underdressed in her denim shorts, tank top, and flip-flops.

"I've sent someone to get him his supplies," Lucy said. "The cat. What's his name again?"

"Nutty. What kind of supplies?"

Lucy paused and looked back at her. "Every cat needs a comfortable commode, right?"

Stan smiled. "This cat probably needs one bad."

Lucy led them down that hall for what seemed like a mile. She finally stopped in front of a wooden door with brass knobs. She threw the door open with a grand sweep of her arm and beamed. "This suite should suit you. There are three floors. Kitchen on the first, living room on the second, and two bedrooms on the third. One has a king bed, the other has two queens. If you don't want to share a bedroom, there's a delightful pull-out sofa in the second-floor living room. As welcoming as the softest bed."

Stan stepped into the suite and looked around. They were in a foyer larger than the one in her own little Victorian house. To her right, a fully equipped kitchen. The first floor also had a full bathroom. A short staircase led to the second floor.

"There's also a small office on the second floor," Lucy said. "Bathrooms are on each level, and both bedrooms have their own bathroom. There's also an elevator."

"I'll take the single bedroom," Maria said. "Age probably has preference, right, girls?" She looked at Stan and Therese, waiting for them to challenge her. Stan didn't care. Therese still hadn't uttered a word. Maria looked disappointed to avoid a fight and promptly disappeared upstairs.

Lucy watched with amusement. "Please let me know

if you need anything else. I hope you'll enjoy. And there's Miguel now, with Nutty's supplies." She waved at the man waiting at the door. He wore overalls and boots and carried a small wooden box that looked hand carved, a bag of cat litter, and another bag full of supplies. He bowed slightly.

"Bed and commode for the gentleman," he said, with the slightest trace of a Spanish accent. "Which room would you like it in?"

Stan glanced at her other roomie. "The second bedroom. Therese, is that okay with you? I'll need to leave him closed off in a room while I'm out of the suite."

Therese let out a loud sigh. "Whatever," she said in a whiny, high-pitched voice with a noticeable New York accent. So much for that exotic accent her features suggested.

"Okay, then," Stan said to Miguel. "The bedroom it is."

Lucy nodded approvingly as Miguel bustled past them. Another knock on the door sounded, and the bellhop appeared with the luggage. "You can take those right to the bedrooms," Lucy said, then turned to Stan and Therese. "I'll leave you, then. I do hope you're comfortable. We'll send dinner up shortly—for you ladies and Nutty. My condolences on the loss of your friend."

Stan almost told her Pierre wasn't her friend, but thought better of it. "Thanks. And Nutty thanks you, too."

Lucy nodded and exited the suite, closing the door behind her. Miguel appeared and beamed at her. "The commode is set up in the bedroom." He bowed again, then backed out of the room.

"Thank you," Stan called. She locked the door behind him and turned to Therese. "Are you going to take the other bed in the bedroom? Or the living room?"

Therese rolled her eyes. "I totally *don't care.* I'm going out anyway. This is the lamest day ever!"

"Oh," Stan said. "Are we allowed to leave?"

"*Allowed?* It's not like Shel is your dad or anything. Like, we don't have a *curfew*," she scoffed, and flounced out of the room. Stan heard the bathroom door slam seconds later.

Shel? Stan shook her head. By this time she agreed with the detectives' unspoken assessment: these people were all crazy. "Come on, Nutty." She led him upstairs, took his harness and leash off, then showed him the litter box. He made a grateful beeline inside. Stan ran a hand over the wood, admiring it. She could definitely use something like this at home.

While she waited for Nutty to finish, she looked around the room. Fit for royalty, done entirely in reds and deep, mustardy yellows. Red velvet curtains covered all the windows, and the plush golden carpet welcomed her feet like a hug when she gratefully slipped her flip-flops off. The bed looked a heck of a lot bigger than queen-sized, and oh, so soft.

Stan heard Maria's door open and a minute later she appeared in the doorway. "Would you like a cannoli?" She held out a Tupperware container. "Homemade from my restaurant just this morning. I brought them with me in case of emergency, and good thing, right?" She held the carton out.

Stan still felt queasy. "Thanks, but I'm not feeling very hungry right now," she said.

Maria sniffed. "I knew it. You're one of those skinny girls. My restaurant *hates* the skinny girls. Come to an Italian, award-winning kitchen and eat salad. *Stunod!*"

Stan recognized the word—Italian for "stupid"—and her eyes narrowed. But before she could respond, the bathroom door flew open and Therese came out. She wore a skirt that barely covered her tiny butt, over-the-knee high-heeled boots, and a low-cut gold top. She glared at the two of them, then wrinkled her nose at the cannoli.

"Ew," she said. "That'll make you fat just looking at it." And she swept out of the room and into the elevator. A moment later the door to the suite slammed.

"That," Stan said, "would be the *stunod* skinny girl."

Chapter 8

Nutty stayed in the commode for a long time. When he finally emerged, shaking his feet, he walked up to Stan and meowed for his dinner. Perfect timing, because someone knocked on the door. She went down to the kitchen and peered through the peephole. Room service. With a huge cart.

She opened the door. The man bowed and wheeled the cart inside. He set up a line of covered silver plates on the expansive counter, then added a row of smaller silver plates. "For the cat," he said, then bowed and wheeled the cart out.

Stan peeked under the silver tops. Lasagna. Right up Maria's alley. The next one contained a white fish in a buttery-looking sauce. She moved down the line. Green beans. Rice. Salad. Prime rib, for crying out loud. Desserts overflowed from the final plate. In a smaller set of the same silver-lidded plates Nutty had his own servings of fish, tiny pieces of shrimp, and some broccoli florets.

She took pictures of the spread to show Jake, then made Nutty a plate. On second thought, she selected rice and salad for herself, then locked herself in the bedroom. Nutty attacked his food with a vengeance, pieces of fish flying out of the bowl. She ate a couple spoonfuls of rice and put the plate aside, flopped on the bed, and dialed Jake's cell phone. While she waited for him to answer, she closed her eyes and imagined they were in her cozy house instead. She and Jake would be lounging around her den, reading or watching TV, the dogs and cats inhabiting their favorite spots. Scruffy, her schnoodle, would be tucked on the couch next to them. Henry, her pit bull, would be in his bed, and Jake's Weimaraner, Duncan, would be on the floor at their feet. Nutty would have claimed the back of the couch, and Benedict, the orange cat and her newest addition, would've staked out the window seat. Candles would be burning. If the TV wasn't on, they might listen to a jazz CD while eating take-out sushi. Or maybe they'd cooked a nice meal together. If Jake had to be at the bar, she'd go too and hang out for the evening. Since he'd added an oven for her use, she could use the time to bake, or simply relax and enjoy the atmosphere if she was caught up. But business had been booming and she usually had plenty of orders to fill.

The phone picked up on the fourth ring and a woman's voice answered. It wasn't Brenna, Jake's other sister, who worked as Stan's baking assistant, and also worked at the bar a few nights a week. Stan didn't recognize this voice and was momentarily startled into silence. "Hellooooo," the woman shouted again. "Anyone there?"

Stan's eyes narrowed. She resisted snapping out a *Who the bleep are you* and settled for, "Is Jake there?"

She could hear laughter and glasses clinking in the

background. "Jake? Sure thing, one second." A minute
later he came on the line.

"McGee."

"It's me," she said.

His voice immediately warmed. "Hey, babe. How's it
going?"

"Who was that?" Despite her best attempts at a neu-
tral tone, she could hear the snark come through and
tried to tone it down. Tired, she told herself. Stressed.

"Shannon. One of my waitresses. She needed to call
someone a cab."

"Oh." Now she felt stupid. And she could feel him
grinning on the other side of the phone.

"You miss me?" he asked.

"Of course I miss you. And the dogs. And Benedict.
How are they all?" Just thinking of them all made her
teary. And then she was weeping.

"Stan?" He sounded alarmed now. "What's wrong?"

"Everything," she sniffled. "I'm sorry. You're
working. . . ."

"Hang on." The background noise on Jake's end
faded away. She heard the sound of a door closing.
He'd probably gone up to his apartment. She was grateful for the quiet, and for his full attention. Restless, she
pushed herself off the bed and paced the room.

"Okay. Sorry. I needed to get out of the pub. What's
going on? Is Sheldon being a jerk? Are the other chefs
not being nice to you?"

His line of questioning made her smile through her
tears. She found a box of tissues next to the bed and
blew her nose. "I wish those were my problems. One of
the chefs is dead. Someone killed him."

Silence on the other end. Then, "You're kidding,
right?"

"Nope." She opened the balcony door and stepped

out into the night. Her room overlooked an area of the parking lot directly behind the hotel. She knew the ocean waited just beyond the parking lot, but the darkness made it too hard to see, keeping the comforting sight out of her reach. Just like Jake.

"How?"

"Someone slit his throat."

He sucked in a breath. "And you saw him?"

"I found him. In the backyard at the house we were supposed to be staying in." Below her, a couple of people exited the hotel's back door, laughing. She saw the flare of cigarettes as they strolled the parking lot, talking and smoking.

"Where are you now? I'll come get you."

"You can't," she said.

"What do you mean, I can't?"

She explained Sheldon's plan to entertain the investors despite losing Pierre. "So we're here, and we're cooking. The show must go on, apparently. We're in a hotel. The Newport Premier. And if we don't end up with a Food Channel contract on Monday, we all might be in danger of being murdered." She leaned on the railing. Another figure hurried out of the hotel. She recognized the long hair and heels. Lucy Keyes. Lucy hurried to a silver SUV parked directly under a floodlight, climbed in, and drove away. Stan left the window and went back to sit on the bed.

"That's absurd," he said. "Listen to me. If you don't want to stay, you don't have to. You don't owe this guy anything. All he does is pop up and disrupt your life. Screw him, Stan. You can open a shop on your own."

Jake wasn't a huge Sheldon Allyn fan. There weren't many people he didn't like, but Sheldon had made the list. Aside from Sheldon's flamboyant, demanding nature, Stan suspected Jake worried Sheldon's fancy lifestyle would eventually coax her away from simple, quiet Frog Ledge. It would never happen. She had no desire to live the Famous Chef Life Sheldon boasted about. It clearly hadn't worked out for Pierre. But Jake needed more convincing.

"I know I don't owe him anything. But I want to make the shop work, and I think he can help me do that," she said. "I promised I'd see this through, and it will benefit all of us if it goes well."

He sighed. "I don't like it, Stan. Do they have any leads on who did it? If it's not safe I don't want you staying there out of some misguided allegiance to this guy."

"I'm sure it's perfectly safe. There're a lot of cops on it. We're in a public place. And I don't have an allegiance to Sheldon. I just like to finish what I start. You're the same way."

She had him there. Reliability was Jake McGee's middle name. There was no way he could fault her for the same. "Honestly, don't worry. It's only three days," she reasoned, pushing away the stubborn thought that kept running through her head: *a heck of a lot can happen in three days.* "It will be fine."

After they hung up, she realized her stomach growled. Talking to Jake had helped rekindle her appetite. Maybe she'd go down and get more dinner. It wouldn't hurt to ask Maria to join her. Slipping her feet into her flip-flops, she left her room and went to Maria's door. She rapped three times and waited. No answer.

"Maria?" she called.

Nothing.

She tried the knob. The door opened. The bedroom appeared empty. Maria's cannoli container sat forgotten on the night table. "Maria, you here?"

Nothing. She peeked further into the room, afraid of what she might see. She couldn't take another dead person. But the bedroom was definitely empty. The bathroom door stood open, demonstrating that it, too, had no occupant, alive or dead.

Maria must have gone out. Maybe the dinner here wasn't to her liking. Shrugging, Stan shut the door and went downstairs. It wouldn't do to let good food go to waste.

Chapter 9

After Stan ate, she turned on the TV in her bedroom and promptly fell asleep in her clothes. She woke up a couple hours later, pulled her pajamas out of her suitcase, washed her face, brushed her teeth, and crawled between the covers. Nutty was fast asleep on one of the pillows. He'd had a long, hard day, too.

She switched off the lamp and slept like the dead until someone banged on her door. She jumped up, on full alert, and flung her covers off. Simultaneously, her cell phone rang.

"What the . . ." She fumbled on the nightstand for the phone while trying to climb out of bed, not sure which to address first in her bleary-eyed state. She found the phone first and answered. "What?"

"Stan, it's Sheldon."

"Sheldon?" She glanced at her clock. Two-fifteen. "What's up?"

"Open your door."

"My . . ." She crossed to the bedroom door and flung it open. Sheldon stood there, still in his silver suit, although his feet were bare. His toenails were painted purple. That was about the only other color associated with him. He looked pale and drained, and his normally perfectly coiffed hair stuck up every which way. "What's wrong? How did you get into the suite?"

He ignored that question. "I need your help." He reached for her arm and started to drag her out the door.

"What? No!" She jerked her arm away. "Help doing what? It's two in the morning! Don't you sleep?"

"Sleep?" He barked out a laugh. "After what happened yesterday? No. We need to do some damage control and I don't think Tyler is up to it, quite frankly. He's fabulous at getting us good attention. Crisis communications? Not so much. But I don't usually have crises." His expression changed to pure puppy dog. "I know public relations and dealing with the media is your other expertise. Would you please consider helping me? Helping us?"

Stan dragged her fingers through her tangle of blond hair. She felt like a zombie and did not want to have this, or any, conversation until she'd gotten another eight or so hours of sleep. And she sure as heck didn't want to relive her former career. But Sheldon didn't look like he'd let her off the hook easily. "Sheldon. I got out of that business. I'm rusty. It's been a year and a half—"

"Nonsense," he interrupted. "If you have a talent, you don't simply lose it."

"It's two in the morning," she said again. "Is there really that much going on right now? Was Pierre's family notified yet? Has this even hit the news?"

"We need to be prepared," he said. "And right now we're not."

Why didn't I let Jake come get me when he offered? Stan

closed her eyes briefly, hoping to wake up in her own bed and find this was all a dream. But when she opened her eyes, Sheldon still stood in front of her. And if she didn't help with the PR, it might be an even longer weekend than she'd already anticipated.

"Fine. Let me get dressed."

"No need." He took her arm again. "You look lovely. Let's go."

Stan glanced down at her cat pajamas and sighed. With a helpless look behind her at Nutty, still sound asleep on his pillow, Stan let Sheldon tug her out the door and close it firmly behind them.

Chapter 10

"I had no idea this place was so big." She hurried to keep up with Sheldon. They'd taken the elevator to the first floor, crossed to another wing of the hotel, and gotten back in the elevator to the fourth floor. Now they were hurrying down a hall that appeared to be the length of the Daytona 500 if the track were in a straight line. Luckily, her flip-flops had been next to the door. Otherwise she'd probably be barefoot given Sheldon's urgency. As they power walked, she looped her hair up in a messy bun thanks to the band she'd had around her wrist when she fell asleep. Her mouth felt dry and thick and she wished she'd at least been able to brush her teeth.

"You've never been?"

"Just to parties. I grew up around here, remember? I never had a reason to stay in a hotel here. You knew that. You told the others, didn't you?"

He gave her a strange look, then shrugged it off. "Yes, of course," he said, stopping in front of room 423. He inserted his card into the slot. The light flashed green and he shoved the door open.

Tyler sat at the kitchen table. His morose expression

from earlier had darkened to explosive as he banged away on his MacBook Air keyboard, a cup of coffee at his elbow, rock music blaring out of the speakers. The ugly side of public relations. It was all fun and games until the scandal hit. She knew it well—she'd lost her own job to a scandal. When the president of the financial services company she'd worked for had been caught with his competitor's wife, there was no amount of PR that could've spun that story. So they got rid of her and her top staffers.

She felt a pang of sympathy for the kid. He looked all of twenty-five years old, if that. This was probably his first real gig, and really, how scandalous could cooking be? Unless you counted the illicit affairs, but those went on in every industry. They were hardly even news anymore.

"Tyler. You met Stan today. She was in public relations in a previous life. She's going to share her expertise. Could you please turn that music *off*?" Sheldon turned to Stan. "Can I get you something, my dear? A drink? Coffee?"

"How about water," Stan said. "Hey, Tyler."

Tyler grunted and jabbed at a button on his keyboard. The music abruptly stopped. "Are you taking over?"

"No. I'm here to help," she said firmly. "What's going on? Where are you stuck?"

A loud snore came from the living room area. Stan glanced at Sheldon as he came over with a tall glass of ice water.

"Joaquin," he said apologetically, setting the glass down. "He needs his sleep."

"We all do," Tyler snapped.

"I understand that, my dear boy," Sheldon said, an edge to his voice. "Why don't you share with Stan your strategy, and then you can take a power nap while she enhances it?" He moved to the bar area and chose what looked like a brandy. He poured, drank, and poured again, clearly at peace with making this kid work all night.

"Great." Tyler shoved the laptop toward Stan. "There's my strategy. When the news breaks, we say that we're devastated by the loss of our friend and colleague and we have every confidence that the police will bring the killer to justice. Meanwhile, we'll raise our cake pops or insert-favorite-pastry-here in his honor."

Stan looked at Sheldon. "That's a perfectly acceptable statement. What's the problem?"

He frowned at her. "There will be questions about why he was at my house before the event commenced."

"Okay. What's the answer?"

"Yeah," Tyler said with a sneer. "What *is* the answer?"

Sheldon shot a look full of daggers at Tyler, who spread his hands innocently and said, "You know that'll be the first question. Once you figure it out I can work with it. Until then, I'm going to bed." Tyler shut the laptop with a snap. "Good luck," he said to Stan, and flounced out of the room. She heard his footsteps on the stairs, then a door slammed shut elsewhere in the suite.

Stan wanted badly to lower her head to the table and bang it a few times. Somehow—and she really had to engage in some self-help practices to figure out why—she ended up in situations like this more often than she cared to count.

"Sheldon," she said. "Please tell me what I'm doing here."

Sheldon's full lips pulled together in a pout. "I just told you. I need crisis communication help. I shouldn't hire people so young. They have no *sensitivity*."

"Oh, cut the crap." She figured she looked almost as surprised as Sheldon—too many years of corporate politeness and politics usually prevented her from outbursts—but it felt good. The combination of exhaustion and trauma had made her bold, and she'd just been yanked out of bed to do someone else's job. No wonder she'd taken so much solace in making pet food over the past year. She could do it alone most of the time and the only personalities she had to deal with were picky cats. Heck, the dogs ate anything she served them. She'd take that over people any day. "What is the answer, Sheldon? Tyler's right. Neither of us can help you if you can't tell us."

They stared at each other for a full minute. Stan pushed her chair back and started to rise when Sheldon let out a long-suffering sigh and leaned back in his chair.

"Fine," he said. "Fine, fine, fine. I don't know why Pierre was at my house. I have no idea how Pierre knew to *find* my house. I've kept this address very mum. Even my staffers didn't know it until they got to the locations where you all were being picked up. I sent them a text, all at the same time. You can check our phones. So I have no good answer."

"If it's the truth, that's your answer. But it's a convenient answer."

"My dear," he said haughtily, "it's the truth. I don't care if it's convenient."

"So you didn't tell him."

"Of course not! He received the same invite as everyone else. He was supposed to ride with Maria, in Therese's car. She called me in a panic that he hadn't arrived and Maria was getting . . . cranky. I told her to come over, and that's when I called and left the address on his voice mail."

"So he planned to come? He RSVP'd?"

"He did."

"So how did he get here, Sheldon? Where was his stuff? Did he have anything with him?"

They stared at each other until Sheldon shook his head, slowly. He tipped his chair on its back legs and rocked. "I'm telling you, I don't know. It's even more of a mystery because Pierre and I . . . had been on the rocks lately. We hadn't really spoken in more than a month, and this retreat came up after that . . . last conversation, I'd hoped we could repair our relationship during this time." He let the chair fall.

The desire to beat her head against the wall grew. "I changed my mind. I'll have a glass of that," Stan said, nodding at the brandy. She told herself it could still be considered nighttime. Drinking in the early morning sounded much worse.

Sheldon rose, poured, and handed it to her. Stan drank it in two swallows, felt the liquid warm her throat. She held out her glass for one more shot. "What were you on the outs about?"

Sheldon held up a finger, went to the doorway leading to the living room, and peeked in to make sure Joaquin was sleeping. He moved back into the kitchen and sat at the table, speaking in a low voice regardless. "Pierre wanted me to fund a second pastry shop in Los Angeles. But his New York establishment . . . let's just say returns have been slow over the past six months."

"You said no."

"I didn't say no. But I hadn't decided for certain yet. He didn't like to wait."

Stan pulled Tyler's computer over, opened a fresh document, and began typing notes. "So he was mad at you."

Sheldon's lips tipped up in a tight smile. "Not just me. Pierre enjoyed being mad at the world."

"Why?"

"Because he wasn't where he wanted to be in his career. He'd been on such a fast track, but his upward progress has petered out recently."

"But right now he was mad at you. So why would he come to this event?"

Sheldon shrugged. "We still worked together, my dear. When you and I have occasional tiffs, I expect we'll be able to work through them."

"Working through them is one thing. A weekend away together is another. Unless he had a carrot dangling in front of him." She picked up an abandoned pen from the table and clicked it open and shut, open and shut. "Did you tell him about the endgame?"

He sent her an apprising glance. "You're very astute."

She rolled her eyes. "What, did you think I just fell off the proverbial turnip truck? Give me a break, Sheldon." She'd never understood that saying, or what turnips had to do with being savvy, but it seemed to fit this situation. "Look. I'm not starstruck like the rest of these guys. I want a shop in Frog Ledge, sure, but I'm doing fine without one. So just be straight with me and let's get this done, okay?"

Sheldon's smile faded. "Fine. Yes, I mentioned the contract. He warmed up immediately and agreed to come. But then over the next few days he had a lot of questions about it. Which I couldn't answer, because I don't have a contract yet."

"What kinds of questions?"

Sheldon shrugged dismissively. "Like who would be named specifically, what the terms of the show would be, how often he would appear."

"Seems preliminary." Unless Pierre'd been familiar with the concept and knew of some potential loopholes to signing on. She narrowed her eyes as a new thought dawned on her. "Unless he thought that you would be the only one getting the contract, with the discretion to parse out spots as you feel appropriate."

"He may have thought that. It's not exactly how it would work," Sheldon said. "Sheldon Allyn Enterprises is—God willing—getting the contract. As part of that, a variety of food would be addressed, which is where you all come in."

"But it wouldn't be us, per se," Stan said. "So if one of us screwed up, you'd just need to have *someone* doing pastry, or vegan, or whatever."

He shook his head, a glimmer of a smile returning. "You'll certainly keep me at the top of my game, my dear. Very perceptive, for someone who doesn't know this business well."

"Again. Turnip truck. I'm not going to out you to the rest of them," she said, anticipating his next question. "I don't even know them."

"Ooh," he said, rubbing his hands together. "This is shaping up to be just like *Survivor*!"

"Focus," she snapped. "So Pierre tried to play hard-ball. What happened?"

Sheldon sobered. "He had no loyalty, that's what happened. He felt I wasn't doing enough for him, even though I helped him get to where he is today, his own flaws notwithstanding. Do you think he'd have been able to fund a bakery in *New York* without my influence?"

"I have no idea. I didn't know him, remember?"

Sheldon glared at her. "Well, he wouldn't. Trust me. Then he threatened to walk away from his shop and go into business with a competitor, if I didn't get him his own TV contract. A competitor who has, according to Pierre, more money and clout."

"Which would've hurt your wallet and your reputation," Stan said.

"Precisely. So we were at somewhat of a crossroads. But I gently reminded Pierre of a few times I'd covered for him. He didn't like that."

"Covered for him how?"

"He'd been in a few scrapes with the law," Sheldon said.

"For what?"

"Most recently, controlled substances. There were other unsavory pieces of his past as well. Due to my extensive network, I was able to get him . . . off the hook."

"So you blackmailed him in return for the favor."

"My dear, I don't blackmail," Sheldon said. "I merely reminded him of all I've done for him."

"What does that mean? Did you threaten to kill him or something?" She narrowed her eyes at him. "My God, Sheldon, did you kill him?" She looked around for a weapon, just in case.

"Did *I* kill him? My dear woman, is that what you think of me?" He pressed a hand to his heart, apparently crushed by her question. "I most certainly did not. Pierre was my first protégé. I adored him. Never a more talented pastry chef have I ever met. For human pastry, of course," he said hurriedly, remembering his audience. "I am completely devastated that he's left this world. I can barely comprehend it." He rose and poured more brandy as if to accentuate his point.

"I simply told him he darn well better not miss this dinner, because it would have negative repercussions on both of us."

Stan absorbed that information. "Who's this competitor Pierre was working with?"

"He didn't name drop. Which led me to believe he might be hedging. But I've been putting out feelers and learned he had been spending an inordinate amount of time with Frederick Peterfreund."

"Who's that?"

Sheldon gazed at her with a fatherly smile. "You're so refreshing. Frederick is young. Cutting-edge, they say." He made a face. "He's tough and loud and looks more like a Hell's Angel than a refined chef working with elegant pastry. As a matter of fact, he rides his motorcycle to each kitchen with a backpack full of pastry-making paraphernalia. Very crude, but I suppose that's his brand. His schtick is saving dying pastry shops. He's weaseled his way into TV already. He worked on a new show last year with some up-and-coming chefs. *Kitchen Cutthroat?*"

Stan shook her head.

"I'm delighted you didn't contribute to the ratings. Quite tasteless. However, he's gaining fame."

"So Pierre aligned with him. Where is this guy?"

"Los Angeles, mostly. I think he dabbles in New York."

"And he knows Pierre had ties to you?"

"Of course. Everyone does." Sheldon puffed out his chest.

"Do you know Frederick?"

"We've met." Sheldon's expression indicated he'd have found meeting Genghis Kahn more enjoyable.

"Could he have killed Pierre? Found out where you lived and lured him here?"

Sheldon sighed. "I have no idea. He doesn't seem like a very nice man, but that could all be an act. I still don't know how either would've known about the house, or even known about a house to look for."

"Do you own it?"

"I do. Sort of."

"Sort of? What does that mean?"

"I did buy it, but not under my name. I didn't want the publicity."

"So who owns the house on paper?"

"My sister. Candace Kramer. She lives in Virginia."

Stan tapped her nail lightly against the shift key on the computer. "Did you tell the police who owns the house?"

"Of course I did. I have nothing to hide." Sheldon spread his hands wide. "They can also simply read the deed. It's not a secret."

"Who else knows?"

"No one," Sheldon said firmly.

"Would your sister tell anyone?"

"My sister doesn't give a hoot about what I do. All she cares about is making sure I pay the taxes."

"You didn't have anyone from your business helping with the negotiations or anything? Or the decorating? You're telling me there's no one who knew about this place?"

"Nobody. I wanted to be completely out of the public eye. I hired everyone anonymously when I needed work done. I own other property in Providence that people know about. No one needs to know everything about me. Although now that's over. Once this gets out, it'll be headline news. I'll have to sell it, I'm sure."

"Yet Pierre somehow figured out where this house was, showed up here, and got himself murdered."

"I wouldn't put it past Pierre to have been concocting his own scheme all along," Sheldon said. "Something must've happened, and it backfired. One thing you should know about Pierre." Sheldon leaned forward, eyes steady on Stan's. "He always had a plan B. Always."

Chapter 11

After two more hours of crisis communication planning and settling on some alternate statements based on the direction the news took, Sheldon retired for a few hours and Stan headed back to her suite. It was four forty-five when she finally fell back into her bed. Until another pounding on the door woke her. This time, at least, she could see daylight through the curtains. When she flung the bedroom door open, Maria stood there, wrapped in a bathrobe. Her wet, and therefore flat, hair had shaved a few more inches off her and she had to look up at Stan. Whatever yesterday's silvery sheen had been, she'd washed it out, leaving her hair a mousy brown.

"Sheldon called. We're going to be meeting in the lobby at one o'clock to discuss our plans for the week-end."

"What time is it now?"

"Eight."

"Oh. That probably could've waited, couldn't it?" she asked.

Maria glared at her. "I did what he asked and am notifying all of you. Where's Therese?"

"I have no idea. She went out last night. Did you check the bed in the living room?"

"No. Oh, there's my little man!" Maria's tone completely changed to a croon as she dropped to her knees to greet Nutty, who'd wandered over. She gathered him into her arms as he head butted her. "Are you hungry, little man? I'll take you downstairs for breakfast. Your mother apparently still wants to sleep." Her tone indicated her disgust with that desire.

Since she couldn't tell Maria that she'd spent half the night trying to help Sheldon with potential damage control, nor did she feel the need to explain herself anyway, Stan ignored the comment. She waved to Nutty, smushed into Maria's neck staring desperately over her shoulder, and kicked the door halfway shut. He would find his way back.

She couldn't fall back asleep, though, as much as she wanted to. Sheldon's story about Pierre, their disagreement, and the elusive Frederick what's-his-name plagued her thoughts. The whole thing sounded compelling enough—power, control, fame, fortune. She couldn't help but wonder what else. As her gram used to say, every story had three sides: yours, mine, and the truth. Right now, both Pierre's side and the truth were missing.

A long hot shower and some clean clothes helped her state of mind. When she emerged from the bathroom, Nutty hadn't returned and there was still no sign of Therese. She went downstairs, following the scent of coffee. Maria and Nutty sat together at the table. Nutty actually sat on the table, a person-sized plate of fish and meat in front of him.

"What?" Maria asked defensively at Stan's raised eyebrow. "It's surf and turf."

"That's great," Stan said. "Is there coffee?"

Maria pointed at the counter. "I just filled up the French press."

Whoever had dropped off the ginormous dinner last night had returned with breakfast. Stan made a grateful beeline for the java. Once she'd had a few sips, her head cleared the rest of the way. She perused the silver-topped serving plates and selected some eggs. "Did you eat?" she asked Maria.

"I did. Sausage, eggs, and coffee cake. I could hardly eat anything after yesterday."

Stan sat at the table, too. Maria studiously avoided her eyes. Stan sighed inwardly. They were stuck with each other for a few days. May as well be friends. "Listen, Maria," she said. "I'm really sorry I didn't recognize you when we met yesterday. I'm not up on my famous chefs these days. Too much to do with my new business. I'm sure you understand." She flashed her best dazzling, apologetic smile. "Can we start over?"

Maria regarded her suspiciously for a moment, then broke into a big smile. "You are forgiven, *bella*," she said. "And I take back the *stunod* comment also."

"Thank you," Stan said.

They drank coffee in companionable silence while Nutty nibbled on his food. Stan noticed a pile of folders on the table. "What are those?"

"The packets that Sheldon had prepared for us. About the restaurant and the investors."

Stan vaguely remembered someone mentioning that yesterday before everything went downhill. She'd have to take a look later. "I take it Therese isn't here?"

"No. And Sheldon is not going to be happy about it. These kids. Sheldy thinks that he's cutting-edge, hiring the little ones. They know the technology, he says." She threw her hands up in despair. "But they don't care about anything. No respect for their elders, either."

Sheldy? Stan bit the inside of her cheek to keep from laughing. But then she thought of poor Tyler and Sheldon's comment about the young ones having no sensitivity. She wondered how Tyler had fared this morning. If he'd been roused from sleep to get back to work. "Hey, have you heard anything on the news? Was Pierre's family notified about his . . . death?"

Maria sobered. "I have no idea. Let's look." She turned on the small TV on the counter and changed the channel to the local news.

They watched a weather report and a story about a car crash on I-95 before the anchor said soberly, "A murder last night in Newport has residents on edge. A man was found dead at a home on Sunset Avenue. His identity has not yet been released. Tammy Lynch is reporting from police headquarters. Tammy, what's new with this case?"

Tammy Lynch gave a fluffy report about the murder (still unidentified man who did not live in the house), the neighborhood (affluent and quiet), and local crime (on the rise since the beginning of the year) before they switched to an update on two teenagers on an alleged crime spree spanning New England. Maria switched the TV off with a sigh of relief.

"Well," she said. "At least they're not camped out in front of the house."

"Maybe the police didn't find Pierre's family yet. Do you know them?" Stan asked.

Maria shook her head. "Pierre didn't talk about his family much. I think they embarrassed him. I heard he's from a very small town in Michigan or something."

"Interesting. Is Pierre his real name?"

Maria snorted. "Ha. I would bet my mother's special

sauce that he hasn't thought of his real name in many years."

"Do you know it?"

"No. It's likely a highly guarded secret. Everything is about image in our world, you know?"

Stan shrugged. "Not really, but I figured as much."

Maria studied her. "You have no interest in the TV shows, do you?"

"Nope," Stan said.

"Yet you're here."

"I'm interested in working with Sheldon," Stan said. "And once I've committed to something, I usually see it through. Unless things get too out of hand."

"Well, they're already plenty out of hand," Maria said. "You'd better get used to it."

Stan went upstairs to her room and did a Google search for Candace Kramer. She found two in Burke, Virginia, both with public phone numbers. She called the first one and got a ninety-something woman who couldn't hear. She finally had to hang up. The other number dumped her into a voice mail with a woman's voice. She sounded normal. Stan left a cryptic message that she knew Sheldon and needed to speak to Candace immediately. She had no idea if the woman would call back, but it was worth a shot.

At noon, Therese showed up, still wearing her outfit from last night. Stan had returned to the kitchen for more coffee. Maria had never left it. Therese grunted at Maria and Stan and headed upstairs. She returned at ten to one, showered and looking like a typical twenty-something with beige capris and a white T-shirt. Her long brown hair had a wave to it from her shower, and she wasn't wearing the extreme makeup from last night. Her face still had the look of someone sucking a lemon.

At precisely one o'clock the three of them trooped to the lobby. The atmosphere reminded her of those days in corporate America when something had gone wrong and heads were about to roll. She'd escaped from that . . . hadn't she?

Marcin darted over to Maria and whispered something in her ear. She looked at him with alarm, then pulled him into the corner. They whispered furiously back and forth for a bit, then Maria came over to Stan.

"Have you seen Kyle?"

Stan shook her head. "I haven't seen anyone but you and Therese."

"He never came back to their room last night. No one can reach him on his cell phone."

Stan frowned. "Is that normal for him?"

Maria thought about that. "I have no idea."

Stan didn't say anything, but little alarm bells were going off in her head. One dead chef, and another conspicuously absent and not answering his phone. Of course, Kyle was an adult and could've gone out to party last night. He could be passed out at someone's house with no sense of time. Those things probably happened regularly in his world. She thought of him and Lucy Keyes, whispering in the lobby when they'd first arrived.

"Hey," she said, as another thought dawned on her. "Where was Therese all night? You think they were together?"

Maria's big eyes bulged. "Dear Lord, I hope not," she said. "I would've thought such a good-looking boy would have better taste than that stick figure."

Sheldon, Joaquin, and Tyler joined the crowd. Joaquin looked alert, rested, and ready to face the day, if not somber. Sheldon looked subdued. Tyler looked a little better than the last time Stan had seen him. Like maybe he'd gotten some sleep after she stepped in. He yawned and rubbed the discs stretching his ears. Those things gave Stan the heebie-jeebies. She looked away. Sheldon met her eyes across the room and motioned for her to join him. She did, with some reluctance.

"How are you feeling?"

"Fine. You?"

"Sad, but surviving." Sheldon observed their group. "Where's Kyle?" he asked.

Stan looked around, feigning surprise. "I have no idea. I'm sure he's on his way down. Did you see the news?"

"I did. I think we're in good shape for now. We should probably regroup tonight. Tyler and I made up."

"That's good," Stan said. "Is he taking it from here?"

"With your help," Sheldon said. "If you don't mind." His tone indicated she had no choice. "I have Joaquin working on a replacement for Pierre. If all goes well, I should have that person here tonight. We're going to cook up a storm! Have to make up for lost time. Now. Where is my vegan chef? Leonardo! What did you do with Kyle?" he called, moving away from Stan.

Stan looked around for Therese to ask her if she'd seen Kyle last night, but Therese was deep in conversation with Tyler. She'd catch her later.

Chapter 12

Lucy Keyes arrived minutes later, wearing another killer suit and leopard print heels. Stan had wondered if Kyle would show up right behind her, but he did not. Maybe he'd just been asking her where the bathroom was yesterday, and Stan had interpreted it as a cozy conversation. Lucy led them to a corner of the lobby near a fake fireplace where platters of sandwiches and bowls of salads had been set out.

"Sheldon and I are pleased to let you know that you'll be staying here for the weekend to plan for your event," she announced, flashing a professional smile at each of them in turn. "You'll remain in your current suites. As for kitchen space, we have a kitchen behind our largest function room that we use for weddings and the like. Since we don't have any functions this weekend, the kitchen is yours. I know you were all looking for community cooking time. We've put out a light lunch for you as you get settled today, and of course my staff is here to serve you anytime. Please see me with any problems." She clasped her hands and looked at Sheldon. "Anything else?"

Sheldon joined her. He took her hand and brought

it to his lips. "What a lovely lady. Thank you for your flexibility and accommodating nature. We are indebted to you."

Lucy smiled and extracted her hand. "Anytime. Enjoy, folks." And she clicked away down the hall.

"What a gem." Sheldon turned to the group. "We are very fortunate, aren't we?"

No one seemed to feel fortunate at the moment. But that didn't deter Sheldon.

"I want us to spend tonight together. Make some food. Laugh. Cry. Get our game plan in place for our big day. I need everyone to get together and *be a team.* We're behind schedule, but I realize yesterday was . . . difficult for all of us. I thank you all for sticking it out." He looked at each of them in turn. "Joaquin is going to go out and gather some items for us that will make our evening enjoyable."

Joaquin flashed them a thumbs-up. Today he wore jeans that were way too tight for his round frame, a tweed jacket that gave him a "hip professor" look, and loafers with no socks. He'd gelled his bright red hair into straight-up spikes. "What shall we have? Any cooking volunteers?"

"Italian," Maria said immediately. "I want to make my mother's marinara sauce. She always used to make it when we were sad." She dabbed at her eyes with her sleeve. "And I want garlic and cheese sausage."

Stan wrinkled her nose involuntarily. Years of meat-free eating made even the sound of sausage sickening. "I can make us a big salad. With grilled shrimp and avocado."

"And I would like to make something special for dessert in Pierre's honor," Joaquin announced. "I'll let that be a surprise and take full responsibility. What would we like to drink?"

"Red wine with Mama's marinara!" Maria thumped a fist onto the bar. "Anything else would make her roll in her grave. And it has to be a hearty red wine, too. None of that boring old merlot business. Get me Shiraz!"

Joaquin noted that in his phone. "Got it. What else, team?"

He wrote down a few other requests and bowed. "I will go to the farmers' market posthaste! Therese?" He waited expectantly for her to put her phone down and join him. "Therese will accompany me," he announced. "Text me if you think of anything else. My number is in your packets we handed out yesterday." He took Therese's arm and they headed out the door.

"That's all I wanted to say right now," Sheldon said. He glanced at his watch. "Please, take the afternoon off. Recharge. Get your heads back together. Let's begin our festivities at eight, shall we?"

"Sounds lovely," Maria said. "I'm going to go find some cannoli!"

Everyone else chimed in with their agreement. Just as they were about to disperse, Detective Owens walked through the door. The light mood faltered again. Stan felt her stomach clench in anticipation. Now what?

Owens smiled. "None of you look happy to see me. Sorry to interrupt," he said to Sheldon. "I'd like one more quick session with each of you. I also have car keys to return. Thanks to all for your cooperation."

Stan held her breath, waiting to hear if anyone's vehicle was being impounded and handcuffs were coming out, but Owens said nothing else.

Sheldon's jaw set, but he nodded curtly. "Of course, Detective. Whatever you need. Folks, please give Detective Owens your full attention. Two people just left on an errand," he said.

Owens scanned the group. "I'll catch them when they return. Everyone else here? Where's your golden boy?"

"Kyle? He'll be joining us later," Sheldon said, casual as ever.

"Good. Hopefully before I leave," Owens said. "And, Sheldon," he said, snapping his fingers. "Do you have contact information for Pierre's family? We aren't having any luck tracking anyone down to notify."

Sheldon looked blank. "I actually don't think I do," he said. "I'll have to ask my assistant, Joaquin. He's keeper of all the records. He's out at the moment."

Owens nodded, then looked over the group. "Who wants to talk first? We can meet right in your suites. I heard you have some nice accommodations."

Chapter 13

Maria went first, since she really wanted to get out for some cannoli time in downtown Newport. Owens came to their suite. Stan grabbed one of the investor packets off the kitchen table, headed upstairs to her room, and quietly locked the door behind her. She tucked the packet in her bag to read later and hoped Therese was fine with the couch for the rest of the weekend, because she did not want to share a room with the disagreeable young woman. She wanted a space no one else could invade. Nutty didn't want company either. He sprawled in the center of the other bed, legs in the air, one paw covering his face. He didn't even stir when she came in.

She sat on the bed, taking a moment to center herself. If she were home, she'd go to the kitchen and bake if she were feeling like this—adrift, sad, anxious. Here, she'd have to share the space with virtual strangers. Any one of whom could've, theoretically, been involved in Pierre LaPorte's murder. At home, she could make herself some of Izzy's coffee or tea, put some jazz music on, and lose herself in new recipes and the feel of dough

between her fingers. Instead, she had to go talk to a cop
about a guy who'd gotten his throat cut. She wondered
sometimes about the way her life had turned out.

She leaned back against the pillows, intending to rest
just for a minute. Next thing she knew Maria banged on
the door and called her name. She'd totally fallen
asleep. Jumping up, she hurried over to open the door.

"I'm coming," she said, trying to smooth her hair
back into place.

Maria stared at her. "You taking a nap?"

"Just resting for a minute. He ready for me?"

"Yes. Be careful what you say," she said in a stage
whisper. "He's looking to pin this on one of us."

Because one of "us" probably did it. Stan managed a
smile and nodded. "Got it. Thanks." She waited until
Maria disappeared up to her room, then shut the door
behind her and walked downstairs.

Owens sat on a stool at the counter, notebook open.
She slid onto the seat opposite him. Stan got the vibe
that behind the all-business demeanor hid a good cop,
one who cared. But he had to figure out who were the
bad guys and who were the good. Her turn to prove
which side of that fence she lived on. She didn't envy
his job.

"Ms. Connor. Thanks for taking the time again. How
are you doing?" he asked.

"Fine."

"Yeah?" His cop eyes searched hers, looking for—
what? Lies? Guilt? A weighty conscience? "That had to
be a disturbing find yesterday."

"Of course it was." She shuddered a little just thinking about it.

"Although, not completely a foreign concept to you."

His casual tone belied his the glint in his eyes. The guy had done his homework.

"Meaning?" she asked, struggling to keep her tone casual.

"Well, you've come across your share of murder victims, right?" He flipped his pad open and read from it. "Carole Morganwick, the veterinarian whom you stumbled upon in her office last year. And you were part of the crowd that found the farmer's body—Hal Hoffman—in a corn maze? And the Frog Ledge town historian."

Stan sat up straight. "So what are you insinuating? They caught the murderer in all those cases."

Owens flipped back to his blank page. "I'm not insinuating anything. Just making an observation. Seems like an unfortunate coincidence it should happen to you again here."

Stan said nothing. Owens let it go.

"So anything else come to mind since we last spoke?" he asked.

"No."

"Any rumblings among the group? Speculation on who would've wanted him dead? Names of people Mr. LaPorte may have had a beef with? Or people who may have had a beef with him?"

Just Sheldon. Stan shoved the thought away. Frederick, the motorcycle-riding chef, came to mind again, but she didn't want to mention him and have it come back to haunt her. Especially since Sheldon had been the only source of that information. "No."

"You know anything about his family?"

Maria appeared again, this time with her purse on her shoulder. She ignored them as she hurried out the door, closing it behind her with a *click.*

"I don't," Stan said. "I'm sorry. I'd never actually met Pierre, remember?"

"You're right. My mistake. Tell me about your business," he said, changing gears.

"My business?"

"Yes. I have a dog. I'm interested in hearing more about what you do."

"What kind of dog?" she asked, feeling her guard drop a bit.

"Rescue pup. He's a Lab mix."

"Rescues are the best. And feeding him organic, human-grade food is the best thing for him." Stan gave him the elevator speech about Pawsitively Organic, her mission, and why she'd started the business.

When she finished he said, "Sounds fascinating. Do you take orders?"

"I do. For both treats and meals. I do parties, too."

"You'll have to leave me your card," Owens said. "So how did you come to know Mr. Allyn?"

"Sheldon heard about my treats through a friend who does rescue. He approached me last year at an event I did. This was during the Carole Morganwick . . . incident, and our conversations never amounted to anything. Then last winter I did a doggie wedding—"

"A what?" Owens interrupted.

"A dog wedding," Stan said, unflinching. She had no shame about hosting that event. The old Stan would've made a joke about it, or worse, offered some apology for doing something that other people found idiotic. "Two rescue dogs. They already lived in the same house," she added.

A smile twitched at the corner of Owens's lips. "Okay. So Mr. Allyn heard about this how?"

"Social media. I had the wedding plans splashed all over Facebook and Instagram. Well, my assistant did.

She loves social media. Anyway, he showed up and asked me if I wanted to give it another go, and said he had big plans for a pet patisserie."

"And here you are," Owens said.

"It wasn't that easy. He wanted me to do it in a real city. I said I wasn't leaving Frog Ledge—that's my town in Connecticut—but I would love to do it there. It took him a while to come around."

"But you didn't back down."

"Nope. I didn't need what he was offering. I wanted it. There's a difference."

Owens nodded. "And something tells me you're not like your colleagues."

She shrugged. "I can't comment. I don't know much about them."

"I didn't think so."

Stan couldn't tell if that was a compliment or not, but decided it was time to change the subject. "Do you know who actually saw Pierre last?"

"I'm the one asking the questions here," Owens said.

"Of course. But maybe it'll help you to talk it through," she said.

"I'm sure it will," Owens said. "With a colleague. One with a badge."

"Did you find a murder weapon?" she asked.

Owens raised an eyebrow. "Why? Do you have a tip?"

"No, but I'm curious."

He regarded her with that look she knew so well from Jessie—the one that said, *Nice try.* "Ms. Connor—"

"Call me Stan."

He frowned. "Again, I'm happy to take any information you have."

"I don't have any. Did any of the cars pan out?"

He set his jaw. "We found nothing of interest in any of the cars."

"What about Pierre's luggage? He had to have luggage somewhere. Any sign of it?"

"You're persistent, I have to give you that," Owens said.

Stan smiled. "I try. Was Kyle's car in the parking lot?"

Owens's eyes narrowed. "Why?"

Stan shrugged. "He's not here."

"Didn't Sheldon say a couple of people went out?"

"Yes. Joaquin and Therese, to buy food." She let the implication hang.

"But he doesn't know where Kyle is."

Stan shook her head. "No one seems to."

"Interesting." He scribbled a note and snapped his notebook shut. "Thanks for your time. Keep both eyes open this weekend, and be careful. Call me if you think of anything else."

Chapter 14

Stan showed Owens out and went back to her room, deep in thought. Had Kyle just gone out and Marcin panicked? He could've been simply overwhelmed and needed to leave this environment. His colleague had been murdered at the house they were supposed to share for the weekend. That was a lot for any of them to absorb. Maybe he'd show up for dinner, apologetic and ready to cook. Stan hoped that was the case.

She locked the bedroom door behind her. Nutty still slept. This time he opened one eye and observed her, then decided he wasn't interested in debriefing and went back to sleep.

Stan grabbed her iPad out of her purse and flopped onto her own bed again, hoping she didn't fall asleep. She needed to find out more about the people with whom she was supposed to spend the next three and a half days. And Pierre, in case there was anything in his past that would direct her with blinking lights to his killer.

She Googled Pierre first. A story about an award for which he'd been nominated last year came up at the top of the feed. The picture accompanying the story showed a dashing Pierre on a red carpet and an elegant, movie-star-looking woman with acres of blond hair. He had his hand on the waist of her tiny, fire engine red minidress. They both smiled at the camera. A girlfriend? She made a note in her notes app to ask around about his love interests. According to the story, he hadn't won the award, which had been for Best Bakeries in NYC. He'd lost to a place called Sugar.

She zoomed in on the picture and studied it. Pierre hadn't simply been handsome. He had a perfectly proportioned face, with strong cheekbones, a well-defined chin and jaw that didn't overshadow his other features but accentuated them. Good hair, not too short, not too long, no obvious product holding it in place. A tiny earring glinted in one ear. In the picture he wore a Cheshire-cat smile with his three-piece suit.

She searched his name and "arrest." Nothing came up. Maybe Sheldon had helped get it squashed. Or maybe he'd lied. She looked up Pierre's bakery. Big potential for drama there—his pastries could have come under fire, or perhaps he'd gotten a bad rating from the health department. But she couldn't find anything other than a couple of five-star reviews on Yelp and someone ranting and raving about his amazing lemon blueberry cupcakes with ginger frosting. Which admittedly sounded pretty delish.

She started a new search and typed Maria's name, taking some juvenile satisfaction in learning that she'd been right. The Italian chef did hail from New Jersey, not Italy. But her restaurants had phenomenal reviews. Maria had been lauded as a chef to watch by *Food USA* and received an award for her marinara sauce; she'd been named an ethnic chef to watch by *International Food Times*; celebrities including George Clooney and Oprah frequented her restaurants. Luigi Rosa was her fourth husband. She'd lost her mother last year and named her signature dish after her: Fettuccine à la Lucia.

Maria had proximity to Pierre, both from her hometown in New Jersey and her restaurant in New York. Stan couldn't figure out from the articles where Maria currently resided, but would bet she hadn't strayed far from her roots. Or her restaurant. So how many of Pierre's fancy pastries had she paired with her fettuccine? Or did she make her own cannoli?

She added the word "scandal" to her search. An interesting headline popped up: RESTAURANT OWNER QUESTIONED IN MOB FAMILY EXTORTION CASE. The three-year-old piece identified Maria as a cousin on her mother's side to the New Jersey Scalia family. Stan's eyes widened. Maria's family had heavy mob ties. Apparently one of the main players, Joseph Scalia, had been picked up in an extortion case. There were questions about how far into the extended family the extortion had gone. Maria claimed ignorance in the lone piece. Stan Googled Joseph and found that he'd been sentenced to fifteen years. That certainly put a new spin on this. Although mobsters tended to shoot, not slice. At least that's what she'd learned from *The Sopranos*.

After bookmarking those pages, she ran through a mental list of her cohorts and decided to search for Marcin next. The search results had just popped up with a photo of Marcin and Leo together on the red carpet somewhere when her phone rang, startling her. She jumped nearly a foot off the bed, almost throwing her iPad in the process. Nutty dove under the bed, awakened by her insane scrambling.

Jeez, Stan. Relax. She grabbed the phone off the night table and answered.

"Krissie?"

Her eyes widened at the voice on the other end. "Caitlyn?" No one called her that but her younger sister. Caitlyn didn't approve of her chosen nickname either—her mother's daughter—and instead had christened her with her own nickname when they were kids. Which Stan hated. But that was typical of their relationship. At four years apart and completely different personalities, they'd always just missed each other's wavelength.

"What's going on? Is something wrong?" It wasn't like Caitlyn to call her out of the blue, and it had been months—maybe longer—since their last conversation. They weren't exactly best buds. She and Caitlyn were only four years apart in age, but it may as well have been a lifetime given their different paths.

"Are you in Rhode Island? I heard you were."

"I am. How did you know that?"

Caitlyn ignored the question. "Are you busy?"

Stan cast a longing glance at her blankets and super-soft pillow. "Not until eight. Why?"

"Can you meet me?" Caitlyn asked. A note of urgency had creeped into her voice. "I really need to talk to you."

"I don't have my car," Stan said.

"I'll pick you up. *Please.*"

Caitlyn Connor Fitzgerald never begged. She'd never had to. Stan couldn't remember her ever wanting for anything. And if she did, someone—usually their mother or Caitlyn's husband, Michael—made sure she had it within the blink of an eye. Unlike Stan, Caitlyn had embraced the rich and privileged lifestyle easily and effortlessly. And if she did need something, chances were she'd reach out to people other than her older sister.

Unless it was serious and not for prime time. Stan had a sudden, disturbing thought.

"Is Mom okay?" she asked. Her relationship with her mother had hit another rough patch last winter, and their contact had been minimal despite her mother's ongoing relationship with the mayor of Frog Ledge. Talk about awkward. Frog Ledge was small enough— her mother's presence made it claustrophobic. But lately she hadn't been around much.

"Mom's fine," Caitlyn said dismissively. "She's away until Sunday. This is about *me*."

"Of course it is." Stan rolled her eyes. *Wasn't it always?* She checked her watch. Almost four. "Sure, I can slip away for a bit. I'm at the Newport Premier."

Caitlyn promised to be there in twenty minutes. Stan dragged herself to the bathroom to freshen up, the familiar family-drama dread settling in her belly. What could Caitlyn possibly need to talk to her about? Why this weekend, of all weekends? And more importantly, how had her sister known she was in town?

Chapter 15

Nutty had moved to the velvet bed with jewel trim strategically positioned on the windowsill. He didn't give her the time of day before she left. Stan made sure he had snacks, left her iPod on playing her cat-calming CD for him, then grabbed her bag and went downstairs. Leonardo and Sheldon sat in cushy chairs in the lobby near the elevator doors, talking quietly. They looked up when she got off the elevator, and Sheldon raised an eyebrow. "Are you walking, or do you need my car?"

Stan gaped at him. She didn't know if she was more surprised that he'd let her borrow the pink Cadillac, or horrified at the thought of driving that beast around. Especially where people might know her. "My sister's picking me up. She needed to . . . give me something."

"Ah. Well, I'll walk you out," Sheldon said. "Be back, Leo."

Leo raised his glass. "Enjoy."

Sheldon waited until they were through the revolving door, then said, "Things have been quiet so far, but I've heard rumblings that we'll need to be aware of."

"Such as?"

He glanced behind him. "I don't want to say it now. We can talk later tonight after our cooking session," Sheldon said.

Great. Another fun-filled night to look forward to. "By the way—what's Pierre's real name?" Stan asked.

"What do you mean?"

"Come on, Sheldon. If he's from some little town in Michigan, he must have given his name a little tweak to get it so French sounding," Stan said. "I'm sure that's why the cops can't find his family. Did you really not know, or were you stalling?"

"Stalling! Never. We simply had to refresh our memories." He smiled. "Joaquin dropped off our food, and I've sent him to the office to see if there's emergency contact information in our files. When Pierre came to work with us we weren't automated, and some of that information is filed away in the basement of our office. What can I say?" Sheldon shrugged. "Short staffed."

Stan waited.

"What?" Sheldon asked.

"His name? If I know it, I can be on the lookout for anyone talking about it. If I don't, I can't help you."

Sheldon didn't like being backed into a corner. Stan could see his brain running quick rationales and calculations before he answered. "It's Pete Landsdowne."

Definitely not a name that conjured up an image of an eclectic French pastry chef. Stan pulled out her phone and tapped the name into her notes. "I'll let you know if I hear anything. Did Kyle get here yet?"

Sheldon shook his head.

"Heard from him?"

Another shake.

"What if he doesn't come back?"

"He'll come back," Sheldon said. "Don't you worry." He blew her a kiss, then went inside.

Stan sat on the bench out front to wait for her sister. She realized she had no idea what Caitlyn drove. She felt a pang of regret about her dysfunctional relationships with her mom and sister. A black Jaguar SUV careened into the driveway and parked in the valet curve. The passenger window whizzed down. "Get in," her sister said.

Stan obliged. The car sped away before she'd even completely closed her door.

Caitlyn waited until they'd exited the hotel's long driveway before leaning over to air kiss Stan. Her Jackie O sunglasses smacked Stan on the temple but she made no move to remove them. "Thanks for coming," she said, before hitting the gas again, jerking Stan back against her seat. The one thing they had in common— aggressive driving skills.

"Not a problem," Stan said, adjusting her seat belt. "You look great. Your hair is different." Stan regarded her sister from the side. Her blond hair was cut shorter in the back, left longer in the front, with red highlighted strands sweeping across her forehead. The colors accented her tanned skin. She wore a casual chic sundress in a vibrant teal. Stan bet on matching shoes and a matching purse somewhere in the car. Caitlyn always looked good. Then again, she spent most of her time at spas or shopping.

"Thanks," Caitlyn said. "You do, too. It's . . . been way too long."

Stan raised an eyebrow. Again, unlike her sister's usual demeanor. Maybe she'd mellowed with age.

"It has. So where are we going?"

"I thought we could get coffee."

"Coffee's good. Where's Eva?" Stan hadn't seen her six-year-old niece since last year, which made her feel like a bad auntie. She sent the little girl a gift every Christmas and every March for her birthday, but without her presence that's all it was—a gift from some faceless person.

"With her nanny." Instead of heading into downtown Newport, Caitlyn drove down Ocean Avenue past First Beach, heading into Middletown. "I thought we could go somewhere quiet," she said at Stan's questioning look.

Stan shrugged. "Fine with me."

Five minutes later, they pulled into the parking lot of a small, happy-looking café. The bright yellow building had a sign out front depicting smiling people standing next to a pile of coffee grounds holding letters that spelled out GROUNDS OF HOPE.

"They support local charities," Caitlyn said. "And the coffee is fabulous." She shoved open her car door and got out, reaching into the backseat for her purse. Stan noted the matching shoes—Manolos, of course. Fabulous shoe taste did run in the family. Stan still loved her shoe collection, even though she didn't dress up nearly as much these days.

Stan got out of the car and followed her inside. Caitlyn took her glasses off, settling them on top of her head. Stan saw dark circles under her eyes beneath the perfect makeup.

Caitlyn went right to the counter and ordered a skinny vanilla latte with an extra shot of espresso. Stan ordered an iced coffee. Caitlyn pulled an American Express gold card out of her purse and handed it to the barista.

"I'm buying," Stan began, but Caitlyn waved her off.

"It's the least I can do for interrupting your weekend. . . . You can add fifty dollars for the Boys and Girls Club," she told the young girl behind the counter with the silver hoop in her lip.

"You rock! Thank you so much. Enjoy your drinks," the girl said.

Stan raised an eyebrow. Caitlyn going to a charity-driven coffee shop? Her sister usually didn't concern herself with those in need. Not that she was mean or unfeeling—Caitlyn simply didn't think of many people but herself and her small circle. Then again, Stan hadn't really seen much of her in the past few years. Maybe she'd had an epiphany and changed her ways.

Caitlyn didn't speak again until they'd collected their drinks and retreated to a table in the back.

Stan's cell vibrated. She checked the readout. Brenna. She felt another pang of homesickness, but pushed it aside. She'd have to call her later. She pressed Ignore and focused on her sister. "So what's up? And how'd you know I was here?"

"I have a situation," Caitlyn said, deflecting the question.

Stan sipped her iced coffee. Delicious, but made her miss Izzy's gourmet coffee. Izzy Sweet's Sweets in Frog Ledge was, next to McSwigg's, her favorite place. "What kind of situation?"

Caitlyn fidgeted a bit in her seat. She'd never been good at cutting to the chase. "Kyle McLeod," she said finally.

Stan's eyes widened. "The chef?"

"Yes."

"The same vegan chef from Florida who's supposed to be at this retreat with me?"

"Yes," Caitlyn said impatiently.

Stan tried to make the connection. "How do you know Kyle McLeod?"

"We'll get to that," Caitlyn said. "The important thing is, he's missing. And I think he's in trouble."

Chapter 16

Stan stared at her sister, not quite sure how to respond. "Forgive me for being dense, but I'm not following you. Let's back up to my first question. How do you know Kyle?"

It wasn't until the blush rose up her sister's neck, slowly turning her pale skin red, that she caught on. "Caitlyn."

"We've been seeing each other," Caitlyn said evenly. "And I don't want to hear it if you're going to criticize me."

Stan's gaze dropped to her sister's left hand and the giant diamond ring and matching wedding band. Caitlyn curled her fingers defensively. "Michael and I . . . have been having problems for a while now."

Don't judge. Do not judge. "Okay," Stan said carefully. "Where did you meet him?"

"He's been spending time in the area. Working with that weirdo chef guy."

"Sheldon Allyn," Stan said.

"Yeah. Him. You're working with him, too."

"Sheldon and I are working on a business plan," Stan

said. "But I hadn't met Kyle or any of the other chefs before this weekend."

Caitlyn nodded, running her finger around and around the top of her coffee cup lid. "Kyle's opening a new restaurant with him. He's been here looking at locations, working on menus, the whole nine. And teaching at Johnson and Wales one semester a year. That's where I met him, a year or so ago. I took his basic cooking class." She smiled wryly. "I thought I could get Michael interested in me again if I was a better cook. So lame, right?"

Stan felt sorry for her. "Not at all."

"I found out later Kyle's vegan. How funny is that? He wasn't thrilled about the menu for the class. But anyway, he was very sweet. One night I stayed late. I was having trouble with my lemon meringue pie. We got to talking . . . and the rest is history."

"Why did he teach the class if he didn't want to?"

"Maybe he needed the money, or was doing someone a favor. I didn't ask," Caitlyn said. "Honestly, I hadn't heard of him as a fancy chef or anything, so I didn't know."

"So he lives here?"

"No. He lives in Boca Raton. With his wife." She made a face. "He spends a semester or two here, but I think he had plans to be here more because of the restaurant."

Good grief. Caitlyn had always known how to do drama well. "Okay," Stan said again. "So Kyle's married, you're married—I'm just stating the obvious," she said when Caitlyn opened her mouth in protest.

"Our marital statuses are not the point. The point is that other chef got killed and now Kyle is missing."

Stan's body tensed, going on high alert. "How do you know about anyone getting killed?"

Caitlyn sighed. "He told me. He called me after it happened. While you were waiting for the police. He was pretty upset."

"Was he afraid? Did you get the sense he thought he was in danger?"

"I don't know. He was . . . upset. In shock, I think."

Hopefully not because he killed Pierre and was trying to figure out how to cover it up. Stan pushed the thought away. "So why do you think he's missing?"

"Because . . ." Caitlyn glanced furtively around the café, gauging the hearing distance of the few other customers. "We were supposed to meet last night and he never showed up. That's not like him."

"What time were you supposed to meet?"

"Ten. He figured that would be enough time to get done with everything. He said he really wanted to see me."

"Where were Michael and Eva?"

Caitlyn's eyes dropped to the table. "Michael's traveling. The nanny lives in, so Eva's no problem."

"Where were you going?"

"We were meeting downtown. We've been finding new places to meet, not going to his apartment much lately."

Stan sat up straight. Of course. If Kyle spent that much time here, he needed a place to live. "Where's his apartment? Have you checked there?"

"He has a place right near the river in Providence. I called, but no answer," Caitlyn said. "I didn't have time to drive all the way to Providence. My nanny had a doctor's appointment this morning. I don't have a key anyway. But I'm telling you, something's wrong."

Something was definitely wrong. Pierre was dead and Kyle's absence screamed either *guilty* or . . . "Why don't you have a key?" Stan asked.

Caitlyn shrugged. "He had to get the lock changed last month. Like I said, we haven't been spending time there lately."

"It's his place?"

"Who else's place would it be?"

Stan didn't answer that, but she wondered if Sheldon might be financing this venture also.

"Krissie. I need to find him." Caitlyn looked desperate.

"Do you think he's in trouble because you haven't heard from him? Or is there another reason?"

"Are you kidding me? Someone killed his buddy. Why wouldn't he think he was in trouble?"

"They were buddies?" Kyle hadn't given any indication he and Pierre had been close in that whole half hour she'd spent with him.

"Well, if they're spending the weekend together I figured they were," Caitlyn said.

"Not necessarily. I'm spending the weekend with them and I don't know any of them. I'd never even met the dead guy." That image of Pierre in a pool of blood flashed through her mind again, turning her stomach. "Finding his body would've been even worse if I'd known him."

"You found his body?" Eyes wide, Caitlyn leaned forward. "That's horrible. Was it horrible?"

"Of course it was horrible. Did you know the man who died? Did Kyle ever introduce you?"

"No. I never met any of them. Do you think it's some plot to kill the chefs?" she asked.

"Thanks," Stan said. "Did you forget I'm one of the chefs?"

No answer to that. Stan could see the wheels turning in her sister's head. "Well, you're not missing," Caitlyn said finally.

This conversation was starting to make her head hurt.

"Did you check the hospital? I hate to say it, but maybe he was in an accident."

"Thought of that," Caitlyn said. "No one with his name or description was admitted. Plus he had no car. I was supposed to pick him up."

"Does he have a lot of friends around here? Would he have asked someone else to come get him?" Stan asked.

Caitlyn shook her head. "He was always so busy with the restaurant deal. He worked so hard on it, plus trying to manage his place in Boca, too. No, he didn't just go out to a party and forget we had plans. Kyle would *never* do that to me. If he says he's coming, he'll come. Unless . . . he can't."

Whatever else her sister held back, she was telling the truth about that. Or at least what she believed to be the truth. "So what can I do?" Stan asked.

"I need you to help me find him."

Stan leaned back in her chair and looked around the café. There still weren't a lot of people in it. A young couple talked softly over a muffin they shared. The girl looked pensive, the guy brooding. They reminded her of the Hemingway story "Hills Like White Elephants." A man wearing a leather cap read a newspaper on one of the window stools. Stan could see his face in the reflection of the window—frown lines, bushy eyebrows, and a goatee. His eyes met hers. He looked away first.

She refocused on her sister. "What do you think I'll be able to do that you can't?"

"I don't know. You're in with these guys; they have to know something."

"No one seems to know anything." Stan checked her watch. It was almost seven. "I'll see what I can do, Caitlyn. Look, we're all here for this big event. It's still moving forward, despite the fact that we're down one chef. There's still a chance Kyle could show. I know Sheldon believes he'll be back. And Sheldon holds the purse strings. He may answer him. I'll keep my ears open, but I can't promise anything."

She hoped that would be enough, but Caitlyn didn't look satisfied. "I'm telling you, he's in trouble," she insisted. "I know some places where he hangs out, but it's hard for me to be everywhere because of Eva. Maybe you can ask some questions. Make some calls. I have names." Caitlyn slid a sheet of paper across the table. "These are his colleagues at the school. And his wife's number is on there." She wrinkled her nose and tapped at a name. Dahianna McLeod.

Stan looked at her in amazement. "You want me to call his wife? And say what? My sister, who's been sleeping with your husband, is worried because he missed a rendezvous?"

Caitlyn drew herself up into that haughty pose Stan knew so well from her mother—shoulders back, chest puffed, head high, lips pressed in a thin line. "You don't need to be vulgar," she said, sounding exactly like Patricia. "You're working with him this weekend. Everyone is concerned for his whereabouts. Has she heard from him? That's what I meant. I tried his house last night. I blocked my number and hung up when *she* answered. I know I shouldn't have called. I just hoped he might answer so I could hear he was okay. Although in retrospect, it was a little crazy to think he'd made it back to Florida that fast."

It did sound crazy, but one never knew in this celebrity foodie world. "Does he have access to transportation that could do that? Like a private plane or helicopter?"

Caitlyn laughed. "Not that I know of. He wasn't that famous." She sobered. "Yet. He totally could be. His specialty is so necessary. More people should be vegan, don't you think?"

The last Stan knew, her sister had been the furthest thing from vegan, but she didn't say that.

Caitlyn snapped her fingers. "But that reminds me. Here's his license plate number." She grabbed the paper and scribbled it, then slid it back to Stan. "He drives a black Jeep. Just in case."

Stan folded the paper and slipped it into her bag. "I have to get back, but I need you to make a detour on the way."

"To where?"

"Downtown. The parking area. I need my car."

Chapter 17

Free at last. Her own space made all the difference, even if it was just a car. Still sitting in the open parking lot, Stan cranked her sunroof open and breathed in the ocean air. Nice to have some distance from the alternate universe she'd fallen into yesterday after arriving at Sheldon's Retreat for Top Chefs. She considered driving straight to Frog Ledge, and would've done it if Nutty wasn't still locked away in the hotel. Instead, she sat and processed the recent events.

One man murdered. Another missing. And her sister, smack in the middle of it.

She hadn't expected Caitlyn's bombshell. Her sister had married young—young to Stan, anyway, although twenty-five seemed perfectly acceptable to most people—but she'd always seemed content. At least until now. Or however long she'd been screwing around with McLeod.

A motorcycle revved nearby, shaking Stan out of her thoughts. She started her car, but before she drove to the exit she cruised the parking lot. In the back, the very last space closest to the docks, was a black Jeep.

She compared the license plate to the one Caitlyn had scribbled on the back of a receipt to the Coach store. Bingo. Leaving her car running, she got out and investigated.

Which meant walking around the Jeep and trying the doors. As expected, they were all locked. She cupped her hands around her eyes and peered through the driver's side window. Spotless interior. It looked brand new. The leather seats gleamed. A travel coffee mug sat in the cup holder. A sweatshirt hung over the passenger seat back. Otherwise, nothing out of place. No map to where he might have gone. No note confessing to killing Pierre, or ransom note left by a crazed kidnapper. No suspicious luggage or bags that could belong to the dead man. Of course the police had already searched their cars.

Stan got back into her car and drove slowly back to the hotel. What if Kyle *had* been taken? Who could've pulled that off? Kyle was a decent-sized guy. He wouldn't have gone without a fight if he didn't want to go in the first place. Unless a weapon or a very big, scary person was involved.

But she had to play devil's advocate. If Kyle had killed Pierre in the heat of the moment, he could've panicked and taken off. He could've walked to Ocean Avenue and caught a cab, called someone, heck, rented a bicycle. She remembered his cryptic words about hoping their activities this weekend wouldn't get them thrown in jail, and how she should expect the unexpected. Sarcasm, or foreshadowing?

The street leading to the hotel had no unusual activity. No media trucks yet, so obviously Pierre's name and the connection to Sheldon and crew hadn't broken yet.

No news was good news. Cars jammed the parking lot, and people in various stages of fancy clothing wandered around the lobby when Stan swung in. It was seven fifty-nine. She didn't bother going upstairs first—Sheldon would probably throw a fit if she showed up late. Instead, she stopped by the front desk and asked for directions to the secret kitchen.

"Oh! You're part of Sheldon's party." The clerk, a twenty-something who towered above the counter like a basketball player, grinned at her. His sparkling white teeth gleamed against his dark skin. "I'll take you. Ralphie, cover?"

His companion, an older, sour-looking man, nodded.

"You guys gonna be making some phat food, huh?" He bounced along down the hall. Stan had to work to keep up with his long-legged gait.

"We are," she said. "You should stop by and sample."

"Dude, I'm so *there*." He rubbed his hands together in glee. "We get Sheldon's pastries shipped in sometimes for events. Sometimes Lucy gets them just for the heck of it, 'cause she loves us." He winked at her. "Make sure you save me some." He led her to the main ballroom—an exquisite room that could easily seat five hundred or so guests—in the back of the hotel. It overlooked a small pond and a beautifully landscaped grass area. A large tent had been set up for a party. In the back of the room a door paneled exactly like the walls hid in plain sight. He pushed it open and held it for her. "Ta-da! And that large table out here is for you guys to use." He pointed to a table with place settings on it. "In case you want to eat together."

She smiled. "Thanks so much."

"Anytime, miss. I'm Jamal, if you need anything else."

"Thanks, Jamal. Hey, before you go, were you working last night?"

Jamal shook his head. "I'm working the whole weekend, so I had last night off. Why? Everything okay with your service?"

"It was perfect," Stan assured him. "I'm asking because one of our friends left and hasn't come back yet. We wondered if anyone saw him leave or knew where he might have gone."

"Hmmm," Jamal thought. "I could ask Sheila. Or Lucy. They both worked last night. Lucy's all over the place, but she may know. What's the dude's name?"

Lucy worked last night? Stan wondered why she'd left the hotel so early. She'd seen her from her window around eight, getting into her silver SUV and driving off. Maybe she'd gone to get something to eat on her lunch break and come back. "You know what? Don't worry about it. I can ask Lucy myself. But thank you so much."

"You sure?" Jamal asked. "I don't mind."

"Positive," she said.

Jamal nodded and went back to work. Stan entered the kitchen. Only Maria and Joaquin were there, laughing over a cutting board full of veggies. "Hey," she said.

They both turned. *"Bella!"* Maria exclaimed, coming over to hug Stan. "We missed you!"

Stan hugged her back warily. She thought Maria had a couple of personalities going, but she'd take the friendly one any day over the one calling her a stupid skinny girl.

Joaquin winked at her. "Totally. But she just went and stole your cat to make up for it."

Stan registered Nutty in a corner of the room, ensconced in his own chair—a fluffy white cat bed on top of a silver swivel base. He glanced at her, his tail flicking disinterestedly, then looked away and continued nibbling at the food in front of him. The plate looked suspiciously like china.

"Wow, look at you getting star treatment," Stan said. "Are you here to test my food or theirs?"

"Both!" Maria beamed. "He's too skinny. He needs to fatten up."

Spoken like a true Italian. Stan didn't agree, but she bit her tongue.

"I hope you don't mind I borrowed him," Maria said. "He sounded so lonely, howling in there!"

"He was howling?" Stan felt guilty. "My poor guy. Of course I don't mind." She hurried over and gave him a kiss. Nutty barely noticed.

"Everyone should be down any minute now." Maria checked her watch. "And Sheldon has some big news!"

Everyone else showed up together at eight on the dot. Aside from Kyle, Therese and Tyler were absent. Sheldon took Nutty's stool and moved it to a more prominent position, then sat on the counter, next to it. He looked more like himself wearing a purple suit, lime green tie, and his silver shoes. He still looked tired, but had covered it with some makeup. His hair was swooped and gelled into a wave atop his head.

"Welcome to our first official planning session!" he exclaimed. "Since we didn't get to do this last night, we're going to have to work a little harder today. But I know you're all up to it. I'll tell you what I'd like to do. We're going to give three menu options to our guests on Monday, and we're going to spend the rest of the weekend perfecting them. Aaaannnnnddddd"—he drew the word out to prolong the moment—"thanks to Joaquin's dedication and charm, we're going to welcome a new guest, Vaughn Dawes, to help fill the enormous hole Pierre has left. Vaughn is due to arrive late tonight, isn't that right, Joaquin?"

Joaquin nodded. "Therese is on her way to pick her up at the airport. She declined a car service and opted for a taxi, but I don't feel right allowing that. We should provide her with star treatment."

"Fabulous, my dear boy," Sheldon said, rubbing his hands together. "I am *so* grateful to you for holding me together!"

"That's great," Stan said. "Where's Vaughn coming from?"

"She's out in LA," Sheldon said.

"LA? Wow. That's a haul."

Sheldon's eyes narrowed. She'd probably get her hand slapped for questioning him later. But why *was* he sending for someone from clear across the country? Couldn't he use his own bakers from Every Sweet Thing? She filed that under her mental list of Odd Things Sheldon Was Doing.

"She's worth it," he said shortly.

"I'm sure. But what about someone from your shop?"

Silence. Then he laughed. "My dear, these aren't fruit puffs for Aunt Rosie's birthday party. These are serious menu items for very rich people. Trust me, we want Vaughn." He started to say something else, but Stan interrupted again.

"Have you heard from Kyle?" she asked.

Leo and Maria exchanged looks. Like they were cringing for her.

"I have not," Sheldon said. "But I'm confident whatever business he had to attend to will be finished soon and he'll join us for this important event."

Fabulous nonanswer. Sheldon would've been great in corporate America. Stan opened her mouth again, but Sheldon cut her off.

"So," he went on, focusing on the others, "tonight I'd like to brainstorm menu items. Maria is cooking us a sauce while we do so." Maria bowed at the waist, still brandishing her large knife. "Joaquin and Therese retrieved all the items on the shopping list, so we are indebted to them. And if we'd like to start cooking or baking, we can do so. Whatever ingredients we need that aren't currently on hand, we'll make arrangements to have delivered or picked up tomorrow. Does that sound fabulous?"

"Absolutely fabulous," Leonardo declared. They all nodded in agreement except for Marcin, who looked like he thought the whole thing was anything but fabulous. Stan could think of a million more fabulous things she could be doing, but she was here now. All in.

"Okay, then. Let's discuss our soups."

While the group engaged in a dialogue about soup and other courses, Stan went to the fridge. Joaquin and Therese had stocked it full of goodies from local farms. She took out her salad items and the shrimp to grill, along with fresh blueberries, honey, coconut flour, and oats to make some simple treats for Nutty. It had been a while since she'd had her hands in dough. She thought of Brenna, envious that she got to do all the baking for their orders this weekend, and made a mental note to call her back.

"Are you making cat snacks?" Marcin inquired, coming up behind her.

"Yes. Blueberry. Nutty's favorite."

"Will you be serving those at the event?"

"I'm sure I can put them on the menu. It's always nice to have a simple option for the finicky cats."

Marcin leaned closer, as if fascinated with that option.

"This whole thing is absurd, you know," he said instead, dropping his voice.

"What do you mean?" Stan asked.

"I mean, to make us stay here and go through with this dinner thing is crazy."

He hadn't dropped his voice low enough. Maria turned from her tomatoes and frowned at him. "Did you forget your meds today?"

Marcin looked like he wanted to shoot a death ray out of his eyeballs at her. He turned and left the room without another word.

Sheldon watched him go, eyes narrowing. "Where in the world does he think he's going?" he muttered to no one in particular.

Meds? Stan wondered what kind. These people had more secrets than Imelda Marcos's closet had shoes.

"I guess that means he did. Or maybe he didn't want to take them." Maria stirred the sauce with one arm, and with the other she rubbed under Nutty's chin. Nutty gazed at her with adoring eyes. "I hope your mother didn't mean that you're finicky. You don't look finicky in the least," she cooed at him.

"You have no idea," Stan said.

Maria tsked. "He's a star."

"A star of what?"

"Of our community. He'll be a poster child, for sure. The photographer will adore him."

A poster child? Like Nutty didn't have a big enough head. "He is very photogenic," Stan said. "Will he be part of the photo shoot?"

"But of course!" Sheldon exclaimed. "He's an integral part of this weekend."

Nutty flicked his tail at her as if to say, *See?*

"What if the guest cat is the finicky one?" Maria asked.

Stan didn't want to say how much that worried her. "It's always a possibility with cats," she said breezily. "But I'm sure I can find something tempting enough."

"You had better, my dear," Sheldon said with a nervous laugh. "That cat *must* be delighted!"

Maria snickered. "I highly doubt the cat will be our deciding factor," she said.

Sheldon wagged a finger. "Ah, but you're wrong," he said. "Cat owners are very cognizant of what their pets want. It could very well make or break the deal." He smiled at Stan. "No pressure, my dear."

By the time the menu items were hashed out—Stan offered salmon, chicken, and beef as her main dishes, as well as a choice of vanilla cat-noli, fruit treats, and a strawberry glazed cake for dessert—and Nutty's treats were cooling, Maria's sauce and the grilled shrimp salad were ready. They all gathered around the table with wine. Joaquin had shown off his own pastry prowess by whipping up a strawberry torte for dessert.

"This looks great," a familiar voice behind them said. "Got room for one more?"

Chapter 18

Detective Owens stepped into the room and surveyed the group. "Sorry to interrupt your evening, folks," he said. "Toasting your late colleague, I see?"

Nervous shuffling ensued around the table. He had something in his hand. Stan tried, but couldn't quite make out what was in it.

"Detective Owens! So nice to see you again, although it would be better under different circumstances," Sheldon said. "Can I offer you some strawberry torte?"

"Thanks, but no. Strawberry doesn't agree with me. Looks too much like blood, and I see a lot of that in my world. Speaking of that." His eyes turned steely as they locked on Sheldon. "Your missing chef turn up yet?"

Sheldon shook his head, his face a picture of apology and disappointment. "I'm sad to say, he has not returned. But I'm confident he'll be at the door soon, the picture of remorse."

Owens nodded slowly. "I hope so. Otherwise I'll have to use extra manpower to look for him, and my chief hates when we need extra manpower."

Sheldon cocked his head, confusion pulling his face into an odd expression. "I'm sorry?"

"No, I'm sorry. I'm sorry that when Kyle McLeod turns up, I'm probably going to have to arrest him."

Maria's wineglass crashed to the table, red liquid seeping into the tablecloth. Sheldon's mouth fell open. Leo gaped at the detective. Stan couldn't see everyone else's faces, but she'd bet they were just as shocked. Her sister's face appeared in her mind, pleading for Stan to help her find her boyfriend.

"For what?" she said, when no one else spoke.

Owens's gaze locked on her. "For the murder of Pierre LaPorte. Or Peter Landsdowne, as some know him." He slowly raised the item in his hand. Stan could see through the plastic bag, and the object inside looked . . . menacing. "We found something that looks remarkably like this in a Dumpster behind Mr. McLeod's apartment. Does anyone recognize it?"

They all peered at the bag. No one spoke. Finally Sheldon stepped forward for a closer look. "It's a pizza cutter."

Owens beamed at him. "I wish I had a prize to give you, Mr. Allyn. Yes, it's a pizza cutter. A fancy pizza cutter, not just your average Joe pizza cutter. And I have a YouTube video showing your golden boy chef using something that looked like this very recently."

"Oh, that's hardly evidence pointing to Kyle," Sheldon scoffed. "Do you know how many people use pizza cutters?"

"Most people I know order pizza," Owens said. "Which already comes cut. If you're making frozen pizza and have to cut it yourself, sure. But I did a little research on this. These half moon jobs aren't what I'm going to buy to slice a DiGiorno. These are usually reserved for professionals."

No one said anything for a long minute.

"He *is* a professional," Sheldon pointed out.

"That's what I hear," Owens said. "So why would he throw away one of his tools?"

Another silence. Maria dabbed frantically at the soiled tablecloth with her napkin.

"You are mistaken," Sheldon said. "You see, it would be impossible for Kyle to have committed this murder. He was part of our little game yesterday. Joaquin, tell Detective Owens again what time you met up with Kyle."

Joaquin pulled out his smartphone and called up the calendar. "Of course," he said. "As I mentioned when we first spoke, Detective, Kyle and I rendezvoused at three o'clock at the garage in downtown Newport. We were then together for the rest of the afternoon, right up until Ms. Connor discovered the body. In fact, he was not out of my sight at all." He looked expectantly up at Owens.

Owens nodded. "Thank you, Mr. Leroy. I'll make a note of that. Although it doesn't matter much, because the coroner has determined the time of death to be between noon and two P.M." His gaze hardened. "So Mr. McLeod isn't quite off the hook. If any of you see him or talk to him, I'd highly recommend you advise him to turn himself in. Otherwise, not to worry." He nodded slowly. "We'll find him."

Chapter 19

Stan slipped out of the group in the chaos that followed and headed for her room. She paused at the front desk when she saw Owens leaning against the counter. She approached him.

"Detective?"

He turned.

"Are you sure Kyle's your guy?"

The clerk looked at them curiously. Owens motioned for her to follow him. He moved to a quiet spot in the middle of the lobby. "Have you heard from him?"

"No."

"Ideas where he went?"

"No."

He sighed. "Then why are you talking to me about him?"

"I don't know," Stan said, offering a weak smile. "I just didn't get the murderer vibe from him."

That raised Owens's eyebrows. "Murderer vibe? I wish I had that. It would make these kinds of cases much easier."

Stan flushed. "You know what I mean."

"I really don't, Ms. Connor. But I did find out that

Kyle McLeod's car—or at least a car registered in his name—is still in the parking lot downtown. Which means he either left on foot or got a ride. With whom and why is my burning question."

Stan thought about that. "No security cameras outside the hotel? There have to be in a place like this."

"There are. I'm waiting for the tapes. In the meantime, I hoped one of you might've seen him leave."

"Not me." Stan glanced at the front desk. "Did you try the cab companies?"

Owens looked amused. "Are you looking to change careers? I don't think we have any open positions right now."

Stan went upstairs, locked herself in her room with Nutty, and called her best friend. She'd known Nikki Manning since college when her dog transport had been just a dream based on a couple of road trips saving five dogs. Today, Nikki and her volunteers made two runs each month and rescued hundreds of dogs. She operated out of a farmhouse on twenty acres in another part of Rhode Island. She also knew Stan's family from way back, which made her the perfect ear for Caitlyn's latest drama and the serious turn it had taken.

"So you're not going to believe this," Stan said when she answered.

"Oh jeez. I'm afraid to ask." Nikki sounded relaxed tonight, which meant she was not immediately pre- or post-transport. "Is it about Jake?"

"No. Caitlyn."

"I'm intrigued. Hold on."

An insanely loud grinding sound came through the line. Stan held the phone away from her ear until the noise subsided. "What the heck are you doing?"

"Making a mud-slide," Nikki said.

"My favorite. I'm jealous." Stan pictured her friend in her typical denim shorts and cowboy boots, short black hair standing up in handmade spikes and probably tipped with some crazy color, dogs and cats following her around her messy kitchen.

"You should be. I make mad good mud-slides. If you come over I'll make you one."

"I wish I could. I'm a prisoner for the weekend. Locked away with a bunch of chefs."

"Sounds horrifying," Nikki said. "Now tell me what the prima donna's up to."

Stan filled her in on the events since yesterday—her trip to Newport, her discovery of Pierre's body, Caitlyn's secret and plea for help, and finally, the murder weapon. "So the police are looking hard for her boyfriend," she finished. "But Caitlyn asked me to help her find him. She thinks he's in trouble."

Nikki stayed quiet for so long Stan was afraid she'd fallen asleep from too much mud-slide. "Nik?"

"I'm here," Nikki said. "Don't take this the wrong way, Stan. You've got some murderous black cloud hanging over your head. I have no idea how these things find you. That aside, wow. I didn't think Caitlyn was interesting enough to surprise me, but she's proven me wrong. So is he a murderer, or is he a victim?" She slurped her drink. "No, Scout! No mud-slide for you."

Stan heard a dog whining in the background and smiled. Leave it to Nikki to rescue the pups who liked to drink. "You didn't have to point out the black cloud," she said. "I'm well aware, since I'm the one it's following. I don't know what to do. I told Caitlyn I would help her, but now I'm wondering if she missed a sign or something about this guy."

"You met him?"

"Yeah. We were blindfolded in the back of the pastry truck together."

Silence again. Then Nikki said, "Seriously, *that* I don't want to know about."

Stan giggled. It did sound absurd. Most of the events since yesterday had been absurd. Then she sobered. They'd also been tragic. Someone had died.

"Did you get a bad vibe?"

"I didn't," Stan said. "But maybe the blindfold could've skewed my intuition."

"It's possible," Nikki said. "Or maybe he didn't kill the guy. Maybe he is in trouble. Anyone call his wife?"

"Besides Caitlyn? I'm presuming the police did," Stan said. "But the cops won't tell me, obviously."

Nikki choked on her mud-slide. "Caitlyn called his *wife*? Is this an open relationship or something?" she asked when she could speak again.

"No, she hung up when the wife answered." Then a light dawned. "Hey. Do you know any cops around here?"

"I know a state trooper, but haven't talked to him in a long time. Not sure he would be much help if the locals aren't interested in him poking around."

"No." Stan thought about that. "And my sister doesn't want any publicity."

"I guess not. What is she thinking? Doesn't she have, like, everything she wants? Isn't she married to some fancy rich boy? Not to mention her own cash. And what about her kid?"

Nikki had a good point. To the outside world Caitlyn did have everything. Including her own trust fund if Michael's salary wasn't enough. As for Michael, a big-deal insurance guy, Stan knew financial services well enough to know that the higher up you were and the more money you made, the worse the hours. Maybe he did work too much. "She thinks as long as Eva doesn't know anything it's fine. And I guess she doesn't think she has everything she wants. Or maybe she really is bored and this is one of those cliché affairs. At least it's not her pool boy or something."

Nikki snorted. "So he's cute?"

"He is. Charming, too."

"Yeah, that's trouble."

"So what do you think? Should I look for this guy? She gave me a list of phone numbers."

"Doesn't sound like he wants to be found. Don't you think the cops would've found him by now if he was nearby?"

"I don't know. He's probably got lots of friends. Maybe he's hiding out with someone."

"Or maybe he went home to his wife and she's pretending he's not there. Or maybe she killed him."

"He couldn't have gotten there that quickly."

"Why don't you ask Jake's sister? By the way, did you tell him about this debacle?" Nikki wanted to know.

"I told him about the dead guy. Haven't talked to him today," she said evasively.

"You don't want to tell him about Caitlyn, huh?" Nikki slurped her drink.

"That's not true," Stan said.

"Sure it is. She's not you, Stan. He doesn't strike me as the type to be confused about that."

"I know. It's just . . ." She sighed. "My family's so complicated compared to his. They all just love each other. Even when Jessie's driving him crazy, he loves her. And speaking of Jessie, why would I ask her about this? She's a Connecticut state trooper—who doesn't particularly love me."

"Nice subject change. And why wouldn't she help? You helped her out a few months ago. She likes you just fine. Ask her opinion. Seriously," Nikki said. "Aside from telling you to fuhgedaboudit and come home, she might have a pointer or two on how to not get yourself killed."

Chapter 20

Stan hung up and thought about Nikki's suggestion. She and Jessie Pasquale had come a long way from Stan's first days in town when they'd been sworn enemies. Their relationship had gradually evolved to toleration and, at rare times, a certain kinship. If Stan called her, it could go one of two ways. Jessie would appreciate her dilemma and offer her some carefully crafted advice that would consist mostly of "Let the police handle it" and maybe a few tidbits she could actually use, or she'd return to her prior conclusion that Stan was either crazy, meddling, or both. That could set them back a few paces. She preferred to think they'd come far enough for option one, but she'd have to ponder it more.

The rest of the suite was silent. Claustrophobic, despite its size. She had no idea if Maria or Therese had returned. She had to get out of here for a bit, even just outside for some air. She grabbed a sweatshirt and a pair of sneakers and hurried to the elevator, unable to shake the creepy feeling Owens's visit had prompted. If that pizza cutter had been the weapon, she'd never be able to look at pizza the same way again.

The elevator doors *whooshed* open in the lobby and she stepped out. It was quiet now, compared to this afternoon's rush. Only one person worked the front desk. Yummy smells wafted from the restaurant at the other side of the lobby. Voices and laughter filtered out of the cocktail bar area closest to her elevator. Then she saw Marcin at one of the high tables, sitting alone, nursing a drink. He saw her and raised his glass, but his vibe said *Don't come over.*

Definitely a weird dude. She wondered again about his meds. Should he be drinking if he was taking meds? And where was Leo? Maybe they'd had a fight. The insane part of her brain hoped Leo wasn't dead somewhere, too. She lifted her hand in a wave and made a beeline for the revolving door as Detective Genske entered it from the other side. Owens must still be here. Maybe they'd found something on the tapes. She stepped outside and watched her walk to the front desk. The man behind the counter pointed down a hall and she followed his finger. Stan changed her mind and went back inside.

The man behind the counter smiled at her. Unfortunately it wasn't Jamal. This guy looked like Harrison Ford. "Good evening, miss. Can I help you?"

"I'm looking for Lucy Keyes," Stan said.

"Lucy is in a meeting right now," he said.

Stan frowned. At nearly eleven at night? "With the cops?"

The clerk pursed his lips. "I'm afraid I can't share that information."

Stan tried a different tact. She turned on her brightest smile. "So do you guys have security cameras outside? It makes me feel so much better to know," she said, leaning closer as if to confide in him. "I had so many problems with my ex." The lie rolled easily off her tongue, and she topped it off with a smile she hoped was just worried enough to elicit sympathy.

The guy seemed unimpressed. "We do." He turned back to his computer.

"So how does that work?" Stan asked. "Does it record everyone who goes in and out?"

"You'd have to speak with the IT people," he said. "I'm not sure how it works. But we can certainly call the police and file a report if someone's bothering you."

"Oh, that's not necessary," Stan said hurriedly. "But thanks." She went outside and walked around back. Maybe she could catch Lucy when she left. She cased the parking lot but didn't see a silver SUV like the one she'd seen Lucy get into last night. She camped out at the back door and called Jake. McSwigg's would still be hopping, but maybe he could take a break. He answered on the second ring.

"Hey, babe." Hearing his warm, husky voice felt like a hug over the phone line.

"Hey yourself."

"What's going on? Any news on the dead chef?"

"No. We expect it'll be public soon. The police have his real name now, so I'm sure it'll be all over the news tomorrow. I got elected to help with the media relations."

"Elected or volunteered?"

"Elected."

"The cops have any suspects?"

Yeah. All of us, with an emphasis on Kyle. "Actually, yeah. A guy from our group left the hotel last night and hasn't been seen since." She didn't mention it was the guy she'd ridden with blindfolded in the back of the pastry truck.

"They think he killed him? Why?"

Stan told him about the pizza cutter and the YouTube video. "There's one other wrinkle with this guy."

"I can't wait to hear it," Jake said.

"My sister is having an affair with him."

Silence.

"Hello?" Stan said.

"I'm here. How . . . ?"

"She called and begged me to meet her. Told me the whole story. She thinks he's in trouble and wants help finding him." She could almost feel his sigh on the other end of the phone.

"I think you know what I'm going to say," he said.

"I'm pretty sure I do." She moved out of the way as a young couple emerged from the door and walked to their car. The girl laughed at something.

"Just in case," he said. "Don't get involved."

"That's what I figured. But I'm already involved."

"Which is bad enough. You don't need to go all in."

"It's my sister," she said. "And my business. Believe me, I don't want to be in this spot either. But . . . I'm kind of in it."

"Okay. Let's break this down," Jake said. "The business part first. What's he really committing to doing for you long term? He puts up capital for the location. Then what?"

"His name," she said simply. "He's got a lot of reach. It would save me about two years of building up my name."

"When did you start your business officially?"

"You know—"

"Just humor me," Jake interrupted. "How long?"

"About a year ago."

"Okay. And how fast have you built up a name?"

"All the dogs in town know me," she said. "And many of the cats. Is that what you mean?"

"I'm serious, Stan. Stop downplaying your success. Since you came to town last year with a few bags of extra treats for the local pets, you're now filling requests for treats around the state. Rescue events, high-end doggie day cares, local food co-ops. You have your own line of meals. You've become the go-to for dog parties, including weddings. You have an assistant, and you're about to expand. And that's with some social media, when you and Brenna have time. Is that about right?"

"Yes," Stan said.

"So that proves your work speaks for itself. You're growing your business organically. If reach is what you're looking for, you put together a thoughtful campaign and you're doubling, tripling your business. Then you open a shop, or whatever you want. My point is, you don't need this guy."

"That start-up capital is nothing to sneeze at," she said.

"You want an investor? I can be your investor," Jake said.

She pulled the phone away and looked at it before putting it back to her ear. "You what?" she said.

"I can be your investor." In addition to his pub owner status, Jake dabbled in development, including investing in projects he thought were good for Frog Ledge.

"But . . . you don't invest in businesses. You invest in real estate."

"I take on whatever project feels right. If a business gets me excited, I'll invest in it."

"And pet food gets you excited?" She could hear the doubt in her own voice and hated it. Confidence had never been her strong suit. In her corporate days, she'd subscribed to the fake it till you make it mentality. Even outside that world, she still had trouble feeling like she'd made it.

"Of course it does. And I'm excited about *you*. I know how committed you are to Pawsitively Organic. It's a win-win."

"I guess," Stan said slowly. "Jake, are you just saying this so I'll come home and forget about Sheldon?"

"I'm saying it because it's true. And if it makes you come home and forget about Sheldon, even better. Look, I want you to be happy here in Frog Ledge. I know it's a small town and it's not totally what you're used to."

"I *am* happy in Frog Ledge. With or without a pastry shop," she said. "It's home."

"Yeah?" Now the doubt had crept into his voice. "I always figure you're going to change your mind. Wake up one day and remember that you miss the city or the ocean or something."

Brenna once told Stan that Jake's last long-term relationship had fallen apart because his ex didn't want to live in a tiny town, and Jake couldn't imagine living anywhere else.

"I'm not changing my mind. We can visit the ocean or the city. I'd miss you more," Stan said. "Remember, I picked Frog Ledge because it felt right. You're not forcing me. I *want* to be there. I can't think of a better place for my business. Plus . . . you make me happy." She gave herself a mental head smack for still sounding like a high schooler bumbling her way through her first crush, even nearly a year after they'd been dating.

But she could feel his smile at the other end. "You make me happy, too. I'm in it for the long term with you, if you'll have me," he said, and left her mouth hanging open while he went on to his second point. "Now let's look at part two of this scenario."

"Part two?" Still mooning over his words, her brain hadn't caught up.

"Your sister. Her request."

"Yes. My sister. I told her I'd put my ear to the ground, but the police were way ahead of me." She didn't mention Nikki's idea to talk to Jessie.

"When was the last time you talked to your sister before today?"

"It's definitely been a while."

"But you're doing this for her anyway." It was a statement, not a question.

She sighed. "I suck at saying no. Besides, like it or not, she's family. Would you do it for Brenna or Jessie?"

"Of course I would."

"You think I'm crazy?"

"You bet," he said. "But it's also why I love you. Be careful, okay? Leave the real investigating to the cops."

"I will." She noticed Lucy then, walking around the side of the building with someone, deep in conversation. "Hey, I have to run. I'll call you tomorrow. And, Jake? I love you, too."

Chapter 21

Stan hung up and hurried over to Lucy. She recognized her companion now. Their bellhop from last night, Jackson. Lucy held a cigarette near her lips, smoke snaking out of it. Their conversation trailed off when they saw her, and Jackson stepped protectively in front of Lucy.

"Hi," Stan said. "I wanted to catch Lucy for a second."

Lucy stepped around Jackson's shoulder. "Hi there. It's fine, Jackson," she said. "You can go back to work."

With a last not-so-friendly glance at Stan, Jackson handed Lucy a set of keys and went inside. Lucy pocketed the keys, dropped her cigarette, and ground it out with her shoe. "What can I do for you? How's that handsome cat?"

"Nutty's fine, thanks. Listen, I just wondered if you had seen one of the guys from our party. Kyle McLeod. He left sometime last night and no one's seen him since. We're all getting worried."

Lucy's lips tipped up in a sardonic smile. "Yeah, the cops who were in here looking for him seemed worried, too."

"That would be Owens and Genske?"

Lucy nodded. "You've met, I see."

"Yeah. They've been questioning all of us in Pierre's murder. Did they get anything off the surveillance tapes?"

"You know I can't discuss that."

Their gazes held, each sizing the other up. This close, Stan could see the cracks in that perfectly applied makeup, the dark circles peeking through her under-eye concealer. Lucy Keyes was human after all.

Lucy finally broke the stare and checked out the parking lot. "Look," she said finally, turning back to Stan. "I haven't seen Kyle since you all arrived last night. I don't know where he went. But if they're look-ing at him for this murder, they're dead wrong."

Stan raised an eyebrow. "You sound sure of yourself."

"I'm quite sure of myself," Lucy said. "I've known Sheldon and some of his people, like Kyle, for a long time."

"Did you see Kyle leave last night?"

"No."

"Do you know if anyone called him a cab, or a car service?"

"Again, no. And even if someone had, we have pri-vacy policies."

I bet you do. "Do you know anywhere he could have gone?" Stan asked.

"Sheldon asked me the same question. I'll tell you what I told him. We give our guests the privacy they desire when they stay with us. The same privacy he ex-pects when he stays here."

"How long have you known Kyle?"

"A few years."

"You know him well?"

"Well enough."

"He wouldn't have stayed here much though, would he? Given that he has his own apartment nearby?"

Lucy cocked her head. "Why so curious, Ms. Connor?"

Because he's sleeping with my sister. "Because I'm suddenly part of this group that may or may not have a murderer in it. I want to know who I'm dealing with. They could be going about this all wrong, Lucy. He could be in danger, too," Stan said, thinking of Caitlyn's insistence. "Have you thought of that?"

Lucy looked out over the parking lot again, as if searching for an answer. "I have. But I don't have an answer for you either way. I haven't talked to him. I don't know where he's gone. I certainly hope he's okay. As for the rest of you, the police are going to stick close until this is solved, so be vigilant and we'll do the rest. Believe me, everyone's taking this very seriously."

"That's good to know," Stan said. "If you hear from Kyle, will you tell someone?"

"Of course I will. Listen, Ms. Connor, I have to run. And if Kyle shows up here, we'll certainly tell him that you all are looking for him. But that's really all I can do." She turned and hurried away, her turquoise heels sounding more like jackhammers in the quiet lot. But she didn't go to the silver SUV, which was nowhere in sight. She went directly to a blue Honda, fumbled with the lock, and finally slid in. The car pulled out quickly and disappeared into the night. Stan frowned, remembering the keys Jackson had handed her. Lucy didn't look the type to drive a Honda. Plus, she hadn't been driving the Honda last night. Had to be Jackson's car.

Why was Lucy driving Jackson's car? Where was her own?

Impulsively, she dialed Jessie Pasquale's mobile. Jake's sister answered on the first ring.

"Pasquale."

"Hey. It's Stan."

A beat, then she said, "Hey, Stan. I thought you were away this weekend?"

"I am. But I wondered if you might be able to do me a favor."

"What kind of favor?" Jessie's tone had turned slightly guarded. Stan didn't blame her. She'd developed a bit of a reputation around Frog Ledge.

"Do you have any way of finding out what kind of car is registered to someone? Like by their name?"

"Just their name? No reg number?"

"Right."

"Who and why?"

Shoot. She hadn't thought that far ahead. The truth wouldn't do, so she needed to figure something out fast. Jessie's BS meter was well tuned from years of being a cop. And just because Stan dated her brother didn't mean she was entitled to special treatment, as Jessie had not so delicately pointed out on many occasions. "Well," she said. "A friend here was wondering what his ex-wife was driving these days. He, uh, thought he saw her cruising by his house." *Lame . . . so lame.*

"Uh-huh," Jessie said. She didn't need to say she also thought the reasoning was lame. But to Stan's surprise, she didn't turn her down and hang up the phone. "I'll make a call."

"You will?"

"Do you want me to?"

"I totally do. Thank you so much. Her name's Lucy Keyes."

"I'll call you back," Jessie said, and disconnected.

Chapter 22

Saturday morning, Stan woke with Nutty's tail wrapped around her head, tickling her nose. His morning routine. The dogs would be awake soon, too, and they would want breakfast. She stretched, then opened her eyes. And realized she wasn't in her room. Or her house. She was still in Newport. Three days and counting. Pierre was still dead, Kyle still missing. Sheldon wanted everyone cooking today with happy smiles. A new pastry chef would be in the house. The news about Pierre—Pete—would break any second if it hadn't already. She pulled a pillow over her head.

But Nutty insisted that he couldn't wait to eat by pawing at her face and meowing.

"How on earth can you be hungry with all the food Maria's giving you?" She wouldn't be surprised if Maria stole him out of her room at all hours to feed him pasta.

He sat back, tail flicking, clearly offended. She swore he looked heavier than when they'd arrived two days ago.

She reached for her phone to see the time. Not even six. With a sigh, she flipped onto her side and gazed out the window into the early morning light, thinking about the day ahead. Nutty, annoyed by her slight, moved to the end of the bed and turned his butt to her.

Stan forced herself out of bed, put out some treats for her starving feline, and made a mental list while she showered. She wanted to get to the kitchen early, whip up a few dishes, and hopefully buy herself some free time later to make some calls for her sister. Caitlyn would be calling any minute looking for a status update. She dressed and combed out her long hair, working some antifrizz cream through to combat the humidity. She was digging through her suitcase to find the pair of sandals she wanted when someone rapped on her door. Expecting Maria, she got up and opened it a crack.

Not Maria. Tyler. He looked exhausted again, and panicked. "Hey," she said with some apprehension. "How did you get in here?"

"Therese let me in. Can you come to our room? There've been some . . . developments."

"Like what? Did the news about Pierre go out?"

"Just come. Please."

"Can I get my—"

"Now," he implored, yanking her out of the room.

She barely had time to put her shoes on, for the second day in a row. These people were so pushy. She followed Tyler along the same circuitous route she'd traveled with Sheldon yesterday to get to their suite. Tyler used his card to let them in. It smelled like fresh bread and eggs. Joaquin beamed at her from the kitchen. "You're joining us for breakfast?"

"I guess so," she said. "It smells delicious."

Sheldon sat at the table with a glass of orange juice. "Stan. You're looking dapper this morning."

"I was heading to the kitchen early," she said.

"Hoping to get some samples of my food for Monday in the can first thing. What's going on?"

"Two things," Sheldon said. "One, the police released Pierre's name late last night to the press. The first reports are starting to post. I expect Pierre's publicist is going to say some negative things about us in the process."

Stan raised an eyebrow. "His publicist?" She looked at Tyler. "Isn't that you?"

"Tyler is *my* publicist," Sheldon said. "That means he discusses my chefs when we have joint ventures or other news. Pierre apparently had another agenda and needed to find another publicist to push it for him."

"Who's the publicist? What kind of agenda?" Stan asked.

Sheldon's lips were pursed again, signaling his disturbance. "It's all part of the double-timing I told you about before. Exploring his options with that common motorcycle gangster."

Stan could barely keep her eyes from rolling. These guys were so dramatic. And Sheldon had ignored the first part of her question. "Who's the publicist?"

"Her name is Melanie," Tyler said. "Melanie Diamond. Her firm is called Gem Communications, in New York."

"Did you know before now that he had his own publicist?"

"We learned this recently," Sheldon said. "It didn't seem relevant until now. But we should be ready to expertly negate whatever they try to throw at us."

"Okay," Stan said. "But there's nothing yet."

Tyler shook his head.

She suppressed a sigh. "You said there were two things. What's the second?"

Tyler and Sheldon exchanged looks. "Vaughn Dawes."

"The other chef. Right. I forgot about her. Is she here?"

"No, she's not."

"Oh. Is she coming late?"

"She's missing."

Stan frowned. "Missing? What do you mean? Missing like Kyle?"

"We don't know. She drove to the airport in Los Angeles, parked, checked her bag, and vanished. No one saw her after that—well, potentially the people on the plane did, but we have no way of knowing. She never emerged from the gate with the rest of the passengers. Therese waited at the airport until nearly two A.M. to make sure she hadn't missed her connection and arrived late."

"You sure she didn't just change her mind?"

"My people don't change their minds about things like this," Sheldon said in a tone that left no room for argument. "This weekend is the opportunity of a lifetime. And even if she had, she would've called."

"So you think she's in trouble? Have you reported it to the police? Or has her family reported it?"

"We haven't reported it. I don't know if anyone else has. But that's not the point. It's going to leak to the press along with his death. I *know* Pierre is behind this."

This guy had lost his mind. She should pack up and leave now. Take Jake up on his offer. "Sheldon. I know it's been a rough couple of days, but Pierre is dead."

Tyler made a choking sound. Sheldon glared at her. "Don't be smart with me. I know that. He had a whole scheme going on how to ruin me. His publicist is simply picking up the thread now that he's gone."

Joaquin swept in with plates. "Despicable, isn't it?" he

said to Stan. "Scrambled eggs with chives and goat cheese, home fries, and freshly baked bread. I do hope Vaughn is okay. She's a sweetheart." He set plates in front of Stan and Sheldon and went back for his and Tyler's.

Stan used the time to pray for patience. "So you think he set up this whole thing? Left instructions on how to destroy you if he died? Paid her to disappear? Had his publicist stage a kidnapping? What, Sheldon? That doesn't even make sense," she said, answering her own question. "Even if he knew he was about to die, how would he know you would call her to fill in for him?"

"Of course I don't think Pierre expected to die. But if his . . . *vile* co-conspirator is behind this, she coerced Vaughn in some way. Which would mean she's fine, and simply under the influence of a person with ill intent."

Despite having no caffeine in her system, Stan fought to follow Sheldon's thought process. "Did Pierre know Vaughn? How do you know she knew the same publicist?"

"I'm so relieved I don't have to do this job," Joaquin said to no one in particular from the kitchen. "It's way too stressful for me. Even just listening to the strategizing makes me exhausted. And hungry."

Stan didn't know whether to laugh or cry. These guys were like the Three Stooges.

"The food community is small," Sheldon said. "But that's not our focus. The focus is what all this is going to do to us. We have very important peoples' eyes on us. We have to make this . . . *publicist* look like the lunatic she is. Which means we have to *expose* her. Tyler."

Tyler slid in front of the computer. "On it. Thanks, man," he said to Joaquin as he put his plate down.

Stan took a bite of her food. It was phenomenal. "This is great, Joaquin."

"Thank you!" He blew her a kiss. "There's coffee, too."

"Thank God." Stan got up and went into the kitchen for a cup. "How did you find out he had a publicist again?" she called to Tyler from the other room.

"A trusted friend," Sheldon said.

"Care to share who that friend is?" Stan asked, returning with a giant mug.

Sheldon shook his head before Tyler could say anything. "You wouldn't know them."

"And you're sure this person has their story straight? They're positive Pierre was her client?" Stan sat and picked up her fork again.

"Of course I'm sure," Sheldon said, insulted. "My sources don't give me false information."

The food kept Stan from losing patience. "What do you need from me, Sheldon? Because I need to bake. I thought the dinner was pretty important, but if no one is cooking and testing food, it's not going to be as successful as you want."

Sheldon thought about that. "I need you to help spin the Vaughn story. But you're right, Tyler. Take your operation into the kitchen to discuss with Stan while she works. We'll have to tell the others today anyway, so they're prepared for the worst. But you can get some work done now before anyone else is up. God knows the rest of this crew won't be up until lunchtime," Sheldon muttered. "You would think I was running a bed-and-breakfast for wayward chefs."

"By the way," Stan said, scraping the last of her eggs off the plate, "is everything okay with Marcin? He seemed angry last night."

The three of them exchanged a look. "Marcin has some . . . troubles," Sheldon said. "Financial troubles. Mostly due to his illness."

"What's wrong with him? I don't mean to pry, I'm just curious," Stan said. "Anything the rest of us should be conscious of?"

Another furtive look. "He has some psychological issues," Sheldon said finally. "I hate to gossip, but I did notice he's been disagreeable."

Tyler tapped his temple with one finger and rolled his eyes.

"Now, Tyler. We mustn't be mean. The poor man had a nervous breakdown a couple years back. He spent some time in a hospital. It was very hard on Leo. They had just opened a new restaurant, and ended up losing it not long after. Leo was running back and forth trying to manage, cook, be there for Marcin—it was a terrible time. In the end, he just couldn't keep it all afloat. That's why this weekend is also very important to them," Sheldon added. "It's a chance for them to start fresh. I know Marcin is likely worried that this . . . issue with Pierre will derail them again."

Chapter 23

Stan went back to her room before heading to the kitchen. They'd delivered Nutty's full breakfast while she'd been gone, so she made him a plate and brought it upstairs. When she went back down into the living area, she noticed Therese sleeping on the pull-out couch with pillows over her head. Maria was nowhere in sight. Stan trekked down to the hotel kitchen with her recipe notes and perused the cooking equipment while she waited for Tyler.

In the interest of keeping it simple yet giving the appearance of fancy, she planned to do a spin on one of the meals she'd made for her gourmet food line at the new pet clinic in Frog Ledge. Her friend and neighbor, Amara Leonard, and her fiancé, Vincent, had opened the clinic this past spring. The clinic offered a merger of Amara's homeopathic and Vincent's traditional veterinarian practice, as well as a small shelter and adoption area. They sold Stan's home-cooked meals, frozen for convenience, and her freshly baked treats. So far her salmon dish with baby red potatoes, a hearty butternut squash, and jasmine rice was the best seller. She planned to offer that to the Siamese with summer greens instead of squash. For the sake of choice, she'd offer beef and chicken versions also. Not much testing necessary, although the beef could be tricky depending on if the cat preferred rare or medium to well.

The desserts, though, would need some tweaking. The vanilla cat-noli needed to be perfect. So far, she'd only made cannoli for pups. She decided to whip up the strawberry cake first and let it bake while she worked on the cat-noli cream. But first, more coffee. She started some brewing.

Tyler showed up a few minutes later, computer in one hand and a large coffee cup in the other. He sniffed the air. "Sweet. More java." He hopped onto the counter and flipped open his laptop. "Dude, it's starting," he said. "I'm getting Google alerts left and right. Only about Sheldon so far. No calls yet, though." He pulled out his phone to check.

Stan watched him as he raked his hand through his already messy hair. A nervous habit. "Are you doing okay?" she asked as she pulled out a mixing bowl and measured out flour.

Tyler shrugged. "I'm fine. It's no big deal. This job pays good," he said defensively, as if he expected her to question him. "And it's usually not like this. I mean, no one's ever been *murdered* before. It's f-ed up, man."

Stan smiled. "Hey, listen. You don't have to explain anything to me. I worked in a place for ten years that paid fabulous money. Unfortunately it was killing me and I didn't even realize it. They had to fire me before I figured it out."

Tyler stared at her, his mouth slack. "I don't really want to get fired."

"I don't blame you. It's no fun, even when you get a severance package." Stan placed her hands on her hips and scanned the room. "You think they have vanilla beans hidden somewhere?"

Another blank stare.

"Never mind, I'll look." Stan began opening cabinets and poking around. "Shoot, I need a piece of copper pipe."

"What the heck do you need that for? You a plumber, too?"

Stan sighed. "No. I need it to shape the cannoli shell. Never mind, I'll find one. So tell me what you're planning for today. Are we keeping the statement we wrote about Pierre's death?"

Tyler hit a few keys. "I think we should. If that's all they ask about, that's the one we agreed on."

Stan stirred the mix. "Okay. As for Vaughn, I suggest we don't comment until we get confirmation that she's truly missing. That's how I would handle it. We don't even know what happened, and to say anything else makes Sheldon sound guilty." She shrugged. "I would just say we're anxiously waiting for news, and we're hoping and praying she's okay. My two cents."

Tyler nodded admiringly. "You're smart."

"I did it for a long time," she said with a shrug. "Now what do you know about this other publicist?"

"Dude, she's hard core. She's in New York, where Pierre lives. This lady gets the *news* out and then some. I know someone else who's her client and he's in the news every day, almost."

Stan figured that meant Melanie Diamond was either very good at her job or had a lot of great media contacts whose hands she washed regularly in exchange for favors. Or maybe both. "Why is Sheldon so convinced she's out to get him? And who is this mysterious friend who tipped you guys off?"

Tyler shrugged. "I don't know why. Sheldon's not

saying much. To me, anyway." He ignored the second half of her question.

"We need the dirty details if we're supposed to stay ahead of her," Stan said.

"Who's got dirty details? If it's us, I hope we have coffee, too." Leo walked in wearing denim shorts and a red T-shirt that said "Kiss the Cook." Stan figured it would've been too much to ask to get through the weekend without seeing that saying somewhere. Tacky, but it worked for Leo.

"We sure do have coffee," Stan said.

"I think I love you." Leo found a mug, poured, and sipped. He sighed. "Ah. Just what I needed. You two are getting an early start," he said to Stan.

"Yeah, I figured I'd take stock of the kitchen, get some things going, figure out what else I needed so I can go out later. Tyler's working on media statements." She put the strawberry cake in the oven and took out another bowl and the ingredients for the cat-noli cream.

"Yes, I planned to do the same. I thought this cooking thing would be more of a joint effort, but the plan went a little south." Leo shook his head. "I guess we'll do what we have to do and it will all be fine. So tell me about the dirty details." He winked.

What was the harm? Sheldon had said they were bringing everyone into the loop anyway. "I'm helping Tyler with some public relations."

"Oh, that's right! Your first career. Sheldon told us you were multitalented."

"Yes." *And apparently one I can't let go of.*

"She's good at it, too," Tyler said.

"Sheldon is concerned with the news breaking about Pierre that his other publicist is going to put out a negative statement. Given their recent . . . disagreements."

Leo laughed out loud. He had to put his coffee mug

down and bend over at the waist, he laughed so hard. Stan glanced at Tyler. He shrugged.

"Did I say something funny?" she asked.

"Oh, sweetheart, no," Leo said, wiping tears from his eyes. "It's not you. I can just picture Sheldon telling you there's been 'a couple of disagreements' when really it's surprising they've been able to keep up pretenses." He sobered. "I shouldn't joke given the tragic events. But Sheldon and Pierre were not on each other's Christmas card list, let's put it that way. All you have to do is check out their Twitter feeds to understand the passive-aggressive nature of their relationship."

Interested now, Stan laid her mixing spoon down and turned to him. "They battled it out on Twitter? In public?"

"They did it with class, but most people who know them can read between the lines. It wasn't pretty."

"Did they get any backlash in the foodie community?"

"Any that affected their bottom lines? No. They both have large followings. Pierre, especially. He was the best of the best. Everyone knows that." He lowered his voice and looked around. "Even better than Sheldon," he said in an exaggerated whisper.

Stan glanced at Tyler, but he seemed busy on his computer. "Better than Mr. Pastry?" she asked. "Wow."

"Shhhhh!" Leo cast another glance behind him. "We don't want that getting back to Mr. Pastry. The wrath!"

Stan raised an eyebrow. Maybe she had the wrong impression of Sheldon after all. She'd seen him get snarky, but she'd not yet encountered his alleged wrath.

Perhaps Pierre had.

Tyler's phone rang. With a pained look, he jumped down and moved to the corner of the kitchen to take the call.

"Sounds like people may have been jealous of Pierre," she said, opening the oven door to check on the cake. Nearly perfect.

"That could be." One more look over his shoulder at the doorway, then at Tyler to make sure he wasn't listening. "Like Maria," he said in a low voice. "Maria couldn't stand Pierre. She wanted to be Sheldon's number two and no matter how much they fought, Pierre never lost that spot in Sheldon's eyes." He smiled at Stan's raised eyebrows. "Contrary to what Sheldon wants you to think, we're not all besties."

Stan tasted the cream. It didn't have enough zing. And it wasn't creamy enough. "Maria seems very successful," she said, looking around for an electric mixer. That might help.

"She is. But no matter how well she did or how much she sucks up, he always runs back to Pierre. It makes her crazy."

"Do you think Pierre was going to leave Sheldon's enterprise?"

Leo went to the fridge and took out some vegetables. "I don't know that. I haven't talked to Pierre directly in about a year."

"Did you know Pierre long?" she asked.

"We met some years back at a competition in Key West. We worked together on a charity dinner after that, then lost touch for a bit until Sheldon brought us together again."

"You guys get along?" Stan gave up on the mixer and took her spoon back to the bowl, mixing with a vengeance, one eye on Leo.

"Oh, sure. I get along with everyone." Leo smiled, but Stan caught a guarded look in his eye.

"What about Marcin?" she asked. "Is he friendly with Pierre?"

"No," Leo said, and his tone indicated he had nothing more to say about it.

"Hey, guys," Tyler said. They both turned toward him. He'd just finished his call and looked a bit worse for the wear. "That was the AP. They got a tip about Kyle and they're running with it. The police have changed their statement to say that he's wanted for questioning in Pierre's murder. It's going live as we speak." For the first time, the indifferent look was gone from his face. He looked like a scared kid. "Do you really think Kyle did this? That he killed Pierre?"

Chapter 24

Thankfully, Stan had just taken her cake out of the oven, because she forgot all about it as the three of them gathered around Tyler's computer and read the AP news alert.

Reports that Pierre LaPorte, famed pastry chef of La Chocolate Bakery in New York City, has died have been confirmed by his publicist. LaPorte was reportedly in Rhode Island for an event Thursday when he was found dead at a private home on Sunset Avenue.

Police are searching for a colleague of LaPorte's in conjunction with his death. Kyle McLeod, owner of the Green Dream in Boca Raton, had been in Rhode Island for the same event. McLeod has not been seen since Thursday evening.

A picture of Kyle smiling in front of a counter full of vegetables accompanied the article.

Stan looked at Tyler. "The Pierre piece is what we expected. And no Vaughn yet. It's a nightmare for

Kyle, though." Caitlyn must be losing her mind. And Kyle's wife.

Stan's phone vibrated in her back pocket. She pulled it out. Caitlyn. "'Scuse me," she muttered, and went into the empty ballroom. "Hello?"

"Where have you been?" Caitlyn demanded, sounding too much like their mother for Stan's comfort. "Have you seen the news?"

"I have," Stan said.

"Krissie, come on, you have to tell me. Do you know if Kyle's okay? Have you heard anything? What are they going to do to him?" Her voice shook with unshed tears.

"I can't talk right now," Stan said. "Can you meet me later, around lunchtime?"

"I'll be at the coffee shop," Caitlyn said, and hung up.

Stan stood for a moment holding her phone, thinking. Owens must've gotten fingerprints or some other incriminating evidence off the bloody pizza cutter to put out the statement about Kyle. Evidence that he couldn't ignore. But something about it bothered her.

If Kyle had killed Pierre at noon, the earliest time in the window Owens's coroner had estimated, he would've had to drive all the way back to Providence to toss the weapon behind his own apartment, then get back to Newport in the summer traffic. The trip took roughly an hour each way. More if there was traffic, which there likely would be given the Jazz Festival. He theoretically could have made it back by three, but unless he was a master murderer who did this all the time, he'd have to be rattled. The guy who'd been waiting blindfolded in the mobile pastry truck when she arrived hadn't seemed rattled in the least.

Or, he could've hidden the bloody pizza cutter somewhere to dispose of later. After the body was discovered and he slipped out of the hotel, he'd have been under pressure to get rid of it. He would've needed to get back to his car, retrieve the weapon from wherever he'd hidden it, then get to Providence to ditch it. Seemed like a lot of work. Unless he had a vehicle at his disposal. Like Lucy Keyes's silver SUV.

But even if he did, why would he pick his own Dumpster to get rid of the pizza cutter when the Providence River was right around the corner? Maybe he wasn't thinking straight. Again, that didn't fit with the even-tempered, laid-back guy who'd sat with her in the living room waiting for the detectives to return Thursday night.

She wanted to know where Sheldon had been, both before the murder and after they'd returned to the hotel. He'd been forthcoming with Stan about his recent issues with Pierre, but Leo'd made it sound ten times worse. Like they couldn't even stand to look at each other. That didn't sound like someone devastated about his prize student being murdered in cold blood.

Maybe she was being naive about Sheldon. His harmless, quirky personality could all be an act that he was using to his advantage. Jake certainly didn't like him. And unlike the rest of them, Sheldon had unlimited access to this house. If he had killed Pierre, he could've set up Kyle. And then . . . gotten rid of him, too.

She shivered, almost dropping the phone when Maria appeared in front of her. Stan hadn't heard her come in—surprising since Maria was a large woman.

"I made meatballs for Nutty," she said. "Did you see them?"

"I didn't," Stan said, slipping her phone into the pocket of her jeans. "We were catching up on the news."

Maria gasped. "What happened?"

"They identified Kyle as a suspect."

Maria made the sign of the cross. "That's terrible. Why would he do it?"

"We don't know for sure he did," Stan said. "I think they're focused on him because he's not here. It does look suspicious, but we don't know the whole story."

Maria shook her head grimly. "It's terrible. Just terrible. I don't know what Sheldon's going to do about this dinner."

"The dinner?" Stan asked. "He should be more concerned about the murder, in my opinion."

"Oh, I'm sure he is. But now he'll have to find another replacement. By the way, is Vaughn here? Or is she still sleeping?"

"You'll have to ask Tyler. He's in here." She rose to head back into the kitchen.

Maria followed. "What? Was she delayed?"

"Tyler?"

He looked up from his computer.

Stan went back to her cat-noli cream. "Maria's asking about Vaughn."

Tyler froze. "Uh, she's not here yet."

So much for him preparing a statement.

"Did she miss her flight? What's going on?" Maria demanded, hands on hips.

"She's vanished into thin air," Leo said helpfully. "*Poof!*" He pantomimed a magician waving a wand.

"What in the name of everything holy are you talking about?" Maria looked from Stan to Tyler and back to Leo.

Tyler seemed to have lost his ability to speak.

"She never showed up," Stan said. "No one knows where she is. But that's not for prime time."

Maria grabbed at the counter as if having a dizzy spell. "This is terrible. Do you think . . . someone is targeting us all?"

"Oh, don't be so melodramatic," Leo said. "It's a publicity stunt. I'd put money on it."

"That's what Sheldon thinks," Stan said. "But we should consider she might be in trouble. Just like Kyle could be in trouble. We have no idea what happened."

Or Kyle could just be guilty, and kidnapped her, too. But why?

Maria pulled herself together and went to peruse the contents of the refrigerator. Leo continued cutting up veggies and throwing them into a sauté pan. Stan frosted her cake and was just about to wrap it up when Martin finally rolled in. He looked like he'd been up half the night drinking. Leo went over to him, took him by the arm, and pulled him into a corner.

"Are you going upstairs?" Maria asked. "Bring these to my Nutty. It's a special batch. They have no dangerous spices."

"That's very kind of you," Stan said, taking the plate.

"Anything for our furry friend."

"I need to go out for a bit," Stan said. "Anyone need anything?"

Leo returned from his huddle with Martin. "I could use some leeks," he said.

"Are you going to the liquor store?" Tyler looked up, hopeful.

"I could," she said. "Will that help you or hurt you when we need to put together another statement?"

"Help me," Tyler said, and she couldn't tell if it was an answer to her question or a plea. "I need some Shiraz. We drank the other two bottles from last night. Well, Maria did, mostly."

"Hey," Maria said. "It's been a stressful couple of days."

Stan made a note on her phone. "Hey, Tyler. Walk me out?"

He jumped at the chance to leave the computer and obliged. Once they'd left the ballroom and were in the main hall, Stan spoke. "Did you come to Newport with Sheldon on Thursday?"

Tyler shook his head. "I drove up from New York alone. I had something going on that morning. Sheldon was here, in Providence."

"Were Joaquin or Therese with him?"

Tyler nodded. "They both were. We had a staff meeting Thursday morning. I called into half of it. Finalizing plans for the weekend, doing a seating chart for the dinner. Joaquin had to do a final meeting with the Chanler staff to make sure everything was set."

"So they were with him all morning?"

"Most of it, I think. But I didn't get here until one." He looked at her curiously. "Why?"

Stan ignored the question. "Thursday night when we were here . . . Did Sheldon stay in the suite the whole night?"

Tyler instantly looked guilty. "I . . . don't know. I went out."

"Where did you go?"

"Downtown. A bar. There was live music and I just wanted to chill."

"When did you get back?"

"Around two. Right before Sheldon came to get you." He hesitated. "He was just getting in, too. He had the same clothes on that he'd worn that day. And he seemed really agitated."

Chapter 25

With the cake cooling on the counter and Leo whipping up some vegetable miracle, Stan went back to her room and gave Nutty some meatballs. She had a few minutes to try the numbers Caitlyn had given her before she had to leave to meet her sister. She sat down with the phone and pulled out the list. May as well start with the most obvious. She dialed the Florida number and waited, holding her breath, for Kyle's wife to answer. After four rings, a machine picked up. Relieved, Stan disconnected. She hadn't been looking forward to that call.

There were three other numbers on the sheet. Two guys and one woman. She started with the first one, a man named Brett Joyce. Brett didn't answer. His voice mail didn't sound friendly. Stan didn't leave a message. The second guy, Travis no-last-name, answered on the first ring. He sounded like he was jogging.

"Hello, is this Travis?" Stan asked.

"Yes. Who's this?"

She took a deep breath and prepared to wing it. "Hi, my name is Kristan. I'm one of Kyle McLeod's colleagues, and I'm hoping you can help me—"

"Whoa," Travis interrupted. "Did you see the news? That Kyle's in trouble?"

"I did. That's why I'm calling, actually."

"What'd you say your name was again?" Travis asked. He sounded like he'd slowed to a walk.

"Kristan."

"How do you know Kyle?"

"Through school."

"And how'd you get my number?"

Shoot. She didn't have a good answer for that one.

"Through a friend of his," she said. "I'm just wondering if he contacted you or any of your friends Thursday night."

Travis sounded on guard now. "Not me," he said. "How do I know you're not the police?"

"I'm not, but if you know something about his whereabouts, you really should call them," Stan said.

Travis seemed to consider that. "I don't. Did you try his girlfriend?"

So much for discretion, Caitlyn. "I'm not sure who you mean."

Travis laughed. "Are you a girlfriend, too? Sorry. Hard to keep track. Kyle's kind of a player."

Just what she'd been afraid of. "No. I'm not," she said. "But if you have a name, that would be awesome."

"One sec." He took the phone away from his ear, presumably to scroll for a name and number. "Andrea Martin," he said when he came back. He rattled off a number.

Andrea Martin? Not Caitlyn, not even Lucy Keyes. This guy got around. This would be a fun debrief with Caitlyn.

"Thanks," she said. "Any other thoughts on where he could've gone?"

"Nope," Travis said. "We weren't that tight. He lives in Florida, though. Boca."

Stan thanked him and hung up. She tried Andrea Martin's number. No answer. She tried the last woman on the sheet Caitlyn had given her, someone named Lena Cruz. No answer there either.

She grabbed her bag and left the hotel. Heat shimmered off the pavement in the parking lot as the day baked in the sun. Perfect beach day. She should ditch this whole thing, go buy a bikini, and head to First Beach. But since ditching things wasn't in her nature, she stayed on plan and pointed her car toward town.

Her cell phone rang again. She glanced at the readout. Jessie Pasquale. She hit the button for her hands-free system. "Hello."

"So I found a Lucy Keyes with an address in Jamestown," Jessie said.

Near Stan's hometown. And not far from Newport.

"There's a silver BMW X3 registered to that name and address," Jessie continued.

Bingo. "Any other cars?" *Like a blue Honda?*

"No. But I don't think it's the right person," Jessie said.

"You don't? Why?"

"This person has no other names associated with her. Doesn't seem like they've ever been married, so can't be your friend's ex-wife," Jessie said pointedly.

Busted. "Maybe he meant ex-girlfriend," Stan said. "I'll have to clarify. But that's really helpful, Jess, thanks so much." She hung up, tossed the phone onto the passenger seat, and focused on navigating through town. Heavy traffic today. Saturday in Newport during the Jazz Festival, not to mention prime summer vacations. Those who weren't going to the beach would go downtown to shop, or tour the mansions, where they could get out of the heat for a while. She opened her sunroof and all her windows despite the temperature and took in a deep breath of the sea air. She wished she could be one of those people enjoying a beautiful place on a beautiful day. But today, everything—and everyone—around her seemed seedy and suspicious. Including her cohorts, who were full of secrets, from mental illness to jealousy to evil publicists.

Chapter 26

Stan pulled into the Grounds of Hope parking lot ten minutes late. Caitlyn sat in her car out front, alone. Stan went up to the window and knocked. Caitlyn's window buzzed down. Stan could tell her sister's eyes were puffy, like she'd been crying, even behind the dark glasses.

"You're late," Caitlyn said, her voice raw.

Stan nodded. "Sorry. Listen, let's take a ride. Want me to drive?"

"Just get in," Caitlyn said.

Stan had barely gotten her door shut when Caitlyn hit the gas, zooming out of the parking lot. Taking the turn on two wheels, she almost careened into a white pickup truck entering the parking lot.

"Jeez. Take it easy," Stan said, grabbing for her seat belt.

"Why are the police making it sound like Kyle killed this guy?" Caitlyn fumbled for a tissue and blew her nose with one hand, jerking the car from stops to starts as they drove into the heart of Newport.

"They can't find him, Caitlyn. Wherever he is, he isn't coming forward. It looks bad." Stan didn't mention the probable murder weapon found in the Dumpster behind Kyle's apartment. The police might not release that information. Plus Caitlyn would probably throw herself off the Pell Bridge.

"Where am I going?" Caitlyn said.

"Let's park and walk the Cliff Walk. We can get some privacy there." True enough, but selfishly Stan also wanted to be outside. She felt claustrophobic, both with Sheldon and his gang and in this situation with Caitlyn's separate but related problem.

"Walk?" Caitlyn looked stricken. "I have heels on."

"You'll be fine. We'll stay on the paved section." Of the three-point-five-mile trail, the rocky terrain existed at the south side. The north side was paved. She left no room for argument. Caitlyn seemed to sense that she would lose, so she said nothing. She managed to shoehorn her car into a street spot not far from the entrance above First Beach, and they walked there in silence.

"What's wrong?" Caitlyn asked once they'd turned onto the narrow path, passing the back entrance to The Chanler hotel. "Did something else happen you're not telling me?"

Stan waited until a group of giggling teen girls had passed before speaking. "Have you been to the Newport Premier with Kyle before?" she asked.

Caitlyn shook her head.

"Do you know Lucy Keyes?" she asked. "The hotel manager?"

"No. Should I?"

"Did Kyle ever mention her?"

"*No.* Why are you asking me about the hotel?"

"Does Kyle have more than one vehicle?"

"Not that I know of. What's going on, Stan?"

A woman on a power-walking mission powered around

them, giving Caitlyn's shoes a dirty look on her way past. Caitlyn didn't notice.

Stan looked out over the water. This first stretch of the walk was her favorite, with only bushes separating the walk from the cliff's edge and unencumbered views of the sea below. Signs warning "Caution, Steep Cliffs, High Risk of Injury" and depicting people in various degrees of falling were the only indicator that anything bad could happen in such a beautiful place. Tiny, nearly hidden steps in the bushes led up to some of the side streets bordering the walk. "I tried calling those people on your list."

Caitlyn stopped. "You did? Did you get anywhere?" She looked so hopeful Stan felt sorry for her. Even more so given the news she was about to break.

"The only person I could get was Travis. You know him?"

"We went out with Travis and his girlfriend a couple times."

"I asked him if he knew where Kyle might've gone and he asked if I'd tried his girlfriend."

Caitlyn's face paled.

"It wasn't you," Stan said. "The name he gave me was Andrea Martin. You know her?"

"Andrea?" Caitlyn laughed. Not the reaction Stan expected. "What crap." She started walking again, keeping close to the side that bordered the mansions' broad yards. Despite the light foot traffic today, the skinny path drove Stan to fall in step behind her sister instead of next to her, making it difficult to read her expressions. "Andrea used to throw herself at him. She was another student. I know he took her out a couple of times before we got together, but certainly not after. Travis and Andrea were friends; that's why he's saying that. Jerk."

Stan didn't know how to respond to that. She turned to the water, admiring the view. She especially loved the nooks and crannies of the Cliff Walk like the Forty Steps where you could walk down almost into the ocean, it seemed, and feel the spray of the waves. Of course Caitlyn wouldn't want to think Kyle was two-timing her, on top of their two-timing of their own spouses. Plus she got the sense her sister actually cared about this guy. Which surprised her. Aside from Eva and her manicurist, Caitlyn didn't usually attach to people. Even as a kid she'd been more interested in the things money could buy. She'd done well following their mother's lead. Stan had always been more like her father. During family visits to her grandmother—her father's mother—out in California when she and Caitlyn were young, she'd be outside with her gram feeding homemade food to the neighborhood stray cats while Caitlyn had been in the house playing dress up with her mother's makeup and high heels. She'd thought Stan was silly for spending time out on the front porch feeding other people's cats. Stan thought Caitlyn was silly for spending all her time in front of a mirror. It became the standard for their relationship over the years—no animosity, just different values that led them down different paths.

"You said you talked to Kyle after the murder. Did you talk to him earlier that day? Like before he went to Sheldon's?" she finally asked Caitlyn.

Caitlyn thought back, then slowly shook her head again. "No. I tried calling him a couple times, but got no answer. I knew he was leaving for the weekend thing, so I didn't think much of it. I figured he was, you know, packing and stuff. Can we turn around, please?"

They'd made it just past the first right-of-way. From

here on, the paths narrowed even more and fencing protected visitors from a steep fall. Stan did an about-face, thinking. Kyle could have been packing, cleaning his house, all the things normal people did when they got ready to leave for a few days. Or, he could've been doing something much more sinister. Like arranging a meeting with Pierre.

"Have you ever heard of a woman chef named Vaughn Dawes?"

Caitlyn looked blank. "Nope."

"Did Kyle make a lot of pizza?"

"*What?* How am I supposed to know that? He doesn't give me a menu of what he does every night. Once he did a class on vegan pizza, but it was just one recipe in a long line of them. Why?"

"Just wondering." *Wondering if you'd ever seen him use the murder weapon on anything edible.* "Caitlyn, I'd be prepared for the cops to call," Stan said. "They're going to pull his phone records if they haven't already, and you'll be one of his last calls before he vanished."

Caitlyn stopped dead in her tracks. "No. Why would I have to talk to the cops? I had nothing to do with his disappearance!"

"No, but they're looking for him hard. Which means you're probably going to get caught in the crossfire."

Caitlyn stopped walking and hugged herself, looking out over the ocean. The waves broke angrily on the rocks below them, rough despite the current stillness of the air. "I just wanted to be with someone who loved me for a change," she said, so softly Stan could barely hear her.

"I know. I'm sorry, honey." Stan put her arm around her sister. "What happened to you and Michael?"

"We grew apart. He works a lot, and when he's home, well, he doesn't pay much attention to us. He's got his friends, and his sailboat races, and he never has time. You don't know anything about it," Caitlyn said, trying to keep the haughty tone. "Your boyfriend would do anything for you, I've heard." Stan heard the slight catch in her voice, saw the tremble in her hands.

"Jake? How do you know about Jake?"

"Mom told me. She said he really loves you. And that he's supersweet. Oh, screw it." Caitlyn stepped away, wiping at her eyes.

Her mother had said *that*? About Jake? She didn't think a "simple guy"—by her mother's definition—like Jake would've garnered any kind of positive press from Patricia Connor. She would prefer if Stan dated a politician or a stockbroker. By contrast, Patricia adored Michael and his financial powerhouse career.

"Do you think Michael suspects?" Stan asked.

"I don't see how," Caitlyn said. "As I said, he's hardly ever around."

"When he is, are you?"

"Most of the time, sure."

"What about Eva?" Stan asked. They exited the Cliff Walk and paused, waiting for the traffic to let up so they could cross the street.

"What about her? Eva's fine. It has nothing to do with her. He loves Eva."

"It'll have a lot to do with her when her family splits up," Stan said.

Caitlyn thrust her chin out defiantly. "She'll hardly notice the difference. Michael's always traveling. And I know he has girlfriends on the side. So why shouldn't I find someone who actually wants to be around me?" She abruptly turned the corner and began walking back up the street toward their car, her gait surprisingly quick given her shoes. She didn't wait for Stan.

Stan followed more slowly. If her sister would give her a chance to say so, she'd tell her of course she should be around someone who reciprocates her feelings. She just had to make sure it was the right person—something she hadn't figured out for a long time. As she slid into the passenger seat, her cell phone dinged, signaling a text message. Tyler. And he didn't have good news.

Chapter 27

Tyler's text read:

Melanie Diamond put a statement out

She knows about Vaughn

Pierre's family's calling for an investigation of Shel re: both of them

Shel's losing it

Stan wanted to thunk her head down on the dash. Once this weekend was over, maybe she should call an exorcist, or at least go see a tarot reader to figure out how to banish this murderous black cloud from following her around. Enough was enough—and she still needed a piece of copper pipe to make her cannoli shell. Because in between all this drama, they all had to cook a perfect meal on Monday.

She shot back a quick text: **Be back shortly**

"Let's go," she said to Caitlyn. "I need to run an errand, then I have to get back."

Caitlyn obediently floored it, zooming back in the direction of Grounds of Hope, still not speaking.

"Don't be mad at me," Stan said. "I don't want to see you hurt over someone who's not worth it."

"You don't know anything about it," Caitlyn snapped. "He's not a bad person." She swerved into the parking lot and stomped on the brake, barely missing the front of the building that bordered her parking space.

Stan figured she had whiplash by now. She rubbed her neck as she got out of the car. "Will you call me if you hear anything?" she asked Caitlyn.

Caitlyn stared straight ahead. "Sure." She got out of the car and disappeared inside the coffee shop.

Stan sighed and searched in her bag for her keys. A white pickup truck idled next to her car, windows open. As she finally beeped her car open and slid inside, Stan caught a glimpse of the man in the driver's seat, reading something on a tablet. Bushy eyebrows hung over heavy-lidded eyes. He didn't look up. There was something familiar about him, but she couldn't place it.

She sat in her parking space, rolled down her windows, and called Tyler. He sounded like he'd locked himself in a closet to answer.

"This. Is. Bad," he said in a loud whisper. "Sheldon's on a rampage. He's blaming Therese for the Vaughn debacle."

"Therese? Why?" Stan asked.

"Because he's losing his mind. And he's desperate. This bad press could royally derail his plans. He's been working on these investors for *months*. He's accusing Therese of tipping Vaughn off and discouraging her from coming. Therese doesn't even know Vaughn."

Stan frowned. She was getting tired of hearing about the dinner. One person was dead and two were possibly missing, and all these people seemed worried about was impressing some rich investors. "What if something really did happen to her, Tyler?" Stan asked, her voice sharper than she'd intended.

A brief silence. "I hadn't thought of that," Tyler said.

"Doesn't sound like anyone has." Stan disconnected and tossed the phone in her console, leaning her head back against the seat. The coffee shop door banged open and her sister emerged with a large coffee in her hand. She got in her car and peeled out of the parking lot. The white truck next to Stan with the droopy-eyed guy pulled out, too. She frowned. She knew she'd seen this guy and his truck before. If she wasn't mistaken, she'd been with Caitlyn. As she watched her sister turn right out of the lot and the truck follow her, the hair on the back of her neck stood up.

She started her car and pulled out of the parking lot, too, and hit the gas. She was two cars behind. The pickup truck sat high enough that she could still keep an eye on it. She thought Caitlyn would head back to Narragansett and her house, but instead she drove straight down Memorial Boulevard again, then swung left onto Bellevue, heading for the mansion district. The small parade behind her did the same.

Stan felt the first catch of fear in her chest. Maybe this wasn't about Pierre at all. Maybe it was about Kyle, and Pierre had just gotten in the way. If someone had taken Kyle—or done something worse with him—then maybe that person knew about her sister and needed to tie up a loose end. But what could Kyle be doing? And did Caitlyn know about it?

She hit the button on her steering wheel that activated her Bluetooth. "Call Caitlyn, mobile," she instructed.

The system placed the call—getting it right on the

first try, even—and Stan listened to it ring and ring on the other end. Caitlyn didn't pick up.

"Shoot!" She banged the steering wheel out of frustration when voice mail finally answered. "Caitlyn. Pick up. I think someone's following you." She jabbed the button to end the call and hit the gas. The car directly in front of her took a right turn, leaving her one car behind the white truck. Caitlyn's car turned into the long driveway leading to the Newport Premier hotel. What was Caitlyn doing here?

The white pickup slowed, then passed the entrance. Stan took the turn behind her sister. Caitlyn drove up to the hotel and parked. Stan pulled up next to her and motioned for her to roll the window down. Caitlyn's eyes widened when she saw her, but she did as Stan asked. Music blared out. Matchbox Twenty. No wonder she hadn't heard the phone

"What are you doing here?" Caitlyn said, turning the music down. "I thought you had an errand to run."

"I do. But I think someone's following you, so I followed them. What are *you* doing here?"

"Following me?" She whipped around, scanning the parking lot. "Why would someone be following me?"

"I don't know," Stan said pointedly. "But you didn't answer my question."

Her eyes shifted left, then back to Stan. "I . . . just wanted to ask around about Kyle."

"You sure you want the attention?" Stan asked. "The hotel staff probably has to call the cops if anyone comes in and mentions him."

Caitlyn thought about that, tapping a manicured finger against her steering wheel.

"Do what you want. You're the one worried about

getting caught, not me. Listen, have you noticed a white pickup truck in your travels?"

Caitlyn looked at her warily. "No. Is that who's following me?"

"Looked like it." Stan looked around, too, but no white pickup appeared with a flashing sign declaring *Here I am!*

"Who is it? What should I do? You think it's someone looking for Kyle?" Caitlyn looked panicked now. "I can't call the police! What would I tell them?"

"Calm down," Stan said, but her mind raced. It could be a coincidence. Heck, she could be seeing things. But something told her she wasn't, and she'd learned to trust her gut. "Switch cars with me," she said.

Caitlyn stared at her like she'd lost it. "Why?"

"Because if someone's following you, they'll follow me and I can figure out what's happening."

"But then you'd be in danger," Caitlyn pointed out.

"I'll be fine. Give me the keys," Stan said. "You have other things on your mind. I'm at least paying attention."

Caitlyn handed her the keys reluctantly.

"Be careful," Stan said.

"I will." Caitlyn made no move to go inside. "You too."

Stan got in her sister's SUV, adjusted the seat, and drove slowly through the parking lot, one eye on the rearview. She didn't buy Caitlyn's story about coming here. But what was her sister up to?

Caitlyn waited until Stan got halfway down the drive before she hurried inside. When Stan got to the hotel ground's exit, she looked carefully in both directions but saw no sign of the white truck. Maybe she *was* losing it.

She drove to the nearest hardware store for her copper pipe. She used that to make her cannoli shell by wrapping a piece of bread around it. She liked it for that purpose because it warmed evenly and gave her a perfectly cooked shell. She also found an outdoor market and got more strawberries, blueberries, and a piece of fish. She'd make one of the dinners tonight for Nutty. At some point, they would all be expected to cook.

She loaded her purchases into the backseat and leaned against her car, sniffing at the sea air. The sun shone bright and high in the sky, giving the impression of paradise. In the jeweled tones of the day with the sea twinkling in and out of her vision, thinking about murder seemed so out of place. A vision of Pierre's still form on the patio, all that blood, flashed through her brain and she abruptly pushed the images away. She had to get back and help Tyler. That familiar feeling of obligation took hold of her. Tyler would be a deer in the headlights again, trying to figure out how to address this while Sheldon freaked out.

She thought about what she would do if this was still her real job. In light of today's developments and the limited information she had, she'd talk to Pierre's mystery publicist. If he did have a campaign going against Sheldon—and it wasn't all in Mr. Pastry's head—Melanie Diamond would have orchestrated it. And if it had to do with Vaughn Dawes's disappearance, she might be persuaded to talk now that the police were involved.

Stan checked her watch. Enough time to whip up a test batch of cat-noli and talk Sheldon off the ledge. Then she could figure out how to find Melanie Diamond and have a conversation about Pierre and friends.

Chapter 28

Stan got back in the car and used her iPhone to search for Vaughn Dawes before heading back. She was curious about the allegedly missing woman. A number of images popped up—including a photo Stan had seen before. The one of Pierre on the red carpet with the blonde woman.

She should've known. Pierre and Vaughn seemed like the perfect couple, if one judged by outward appearances. But why hadn't Sheldon told her they were an item? He'd either pretended not to know, or he hadn't known. She checked the date on the phone. Last February. Maybe they'd since broken up.

Her phone rang again. Stan smiled when she saw Char Mackey's name flash on the screen. Char would likely be following this story and want the gory details. Char was a huge foodie and loved The Food Channel. She also loved pastry and had been beside herself with excitement about Stan's partnership with Sheldon. Stan knew she harbored a secret desire that Sheldon would open a people bakery in Frog Ledge, too, so she didn't have to drive so far to get his goodies.

"Stan, honey! How are you?"

She pictured Char in the bed-and-breakfast's cozy kitchen, whipping up something delightful and Southern to eat while she cranked the air-conditioning and a Billie Holiday CD. It made her smile. "I'm okay. How are you?"

"How am *I*? Well, sugar, I'm not rubbing elbows with dead chefs, that's for sure! What in blazes are you cooking up now?" Char giggled a little. "Get it? Cooking up?" Then she sobered. "I shouldn't joke. This is serious."

Despite herself, Stan chuckled. "What have you heard?"

"Heard? Honey, it's all over the news. Pierre LaPorte, one of the juiciest chefs around, is dead, another up-and-comer is on the run or missing, the fabulous Vaughn Dawes is missing . . . sounds like y'all got yourself in a speck of trouble."

"Seems that way," Stan said. "I'm so glad you called. It sounds like you know these guys."

"Well, I know them the way groupies know their favorite rock bands," Char said, laughing. "And Pierre was juicy. How could you not know him? Such a shame. Good pastry chef, too. I've been to his place in New York a few times. He didn't make the rags much, other than that stint of family drama that followed him around for a few years."

"Family drama? Like what?"

"Oh, honey. You need to read your rags more often. Pierre and his ex-wife Marianna Russo. Mob ties," she whispered, as if the mob had slipped in and bugged her house. "They were building a restaurant empire. Her father managed the whole thing. Successful too. Then they split. Pierre fired his father-in-law, but Mr. Russo fired him right back. What a mess. The Russos had a lot more money, though, so of course they came out on top. Pierre's been trying to find his footing ever since."

"Wow. How long ago?"

"Probably five years or so," Char said.

"Why'd they get divorced?"

"She cheated on him, according to the rumor mill. Not even the poor dumb schmuck's fault."

Which would've left Pierre bitter—and probably broke. Maybe he'd been threatening his ex-family in a desperate quest for money, if he was struggling like Sheldon suggested. Maybe they hadn't liked that and wanted him silenced. Stan wondered if Sheldon knew the Russos.

"What about arrests? I heard Pierre had some trouble with the law."

"Hmm. Now that you mention it, I think he got in trouble for selling drugs out of the New York kitchen. He somehow managed to avoid any real consequences, though. Or even much publicity. I remember hearing something last year, maybe? Then nothing."

"You knew of Vaughn Dawes, too?"

"Vaughn? Sure," Char said breezily, as if they were friends on a first name basis. "When Ray took me to Southern California for our twentieth anniversary, we ate at all the best restaurants. Including hers."

"She has a restaurant?"

"She did back then—Grind. We were reminiscing about our anniversary dates just last week because we were planning our date for this year. The California trip would've been four years ago. We just celebrated our anniversary this weekend at Jake's, you know."

Four years ago. Pierre and Vaughn may have been an item. Vaughn had a restaurant. Pierre had a divorce bill. "Congratulations. I wish I'd been there." That left-out feeling washed over Stan again. While it hadn't been an official party, it would've been nice to be part of the night. And most things at Jake's turned into a party.

That was the way of the Irish pub. "I thought this woman was a pastry chef. You said she had a full-service restaurant?"

"That's her specialty, but she was trying for the whole nine yards. She brought in this young, new talent as her star chef. I remember noticing it because it had been written up in *Foodie* right before we went. She did a gumbo that the reviewer raved about, so of course I had to try it. So did everyone else. I remember it was busier than a cat on a hot tin roof."

Char was originally from New Orleans. Despite twenty-something years in New England, she still talked, cooked, and best of all, acted like a Southerner. And she made monkey bread to die for.

"So her food was good?"

"Eh. My gumbo's better, but I'm biased. Her desserts were scrumptious, I do have to say. Seems that was her calling. But the rest of it went downhill faster than a hot knife through butter. The chef just wasn't that good, I guess."

"Who was the chef?" Stan asked.

"Oh, let me think a minute." Char paused, searching her memory banks for the information. "He had an interesting name. . . . Felix! That was it. Raymond!" she called to her husband. Stan pictured Ray in his ever-present overalls, just in from tending to the alpacas, and felt that homesickness again. "What was that chef's name at Grind? Paulson, that was it," she said back into the phone. "Felix Paulson. I never heard about him again, after that place closed."

Hmm. Stan scribbled the name of the restaurant and the chef on the receipt from the hardware store and started the car, keeping an eye out for a white pickup as she drove back to the hotel. "So what's the word about her being missing?"

"There wasn't much info. Just that a friend reported she was on her way to Rhode Island, but didn't arrive as scheduled. Foodie tabloids, you know. Not much substance. But it came on the heels of this murder scandal. Did you know Pierre and Vaughn were linked romantically at one time? That's why it's big news, too. I've already heard stories about it being a murder-suicide. All kinds of crazy theories will come out now."

"I Googled her. Saw a picture of them. Murder-suicide? Like she killed him, and now we're going to find her body somewhere?" Creepy. Stan thought about that possibility as she navigated the streets of Newport, avoiding families lugging children and supplies to the beach, kids on skateboards, motorcycles, and everything that screamed summer. Love, lust, and sex. All good murder motives.

"Oh, you bet. It's just like Hollywood, honey. Stories galore. Wasn't she supposed to get there last night?"

"Yes," Stan said slowly. Which would mean a very limited number of people knew that she'd made this last-minute trip. Someone must've tipped off the rags. But who, and to what end? "I won't lie. They all seem nuts."

Char laughed. "I'm quite sure they are. They seem nuts, from what I read in the papers. Always have. I've been following the food industry my whole life. I was almost a chef, you know."

"I didn't know! But I can totally picture it." That fit. Char's cooking skills left Stan feeling like an amateur.

"Long time ago, but I enjoyed it. I went to cooking school and trained under some experts in Louisiana. Had my sights set on a Creole kitchen."

"So what happened?" Stan asked.

"I met my Raymond, and up and left to come north. It was meant to be."

"Did you ever regret it?" Stan asked. "Not Ray, of course, but leaving your dream behind?"

Char laughed. "Oh, honey, I didn't leave anything behind. I cook every day. And I get to share that food with all my friends and the lovely people who stay at Alpaca Haven. I'm still a chef. I just do it my way. Good thing, too. I could never be part of the nonsense that goes on in those celebrity circles. Like what's happened with your friends. I just like to read about it."

"They're not my friends," Stan said immediately, then realized how that sounded. "I mean, this is the first time I've met most of them. Anyway, that's really helpful, Char. Thanks."

"Anytime, sugar. Need to know anything else?"

"Yeah. How to read minds. If I could pick a superpower, that's what I'd take."

"Nah, you don't want that," Char said. "I'd never want to read Raymond's mind."

"No?"

"No. That's a recipe for disaster. I'd much rather be invisible when I wanted."

"That's a good one, too." And might come in handy in this case also. "Hey, Char?"

"Yes, darlin'?"

"Speaking of reading people's minds, have you talked to my mother?" Char and Patricia had become friends of sorts when Patricia first began spending time in Frog Ledge. Char hadn't seemed like Patricia's type, but to this day they spoke regularly. And since her mother had been radio silent for a while, maybe Char had some info.

"I have, honey. She keeps in touch. Y'all haven't?"

"No. Not in a while. I just wondered . . . what's going on with her." God, she hated the awkwardness of her family. She was thirty-six years old, for crying out loud.

Char sighed. "You two are such Yanks."

"What's that mean?" she asked, pulling into the hotel parking lot. Maybe she'd been crazy before, imagining the white truck following her sister. Even driving her SUV, she hadn't seen a glimpse of it.

"You can't just love each other. Always has to be some reason why you're not happy with each other. Your momma is trying to figure some things out."

"With Tony?"

"I think that's a big part of it, yes. She asked me about you, too, last week. I told her the same darn thing I'll tell you. *Call her.*"

"It's gotten complicated again," Stan said.

"Oh, that's nonsense. Listen, honey. I love you, but you're stubborn as any mule. Call your momma. Life's real short. Sometime you'll be sorry you didn't."

Chapter 29

Stan hung up with Char, hefted her bags, and headed for the hotel entrance. Her cell rang again. Juggling, she dug around for the phone. A Connecticut number she didn't recognize flashed on the screen. She picked up anyway. "Hello?"

"Stan? Cyril Pierce."

News traveled fast, even to Frog Ledge. "Hey, Cyril. What's going on?"

"I should be asking you that question," Cyril said. "Actually, I *am* asking you that question. I'm getting a bunch of news alerts about a dead pastry chef, and I heard a rumor this is a guy at your retreat with Sheldon Allyn. The rumor started with Char, so I'm fairly confident it's true."

Stan had to smile. It figured Char would spread the news. She paused outside the revolving door. "Are you looking for confirmation?" she asked. "Sheldon has a publicist, you know. I can connect you—"

"No, I'd rather talk to you," Cyril said. "This is one of your specialties, remember?"

Stan sighed. "Right." She listened to Cyril tapping

keys. "What do you want to know? I probably can't comment."

"That's okay; I'll ask anyway. So Pierre LaPorte, aka Peter Landsdowne, is dead. Foul play. Now there are two other chefs missing from the party. How are you feeling, given that you're in the midst of this drama as it plays out? Is the retreat continuing?"

"Let me take that one question at a time. We don't know for sure about the second chef being missing. That's an unsubstantiated rumor right now. As for the retreat, it is continuing. We have an event planned for Monday, so we're sticking it out despite the tragedy that's unfolded here. This is a dedicated bunch of chefs." Sheldon would like that one.

"The police have declared Kyle McLeod a person of interest. Do you know him?"

"I met him Thursday for the first time."

"Did he get along with the murdered chef?"

"Not sure."

"Do you know of anybody who *didn't* get along with him? Like anyone who's at the retreat?"

"I really don't know. I never even got to meet him." Stan swallowed against the memory of his blood on the white patio stone. She didn't think she should mention the snarky comments she'd overheard her fellow chefs make when they thought Pierre had arrived late due to a diva moment.

"What about Sheldon Allyn?"

"What about him?" Stan asked.

"Did *he* get along with the dead man?"

"They worked together. That's all I know."

"Hmmm." Stan heard Cyril scratching notes on his pad. "What else can you tell me?"

"Not much," Stan said.

"What about Vaughn Dawes?"

"I don't know her."

"She left Los Angeles—or was thought to leave Los Angeles—for Rhode Island. No one's heard from her since. She either never got on her plane to Rhode Island or something happened when she got there."

Cyril simply repeated what she already knew, but put that way, it sounded even more sinister. "I wish I could tell you, Cyril. I don't know."

"Do you think she and Kyle are in danger?"

"I couldn't possibly comment on that," Stan said.

"Do you think you and the rest of the remaining chefs are in danger?"

"We're all on edge, of course, and feeling terribly upset about what happened to Pierre. I have complete faith in the Newport police to find the person or people responsible for this senseless act of violence." She smiled triumphantly. She hadn't lost her touch after all.

Cyril chuckled on the other end of the phone. "You're a master. Now. Off the record?"

"Go ahead." Stan set her bags down and leaned against the wall, enjoying the opportunity to be out in the sun and, though she'd never admit it, have this conversation with the quirky newsman. She and Cyril had bonded earlier this year and she'd grown rather fond of him. Plus, he kept her on her toes.

"I'm closing my notebook and putting my pen down," Cyril said. He made a big show of rustling papers on his end of the phone. "I've heard from a reliable source that Allyn's crazy as a loon. True?"

Stan laughed. "Who, Jake?"

"Not this time. Other sources." His voice sobered. "Stan, there's a good chance he killed this guy. You know that, right?"

"The matter-of-fact way you said that gives me chills, Cyril." Stan rubbed her arms and watched the revolving hotel door. The last thing she needed was Sheldon to walk outside and spot her while they were discussing the possibility of him being a cold-blooded murderer.

"I'm not trying to scare you. I just want you to be careful. He planned this rendezvous and invited everyone. He could've planned Pierre's invite a little differently."

She'd resisted that thought until now. "I don't know, Cyril. I don't know what to think. I can't imagine Sheldon . . . doing that to anyone. There are a lot of people who could've killed him. Including someone who had nothing to do with this weekend."

Cyril made a noncommittal sound.

"When's your story running?"

"I have a version online now. I'll update it."

Which meant everyone in town would be calling her as soon as they saw it. Just what she needed. "Does Jessie know?"

"If she's reading my Web site she does," he said. "I have a new Web site, did you know? It launched this week." She could hear the pride in his voice. "I needed something more professional to go with my new office."

"Look at you, Mr. Fancy. That's great, Cyril. Congrats." Izzy Sweet and Jake were partners in the renovation of an old building in town, with the main floor slated for a bookstore. They'd also decided, after much debate, to turn the ground floor into an office for the *Frog Ledge Holler* operations. The town paper had gotten some huge press and major attention over the winter, which resulted in greater advertising opportunities and an actual revenue stream—a first for the one-man operation. Cyril suddenly found himself with the budget for a small staff. His one-room office above the flower shop downtown wasn't going to cut it anymore, and he'd decided to expand his reach. Izzy had been torn on what to do with the ground-floor space, which held appeal for a number of reasons. Cyril's operations were a perfect fit. "I'll definitely check it out later."

"Oh, one more thing. Someone e-mailed a photo to me. It looks like your missing friend Kyle and a woman."

"E-mailed to you?" Stan asked. "Like, a mass e-mail to reporters?"

"No. Like an e-mail directly to me. Unless this person sent them one at a time to other people."

"What did the message say?"

"No message. Just the e-mail of the photo."

"Why are you telling me this?"

"I wanted to see if you recognized the person. The picture has a date on it. Thursday. Taken some time during the day. Can I e-mail it to you?"

Stan's stomach turned. She had the sinking feeling that her sister's face might appear in her inbox. "Yes. This past Thursday? Like, the night of the murder?"

"You got it. Stand by." She heard Cyril tapping keys, then he returned. "All set. Let me know if you recognize her. And call me back if you want to give anyone an exclusive when this breaks, hey?"

Stan promised, then hung up and checked her e-mail, trying to stop her heart from pounding so hard. She clicked on the picture and Kyle's profile filled the screen. His head was close to a woman's, and he looked to be in midsentence. But it wasn't Caitlyn. The woman's face was partially obscured by long dark hair, but Stan had no problem recognizing her.

It was Lucy Keyes.

Chapter 30

Stan strode into the hotel and up to the front desk. "Where's Lucy?" she demanded.

The clerk, an older woman Stan hadn't seen before, frowned at her. "Pardon me?"

"Lucy Keyes."

"She's stepped out. Can I help you with something?"

Stan wanted to throw her phone at the woman, but worked hard to keep a smile alive. "No. I'll come back." She turned and almost bumped into a Latina woman standing directly behind her. Sunglasses were perched on top of a cascade of dark hair, and her foot tapped an impatient rhythm in her wedge-cut sandal. Her expression indicated that she'd like to rip someone's head off.

"Sorry," Stan muttered, and moved around her. The woman glared at her, then stepped up to the counter.

Stan jabbed the button for the elevator to Sheldon's floor. But she turned back when the woman said in a loud, Spanish-accented voice, "You say she's not here? I say bull! I wanna talk to *Miss Lucy Keyes*. And I wanna talk to her *now*."

The clerk held her ground. "I'm sorry, she's not. I'm happy to take a message—"

"Do I need to make a scene?" the woman demanded.

You already are, the clerk's face said. "Please step aside, ma'am, and we'll see if we can help you further."

Stan walked back toward the front desk, curious now.

"Help me? I'll tell you how you can help me. You bring Lucy out here. You tell her Dahianna McLeod is here." The woman stepped back, nodding with attitude. "She knows who I am."

Stan stepped over to her. "Excuse me. Did you say you're Dahianna McLeod?"

The woman turned on her, fire flashing in her brown eyes. "Who are you?"

"I'm Stan Connor. I'm a chef who worked with Kyle—"

She didn't even get to finish the sentence. She sensed the rage emanating from the other woman, but didn't expect what happened next. Dahianna stepped forward and slapped Stan across the face.

Stunned, Stan stepped back, her hand flying to her stinging cheek. "What the—"

"Ma'am, do you want me to call the police?" The clerk grabbed the phone. Other guests milling around the lobby stopped to stare at the catfight unfolding before them.

"You too?" the crazy woman screeched. "He was sleeping with you, too? Bad enough this one"—she jerked her finger toward the counter—"*Miss Lucy,* who won't come out of her cave. But another one? I'm so embarrassed. I've never been so embarrassed in my life!"

Stan doubted that. *Nice to meet you, too, Dahianna McLeod.* No wonder Kyle'd been seeing her sister on the side. And all the other women. She stepped forward, jabbing her finger into the woman's shoulder. "Don't you ever touch me again. You have no idea what you're talking about, either. I was *not* sleeping with your husband, if that's who Kyle is."

Kyle's crazy wife started shouting something back at her, but a man wearing a security jacket came out of a side door and made a beeline for them. "Ladies. I'm going to have to ask you to leave," he said firmly, grabbing each of their arms and propelling them to the door. "This behavior is unacceptable in this hotel."

"I'm a guest here!" Stan shook him off. "She's the crazy one."

"Leave me alone!" Dahianna McLeod fisted her hands. "I want to talk to Lucy. *Now.*" She turned her glare on Stan. "Since you lost track of him on Thursday night, I don't think you rate as high as that tramp did."

"Hey," Stan said. Just because Lucy had that salon-finished hair every day didn't mean she couldn't rate as high on the hot scale.

The security guy ignored what they both had to say. He went to shove them through the revolving door, but was stopped.

"Thanks, Dennis. I'll take it from here," a voice purred from behind Stan.

They all whirled to see Lucy Keyes. She wore a green pencil skirt, black lacy top, and multicolored open-toed stilettos. And, of course, her hair was perfect.

"You!" Dahianna advanced on Lucy, finger pointed. Her too long nail jabbed at the air. Dennis immediately stepped between them, but Lucy stepped past him.

"Listen, Dahianna," she began, but Dahianna wasn't hearing any of it. She just continued shouting at Lucy, to the point where Stan couldn't understand her.

This was so stupid. Stan'd had enough. Whoever Kyle

was sleeping with or not sleeping with, there was still a murder that needed to be solved. And the fact that two people were missing. "Stop!" she yelled finally.

All heads swiveled toward her. Dahianna actually shut up, too.

"Enough, for the sanity of everyone in this lobby," she said. "I need to talk to Lucy. You'll have to wait." Before Dahianna could respond, she grabbed Lucy and pulled her toward the nearest hallway.

"Dennis, take her somewhere to cool down," Lucy instructed, following Stan. "Then we can decide if we need to call the police. This way," she said to Stan.

They went through a door into a small stairway and down one flight. "In here," Lucy said, nodding toward a door. She flashed an ID at a black box. A button on the box turned green and Lucy pushed the door open. Stan followed her inside. The door closed behind them with a *snick*.

They were in a small office with no windows. Lucy pulled the chair out from behind the desk and motioned for Stan to sit in the guest chair. "Thanks for the reprieve," she said with a small smile. "That one's a little . . ." She tapped her temple.

"You know her," Stan said.

"Of her," Lucy corrected. She reached into her bra and extracted a cigarette, then seemed to remember where she was and didn't make a move to light it, instead twirling it between her fingers. "She's . . . got some issues."

Stan pulled her phone out and opened the e-mail from Cyril. "What's this about?" She thrust the phone in Lucy's face.

Lucy examined it, and her face paled. She handed it

back to Stan. This time, she lit the cigarette. "Where did you get that?"

"It was e-mailed to a reporter I know. Taken Thursday during the day, apparently. Before everything went down."

Lucy shrugged, but her hand shook as she brought the cigarette to her lips. "I told you I talked to him Thursday."

"Are you seeing him?" Stan asked.

Lucy blew smoke and fanned it with her hand, trying to avoid setting off the alarms. "No. Not anymore." She paused. "But he was staying at my house when he was in town."

Stan frowned. "I don't follow."

"Kyle and I were an item for about a year," Lucy said. "Against my better judgment. I broke it off about six months ago, because his . . . home situation became quite precarious."

Six months ago. Caitlyn had been seeing him longer than that. Stan tamped down her anger on her sister's behalf and focused on the woman in front of her. "Precarious how?"

Lucy leaned back and crossed her legs, drumming her fingers on the desktop, and arched an eyebrow at Stan. "You have to ask?"

"Well, he did marry her," Stan said pointedly.

Lucy's mouth tipped up in a smile. "Touché. There's a kid involved, so he's afraid to leave. It's kind of a mess. He's been trying to get out for a while. He migrated here to work on this restaurant. We met, the rest is history, as it often is." She shrugged. "I broke it off, but Kyle's financial situation has been less than stellar. He thought this restaurant with Sheldon would get going faster than it did and he'd have money, but it didn't and he couldn't afford his rent any longer. He let the apartment go and begged to stay with me. I was tempted to put him up here so I didn't have to deal with it, but that was too close for comfort. Plus I need my job and didn't want to put myself in jeopardy."

"Wait. He doesn't have that apartment anymore?"

Lucy shook her head. "Couldn't afford it. Sheldon helped him out for a few months but couldn't keep it up."

"When did he give it up?"

"It's been a month or so now."

"And he lived with you?"

"He stayed in my guest room."

Then why was the bloody pizza cutter in his Dumpster if he didn't even live there? And where was he meeting with Caitlyn?

"What?" Lucy said.

"Nothing. Did Sheldon know he was staying with you?"

"He warned me against getting involved with Kyle," she said with a small smile. "But I figured I could handle it. I don't think he knew Kyle stayed with me. I never told him. I don't know if Kyle did."

"Does he have your car? I know the SUV is yours," she said before Lucy could come up with a story.

"You an undercover cop or something?" Lucy asked with a small laugh. "Yeah, Kyle has it. He knew where I kept my spare keys. I went out to get dinner the night of the murder. He must've seen me get back and figured I'd be here for another four or five hours. He took the truck and left me a message not to be mad, that he'd bring it back." Her smile was cynical. "He didn't say when."

Stan sent her a skeptical look. "You really didn't talk to him after the murder?"

"Nope. Cross my heart," she said, drawing the symbol with the tip of her long nail.

"And the security tapes didn't tell the cops anything different."

"We have a security cam out front, not out back. Nothing showing him leaving out front, so I presume he left through the back door."

"So he did leave on his own. Or do you think he was under duress?"

Lucy shook her head slowly. "He didn't call from his cell phone. There was a lot of noise in the background and I could barely hear him. Just said he'd be back. I haven't heard from him since."

"Are you absolutely sure it was him?"

She thought about that. "At the time I didn't give it a second thought. That's something Kyle would do, quite frankly. But now that you mention it, the connection was pretty bad. I don't know."

"Did you report the car stolen?"

Lucy shook her head. "I figured that would add to his problems."

"Did you tell the police he has it?"

Lucy shook her head again. "And I'm afraid that ship has sailed. It's a little late to 'remember' that now, don't you think?" She used air quotes. "They'll probably get me on aiding and abetting."

Stan looked her square in the eye. "Do you think he killed Pierre?"

"Honestly," Lucy said, "I have no idea what the hell is going on."

Chapter 31

Stan left Lucy in her tiny office and took the back stairs to the second floor, trying to avoid the lobby and Dahianna McLeod. From there, she took the elevator to Sheldon's suite and banged on the door. No answer. She texted Tyler.

Where are u guys?

A beat, then Tyler wrote back.

Sheldon took off. I'm out for a bit.

So much for their SOS that she needed to get back right away. The heck with this. She had cat-noli to bake. She went back to the ballroom and shoved the secret door open, expecting mass chaos, with the rest of the group fighting for the oven. Instead, opera music soared from the kitchen. Curious, she approached cautiously, not wanting to interrupt hotel staff if they'd needed the room after all.

To her surprise, she found Joaquin wearing a neon green apron, surrounded by baking paraphernalia. As she watched, he sang along to some aria, throwing his hand up in the air as he reached a particularly high note. Flour drifted from his hands into the air and landed on his brazen red hair. Spinning around to grab something from the fridge, he noticed Stan and cringed guiltily.

"Oh, dear. Hello there. I was just being a little silly."

"Don't apologize on my account. At least someone's enjoying themselves," she said, throwing her bag on the counter. She thought about pouring herself a drink, but dismissed the idea. She had to stay sharp until she could figure out what was going on around here.

"Bad day?" Joaquin shot her a sympathetic look as he took out milk and eggs.

"You could say that. Where did Sheldon go? Where is everyone else?"

Joaquin shook his head sadly. "I don't know. He was very upset. Tyler and I thought it best to let him have some space." He broke eggs into a bowl and worked to keep a smile going. "I'm not sure where the other chefs are, but they haven't been getting in much practice. It's a shame. Anyway," he said coyly, "if you like apple pie and chocolate fudge cake with mocha creme, your day is about to get better."

Stan's eyes widened. "Get out. Chocolate fudge cake? Mocha creme?"

"Would I lie to you?" He winked and deftly added ingredients into a large silver mixing bowl, pausing to pick up a small red leather notebook off the counter. Stan recognized it. Moleskine. Her favorite kind. He brushed off the flour, flipped to a page, and skimmed his finger down some lines of scribbles, then slid the notebook into his apron pocket. Today his nails were pink.

"Not about that, I hope. I had no idea you were such

a cook. Maybe you could make something for the dinner. Has Sheldon asked you? Or have you talked to him? You know, in case this Vaughn person really doesn't show up?"

Joaquin shook his head. "I'm just playing around. I like to dabble in cooking, and working for Sheldon has reinvigorated my interest. Plus I've wanted to make something chocolaty and delightful for everyone, because I feel like we're all very sad and stressed. Would you like coffee?"

"Always. What's your take on all this craziness?"

Joaquin worked what looked like cocoa powder into his milk mixture and took a whisk to it, his brow furrowed in concentration. "I've worked for Sheldon about a year now, and I've seen a lot of things," he said. "I think Pierre had gotten into some unfortunate situations and this, sadly, is the result."

"What kind of situations?"

Joaquin put his spoon down, looked around, then stage-whispered, "Drugs." He raised his eyebrows knowingly. "He'd been lucky to get his drug bust squashed, but it didn't stop him. I know Sheldon was concerned about the goings-on at the bakery. And Pierre's attitude had been on a downhill slide, too. He was discouraged with what he considered a slipping career, and acted out." He moved to the coffeemaker and loaded beans into the grinder.

So that must be true. Joaquin was the second person she'd heard it from. "Was his career really slipping?"

Joaquin shook his head vehemently. "Only in his mind. He thought he needed to be on the cover of all the magazines to really say he'd made it. But his dedicated patrons would disagree. So many people would only eat his pastries. And he did charity work, which to me is better than any magazine cover. As a matter of fact, as my first real task for Sheldon when I was hired, I organized a bake-off charity event. Pierre was there from the beginning, pitching in, offering his yummies for a good cause. Amazing chef. Such a loss." He finished prepping the coffee, turned the machine on, and went back to the cake.

"How long have you known him?"

"A year and a half or so? That's when I started working for Sheldon."

"Was he seeing anyone? Didn't he used to date Vaughn?"

"Oooh!" Joaquin abandoned his batter and leaned on the counter, chin in his floury hands. "I don't know! Do tell."

"I don't know either. I don't know them, remember? I'd just heard that. Through the gossip mill," she said.

Joaquin looked disappointed at not getting the 411. He finished making his mocha creme and layered it into the fudge cake.

Stan watched. "Can I make my vanilla cat-noli creme the same way? Yours looks fluffier than I can ever get mine and I wanted to try something new for this meal."

"Of course you can! Are you using ricotta?"

"Yogurt. Low fat."

"And how are you mixing?"

"By hand."

"Well, that's the problem!" He snapped his fingers, then looked around. "Ah, there we go." He pointed to the food processor. "Let's whip up your mixture and then we'll put it in there, shall we?"

"Sure." Stan gathered her vanilla extract, almond extract, and yogurt from the fridge. "Maybe I'll add some berries," she decided, pulling out the blueberries. She measured and mixed, then handed it to Joaquin.

"Okay. Let's see now." Joaquin spooned the mixture

into the machine, then lightly pulsed it until the texture turned smooth and creamy. "Voilà!"

"Wow. I never thought to use a food processor because I thought it would get too runny. That's fantastic." Stan tasted it. "Delicious. Thank you."

"Anytime. The blueberries must make it superb." Joaquin nodded approvingly and took two mugs from a cabinet. "I've learned a lot from Sheldon." He poured them each coffee, handed Stan hers, then added milk and sugar to his.

"I'm sure. I was looking forward to getting pastry tips from Pierre, too."

Joaquin nodded, then his face turned serious. "I'm sad for you, that you didn't."

"Yeah, I'm kinda sad about it, too. I'd heard such great things about his work. Did he mentor you, too?"

"Unfortunately, no. He was very busy, and spent the majority of his time in New York, where Sheldon and I divided our time between here and Boston. Sometimes Shel would send the heli to get Pierre—"

"Heli?"

Joaquin grinned. "Sheldon has a helicopter, yes."

Stan raised her eyebrows. "Wow. This pastry thing is more lucrative than I thought." And so much for Caitlyn's belief that Kyle didn't have access to that mode of transportation. If he'd needed to make a fast getaway, would Sheldon have arranged it for him? She made a mental note to mention that to Detective Owens next time he came around.

"You're not kidding," Joaquin said with a knowing smile. "Why do you think I want to be mentored by the best?"

"Good thinking," Stan said. "Did Pierre use it often?"

"When Sheldon summoned." That wry smile again.

"Shel likes to be in charge, if you hadn't guessed. But not lately. Like Shel said, there'd been some trouble."

"Did Sheldon let all his prize chefs use it?"

Joaquin laughed. "Oh, no. It wasn't like that. He only used it for dire situations. Truth be told, Sheldon didn't love the helicopter. He only bought it because someone suggested it. He sent it for Pierre to help him out, get him back and forth quickly."

"Why just Pierre?" Stan asked.

"Aside from Maria, Pierre is busiest," Joaquin said with a shrug, then grimaced. "*Was* busiest. And Sheldon liked to have him available. It did make the other chefs jealous, though. Especially the core group, like the ones here."

"Maria," Stan guessed.

"Well . . ." Joaquin glanced around to be sure no one had come in. "Marcin, more often."

"Marcin? Really?"

"Yes. But any cause he had to be angry at Pierre, he took."

"Why?"

Joaquin sighed. "You heard about Marcin's problems. Unfortunately, I think he partly blames Pierre. For the financial ones, anyway. When Marcin and Leo started their new restaurant, they asked Pierre for help. To do a special dessert of the week or something in hopes of attracting more customers, since they were fairly new at it. Pierre said he would, but he wasn't good at follow-through. One week in particular, he'd given them desserts for their menu and then failed to send the desserts. It was a big mess. Of course, that wasn't the only trigger for Marcin's . . . issues. They were a long time coming, and this just added fuel to the fire. You know how it is when things go terribly wrong, and sometimes you fixate on one thing? I fear that's what happened to Marcin." Joaquin shrugged. "His breakdown happened not long after. I think he always held a grudge against Pierre after that."

"Do you think he could've killed him over that?" Stan asked with a shiver. Missing desserts?

Joaquin shuddered. "I never thought about that. I don't know. I have seen his mood grow very dark lately. It concerns me. And Leo is such a good man, always trying to compensate. I think he's in denial," he finished in a low voice.

Stan thought about that. The story seemed weak as far as motive, but Joaquin was right about people, even those without mental illness or psychiatric problems, fixating on a person or situation they felt had screwed up their lives. Sometimes those stories took a very bad turn.

"I know it sounds crazy," Joaquin said. "But then when he was late on Thursday—"

"He was?"

Joaquin nodded. "At the very last minute, Leo called me and said Marcin had something to attend to, and wouldn't make it at the agreed-upon time. Tyler had to wait for half an hour. Again, I can't speak to where he was," he said, holding up his hand. He laughed nervously. "These terrible police detectives. They have us all suspecting each other."

Chapter 32

Joaquin put his fudge cake in the oven, set a timer on his phone, and excused himself. Grateful to have the kitchen to herself, Stan baked a couple of different sizes of cannoli and filled them with her new, improved blueberry cream. Praying Nutty liked it, she took some samples of that and the strawberry cake to offer him. On the way up she checked in at the front desk. There was no sign of Dahianna McLeod, but Detective Genske sat on one of the sofas in the lobby. She saw Stan and waved, making it impossible for Stan to slip past.

"Hi," she said, veering over.

"Afternoon. What's new?"

"Nothing. Are you here because of Kyle's wife?"

Genske raised an eyebrow. "We were here to meet Kyle's wife earlier. We're back to see Sheldon now."

"Oh," Stan said. "By the way, did you know about the helicopter?"

Genske regarded Stan. "Tell me more."

"Not much to tell, but Sheldon apparently had a helicopter he often used to fetch Pierre." She shrugged. "I thought you should know."

"Thank you. That's helpful. Did you meet Kyle's wife, too?"

"I did," Stan said, her hand going to her cheek as if Dahianna's handprint could still be visible.

Genske smiled a little. "You seen Sheldon?"

"Not since early this morning."

"Huh," Genske said. "He upset about anything?"

"I think he's upset about everything," Stan said. "He's concerned about the publicity on Vaughn Dawes's nonarrival, for one, and the fact that suspicion is being cast on him. Has she officially been reported as missing?"

Genske spread her hands. "I have no knowledge of that. Her family and friends would've reported it locally."

Stan's phone vibrated in her pocket and she pulled it out. Tyler.

The cops are asking for Sheldon!

Genske watched her curiously.

"Okay. Well, I have to run," Stan said. "Have to taste-test my treats on my cat."

"Good luck. Hey, if you see Sheldon, tell him we're looking for him, will you?"

"You got it," Stan said, and turned to go.

"One more thing?" Genske said.

Stan gritted her teeth, but managed to change it into a pleasant smile by the time she turned. "Sure."

"Are you related to Caitlyn Connor Fitzgerald?"

The sigh of defeat almost escaped her lips, but she held it back. "Yes. That's my sister."

"Really? Have you seen her lately?"

"I have actually. We went for a walk this morning. Why do you ask?"

"Just wondering. I've heard her name linked to Kyle McLeod," Genske said, her eyes steely. "But I figured if you knew any of that, you'd have told us. Right?"

"Of course," Stan said in her best I can't believe you even have to ask tone. "My sister is happily married." The lie made her tongue itch as she said it, but she had no idea what else to say.

"Hmmm," Genske said.

Stan ducked into the elevator, relieved when the doors slid shut between her and the detective.

Her relief was short lived. When she got off the elevator and let herself into the suite, Sheldon and Maria were at the kitchen table, nursing coffees and cookies. Homemade, of course. Sheldon jumped up when he saw her. His normal shiny suit and perfect hair were both missing. He wore a pair of jeans, loafers, and a fitted T-shirt, and none of his usual primping was apparent. He didn't even have any makeup on. Things must be dire.

"Sheldon. The cops are looking for you." Stan jerked a thumb toward the door. "One's in the lobby and the other's at your suite. Tyler just texted me."

"Never mind that. Thank goodness you're here. Have you seen? Heard? This woman wants to destroy me! Tyler has been on the phone answering calls most of the day. We've sent out another statement with some adjustments, including a line that we're working closely with the local police to do everything they can to find the killer and, of course, to locate Kyle and Vaughn. But of course there's fallout! My name attached to this . . . this . . . *debacle* is fallout!"

Stan deposited her baked goods on the table. "It's good that you added that statement. I think that's all you have to say. Give it any more attention and you look guilty." She watched him closely for any sign of said guilt, but he was barely listening to her as he obsessively checked his phone, muttering about "having to stop her."

Maria took another cookie. "I can't bear to hear any more," she said to Stan. "This is terrible, what they're trying to do to him. Just terrible." She took a huge bite.

Stan ignored her. "Are you going to talk to the police?" she asked Sheldon.

Sheldon froze. "Why?"

"They have more questions."

"They'll have to wait," Sheldon said. "I have some things to attend to."

"I don't think they're in the mood to wait," Stan said. "I'd go talk to them if I were you."

Sheldon's face lost a little color, but he straightened his sleeves. "Fine. I'll go."

Maria made a sad noise around a mouthful.

Sheldon patted her shoulder. "Please tell everyone I'll be back shortly and not to worry. I want them cooking and baking and conquering the world!" He gave a weak attempt at a Sheldon battle cry, arm raised in a victory fist, but his heart clearly wasn't in it. Stan followed him to the door. He tried to keep his head high, but by the time he'd reached the elevator he looked . . . smaller. Like an old man.

Stan quietly closed the door behind him.

"You want a cookie?" Maria asked.

"Sure," Stan said. "What the heck."

Stan felt no guilt as she munched on cookies, some kind of chocolate chip creation with hints of espresso. While she enjoyed it, Maria got a text from Sheldon that he'd been asked to go downtown with the cops.

"What!" Maria stared at the phone, then at Stan. "He can't go!"

"He has to, Maria. It will look really bad if he doesn't."

"This is preposterous! Sheldon is not a murderer!" She burst into tears and fled upstairs. Stan heard her door slam. She shook her head and finished her cookie. Then she took Nutty's treats upstairs. He was awake, sitting on the window bed watching a bird fly back and forth outside. His regal tail was in full fluff mode.

"Hey, baby. Brought you something." Stan presented the bite-sized cat-noli and cake to Nutty. He approached cautiously, as cats often did with new food, and sniffed.

Stan watched anxiously. He kept sniffing. Then . . . he walked away.

Stan's mouth dropped. He had to be kidding. Strawberry cake? Blueberry vanilla cat-noli? "You're killing me," she said. "How am I supposed to feed this to a Siamese if you won't even eat it?"

He looked at her as if to say, *Not my problem*, then hopped back onto his window. Stan flopped onto the bed and closed her eyes. What a disaster this weekend had been, and there were still two days left. She should call Jake. He would make her feel better. Maybe she should call him and see if he'd pick her up. As if on cue her phone rang. But it wasn't Jake. It was Caitlyn.

"Hey," she said.

"You were right," her sister said in a funny voice.

"About what?"

"A cop showed up here. They know about Kyle."

Stan thought of Genske's question in the lobby and swallowed hard. The detective was probably on her way upstairs to arrest her, too, for withholding information.

"They're taking me in for questioning," Caitlyn said, and her voice broke. "Eva's here, and my nanny, and Michael will know. If he doesn't already. You know how the neighbors talk. It's all over. I can't believe this." She started to cry and hiccup.

"Where are you right now?"

"In the bathroom trying to pull myself together."

"Listen. Tell them what you know. It's not much, right? They want to find Kyle. That's their endgame. Once they understand that you don't know where he is, they'll forget about you. But just to warn you, Kyle's wife showed up at the hotel today."

"What?" Caitlyn's shriek wasn't as effective in a whisper, but she gave it a good try.

"Yeah." Stan didn't mention Lucy Keyes. Her sister had enough to worry about right now. "I'll tell you later. Listen. Go with them but don't say anything. Call Mom's lawyer. I'll come get you. Okay?"

"You will?"

"I will."

"Thanks, Krissie." With another hiccup, Caitlyn disconnected.

Chapter 33

Stan went downstairs and almost bumped into Joaquin, coming down the hallway holding a gorgeous cake.

"Hey," Stan said. "That looks fabulous."

Joaquin smiled proudly. "It did come out extra perfect, didn't it? I hope Sheldon likes it. I feel like he needs a smile."

Oops. He didn't know that Sheldon had gone to the police station. "Yeah, he's not back yet," she said.

"That's okay. He needed some playtime." The elevator dinged.

"He's at the police station, Joaquin. The detectives asked him to go in for questioning."

His face went pale and he swayed slightly on his pink sneakers. Stan reached out to steady the cake. That would be a tragic casualty. "You okay?" She felt bad for Sheldon's three young charges. Between Tyler and his crash course on crisis communications, Therese getting blamed for a leak, and now Joaquin learning his adored boss had been hauled off by the cops, none of them were going to be the same after this weekend.

"Why . . . what do they want with him?"

"Probably to see if he knows why one of his chefs is dead and two more are missing?"

"This is terrible. He can't handle that," Joaquin exclaimed.

"He's going to have to handle it," Stan said. "He doesn't have a choice."

Joaquin looked like he might cry. "He's very sensitive."

Sensitive? "Does he have a lawyer you can call, just in case?"

Now Joaquin looked like he might pass out. "Lawyer?"

"Don't freak out," Stan said, glancing around. A couple of people looked at them curiously as they passed by. "They didn't sound like they were arresting him. But just in case, maybe you should contact one?"

"Good idea. You're amazing. Can you ask Tyler? I need to go set up the table for when Sheldon returns." He shoved the cake at Stan. "Tyler has the computer with all the contacts," he said. "Let's plan on having a special dinner for Sheldon, even if no one wants to cook. We'll order in. But he needs something happy when he returns. Thank you, thank you!" he called as he jogged away.

"No problem," she muttered, and jabbed at the elevator button. She made the trek to Sheldon, Tyler, and Joaquin's suite and raised her hand to knock. Then she realized the door was cracked open.

"Hello?" Peering in, she nudged the door back and opened her mouth to call for Tyler. Then stopped when she saw him. Well, the back of him. The front of him was lip-locked with Therese, whose hair was really the only part of her Stan could see. Yes, she was that skinny.

"Um." She cleared her throat, then cleared it again more loudly when they didn't acknowledge her. "Guys?"

Tyler jumped back, startled. Therese pouted, then sent Stan a nasty look.

"Whoa. Hey, Stan. Need something?" Tyler said, running his hand through his hair. "Shoot, did something happen? Nice cake."

Stan set the cake on the counter. "I do need something, actually. Can you get me the number of Sheldon's lawyer?"

"Lawyer?" Tyler stared at her. "What for?"

"He's at the police station."

"No freakin' way," Tyler breathed. "You hear that, babe?" he asked Therese.

Therese gave him a look, brushed by Stan, and left the room. Stan swore the other girl hissed at her on the way out. Kind of like Nutty when the dogs bothered him.

"Sorry about her. She gets cranky," Tyler said.

"I can tell. I didn't know you guys were an item," Stan said.

Tyler laughed nervously. "I didn't either. I mean, we aren't really an item. We're just, you know. Having fun."

"Were you having fun Thursday night after we got here?"

Tyler's face turned red. "Yeah. So what?"

She shrugged. "I've been wondering where Therese had been all night. So she was with you?"

"Yeah. I really did go to a bar downtown. I brought her with me."

"Did she stay here in your suite? Because she never came back."

Tyler reddened. "Yeah, she did. Is there a problem with that?" he asked defensively.

"No problem. Just good to know."

"Am I calling this lawyer?"

"I'd keep the number handy. And while you're thinking about it, you might want to get a statement ready about Sheldon's trip to the police station. I'm sure that'll be the next headline in the news."

Chapter 34

Stan finally left the hotel for the police station to get her sister. As she started Caitlyn's SUV, she wondered if they'd finished with Sheldon yet. What a disaster. Things weren't looking good all around, yet Stan didn't feel like they were any closer to solving the murder. Plus, now she had to figure out how to tell her sister that Kyle and Lucy hadn't been over when she'd gotten together with him, never mind that Kyle hadn't even been renting the apartment he'd said he was renting while he lived off Lucy. He was lucky he was missing—if he were here, Stan would smack him.

She turned out of the hotel parking lot and drove down the long driveway, finally emerging into the heart of Newport as her mind worked through the puzzle. Something was missing here. A big piece. But darned if she could put her finger on it.

Taking a right onto Ocean Avenue, Stan happened to glance in her rearview mirror and saw headlights right behind her. Tall ones. Like from a truck. Thankfully it wasn't completely dark yet. She kept her eyes on the mirror and felt a jolt of adrenaline when she recognized a white pickup truck, close enough to her bumper it could've pushed her.

Coincidence? Stan doubted it. Nerves soaring, she hit the gas and took off down the street, making a fast left turn with no signal. The truck clearly wasn't expecting it, but at the last minute corrected and made the turn. Stan took another two or three turns, watching the truck the entire time, driving in a big circle to see if it would stay on her tail. It did. Anger replaced fear now. There was enough going on in her world without this added stress. Stomping on her brake, she reached for her phone and dialed 911.

"I'm on Maple Avenue in Newport and a white pickup truck is tailing me," she said when the dispatcher answered. "I've seen this truck three times over the past two days, including earlier today, and I'm feeling unsafe."

"Do you have a license plate number, ma'am?"

"I can't see it," Stan said, kicking herself for not taking it down when she'd seen it in the coffee shop parking lot, or when it had followed Caitlyn to the hotel earlier.

"Okay. Stay in your vehicle, ma'am. I have a unit nearby."

"Should I keep driving?"

"Go slow," the woman advised. "They should be there in one minute or less. What kind of car are you driving?"

Stan told her. "Ask Detective Owens to come, if he's available," she said, then disconnected. A moment later, she saw flashing lights flying up the street behind her.

She pulled over in front of someone's house. The pickup truck did the same. The cop car pulled in sideways and partially behind the truck, blocking him in. She watched, fascinated, as two cops approached on each side of the vehicle, hands poised over their weapons. The cop on the driver's side spoke, then Stan saw hands coming out of the driver's side window, demonstrating that he had no weapon. The officer opened the door, still standing slightly back, and let the driver step out of the car, his colleague coming around the front of the car. The cop had him face the truck and put his hands against the side of the roof. He was tall enough to reach.

Another cop car shot up the street and pulled up in front of her car. The cop got out, conferred with his colleagues, then came over to Stan. She buzzed the window down.

"You placed the nine-one-one call?" the officer asked.

"I did."

"This guy was following you?"

"Yes. For the second time today. Well, earlier he was following my sister in this same car. Did you call Detective Owens? Who is this guy? Is he dangerous?"

The cop turned when one of the others called his name. "One second," he said to Stan, and walked over. She leaned out of the car window to get a better view of what was happening behind her. And frowned. The driver was no longer assuming the position. Instead, he faced the cops. And they were laughing.

What was going on here? Stan shoved the car door open and got out. "What do you think you're doing?" she said to the cops. "This guy was stalking me and my sister and you're standing here having a good laugh about it?"

"Ma'am, not at all," the last-to-arrive cop said. "If we can explain—"

"No wonder people don't feel safe when they get restraining orders or tell you about being stalked," Stan went on, her voice rising, "if this is what happens. I guess it's all just one big boys' club though, right?"

"Ma'am," the cop interrupted, more sternly this time. "This is Ryan Holder."

Stan stared at him. "So?"

Another car pulled up. They all stopped to watch Detective Owens emerge. He walked over, his keen eyes taking in the scene before him. He nodded. "Evenin'," he said, as if this were a normal meeting.

Stan turned to him. "Thank goodness. This man has been following me and my sister around. This is the third time I've seen him since yesterday. And these officers seem to think it's funny. This could have something to do with Pierre."

Owens regarded her calmly. He looked at his colleagues. "That true?"

"No," the cop who had first approached the pickup's driver's side door said. "Well, the part about him following her is true. We don't think it's funny. But we were trying to explain who he is."

"And who's that?" Owens asked.

"Ryan Holder."

Owens showed no sign of recognition either.

"The PI," the other cop said. "Don't you remember? He worked that missing kid case after the dad tapped him? Ended up solving it, hate to say it."

Ryan Holder smiled. He pushed off the side of the car and approached Stan, hand extended. "I'm very sorry to frighten you," he said, those droopy eyes seemingly sincere.

Stan folded her arms, rebuffing him. "Why were you following me? Or did you think you were still following my sister?"

"Your sister," he admitted.

"Why were you looking for my sister, then?"

"I was hired to do so."

Stan groaned inwardly. Of course. A private eye. Only

in her sister's world. All the cops were watching her now, including Owens.

"By whom?" she asked, although she feared she already knew the answer.

"That's confidential information."

"Was it her husband?"

Holder said nothing.

"Great. Fabulous. Did you get what you needed? Although if you were any good you'd know she's at the police station right now."

Holder turned his hands palms up. "Hey, we all have our off days. I wasn't expecting you to switch cars."

One of the cops snickered. Stan shot him a dirty look, then turned back to Holder.

"You should really be more considerate when you're tailing women," she said. "Unless you're trying to scare them to death. Did Michael pay you extra to do that?"

Without waiting for an answer she spun on her heel and went back to her car as the rest of them dispersed to their vehicles and Ryan Holder climbed back into his truck. She'd just cranked the engine on when Owens appeared at her window. "Got a second?"

"Not really. I have to go pick Caitlyn up at the station. I'm presuming she's still there?"

"She is. Genske was talking to her when I left."

"Sheldon still there, too?" Her gaze followed the white pickup truck as it traveled down the street and turned out of her line of sight, the cop cars right behind. Maybe they were all going to the bar.

"He is. I had to put him on hold to come out here. Heard you met McLeod's wife."

She glared at him. "Yeah. She's a gem. My sister in trouble?"

"Not if she didn't do anything. She swears she didn't see or hear from him after he vanished."

"She's freaking out."

"I can tell. McLeod isn't worth it, though. Seems like he's got a few ladies on the side."

She leaned her head back against the seat, feeling suddenly incredibly tired.

"Your sister may have her hands full with Mr. McLeod's wife. I almost wished I had something to hold her on, because you know that woman will go cause some kind of trouble for someone."

Despite herself, Stan wanted to laugh. The whole thing was crazy. "I'm going to get Caitlyn," she said. "Thanks for coming out, Detective. Sorry to interrupt your night."

"Be careful out there, Ms. Connor," Owens said, stepping back. "We still haven't caught the killer."

Chapter 35

By the time Stan picked up Caitlyn, her sister had graduated from freaked out to zombie calm. Which would change when she told her about the PI.

"So, we can swap cars back," Stan said carefully. She took a deep breath and glanced over at her sister. "I was right. You were being followed."

Caitlyn made a pitiful sound. "By . . . whom?"

Stan braced herself. "A PI. Michael hired him, Caitlyn."

Caitlyn closed her eyes. She said nothing, just leaned her head back against the seat. Stan kept driving.

"Where were you and Kyle meeting the last few months?" she asked finally.

Caitlyn opened one eye and looked at her. "Why?"

"Just tell me."

"He took me to a bunch of different places. Fun, new hotels or B and Bs. He said he wanted to keep it fresh." She turned her head to look out the window.

"Had you been to his apartment lately?" Stan asked.

"Not in a while. He didn't spend much time there. He said he'd gotten some crappy neighbors and didn't want me in the building, especially by myself." She still didn't look at her sister. Stan got the sense Caitlyn was trying to deflect something.

"Why did you go to the Newport Premier?" she asked her sister.

Caitlyn sighed. "Why does it matter?"

"It does."

Caitlyn turned to look at her. "To see Lucy Keyes, okay? I'm not stupid, Stan." Her eyes filled with tears. "I knew they had a history. I wanted to know if it was still going on and I . . . didn't think Kyle would tell me the truth."

So Caitlyn had talked to Lucy. Stan wondered if Lucy had figured out she and Caitlyn were related. "So what did she say?"

"That she was just helping him out." Caitlyn's tone was bitter.

"Maybe she was," Stan said gently as they pulled into Caitlyn's driveway.

Caitlyn jerked her shoulder in a shrug.

"Do you want to stay at the hotel with me?" Stan asked.

"No. I need to be with Eva. And I need to face the music."

Stan felt a pang of pity for her sister. Caitlyn wasn't used to this kind of thing. She usually preferred to live vicariously through other people's drama without being the center of attention herself. "Call me if you need me," she said.

They swapped cars and Stan drove back to the hotel, her mind drifting back to the mysterious Melanie Diamond. The more she thought about her, the more she became convinced she held the key. Or at least some answers that might lead to the key. But calling her wasn't going to work. Too easy to hang up, or avoid her entirely.

Face to face, though . . . Stan parked, the plan forming in her mind. Maybe a trip to New York was in order. That way she could visit Pierre's bakery, too, to see if there were any clues. And if she left early enough tomorrow, she could get down and back in one day. Sheldon would be so wrapped up in his problems he wouldn't be worried about who was cooking. She could catch a train out of Providence. And maybe she could recruit some help.

Stan dialed the number three times before she let it connect. She kept hanging up to refine her pitch, sure she'd get hung up on at best, or the death silence, which was worse.

Oh, get a grip. Dial the phone and act like a big girl, or don't ask for help at all. Wing it and go alone.

Since winging it didn't sound like the best idea, she let the call go through. "Hey," she said when Jessie answered.

"Hello again," Jessie said. "What now? Some other friend needs to find out who's driving what car?"

Stan grimaced. She could never tell if Jessie was kidding. She decided to proceed as if she were and laughed. "No. But I did have a different favor to ask. Are you off this weekend?"

Now Jessie's tone became guarded. "I am."

Stan blew out a breath. "I need some help. In-person help." She imagined the mental groan and forehead smacking going on at the other end of the phone.

But to her credit, none of that came through in Jessie's response. "With what?" she asked.

"I need to go to New York tomorrow." She gave her a rushed Cliffs Notes version. "And I need you to find an address for this publicist. I doubt she'll be at her office on a Sunday, and I can't find a listing for her."

Jessie said nothing during Stan's spiel, not even honing in on the parts she'd glossed over, like the fact that the police were looking for her sister's boyfriend in earnest, and that her sister and said boyfriend were both married to other people. When Stan finished, Jessie remained silent for so long Stan wondered if the phone had cut out on her.

Then she spoke. "You know you're getting involved in something you shouldn't, right?"

"Totally," Stan said.

"You have no idea what the real story is with these guys. They could be dangerous. Clearly someone the dead guy was involved with *was* dangerous."

"Understood," Stan said.

"So you just decided to call me and screw up my weekend off."

"Well, when you put it that way . . . yes."

Jessie sighed, long and loud, sounding like a balloon deflating. "My kid wanted to go play mini-golf."

Now Stan felt bad. "I'm sorry. Look, it was a shot in the dark. I thought you might know the best way to get some answers. I feel bad for my sister, and everyone here is scared and worried. But I don't want you to neglect Lily."

"What train are you taking?" Jessie asked.

"I'm going to take a morning train out of Providence. I have to check the schedule."

"Let me know which one. I'll pick it up in New Haven."

Stan almost dropped the phone. "Sorry?" She had expected a lot more resistance than this. Maybe Jessie wasn't feeling well.

"I said, I'll pick it up in New Haven. Down and back in one day, right?"

"Right. Totally. Yes." She hesitated. "Forgive me for saying this, but is there a catch?"

Jessie chuckled. "A catch?"

"Yeah. I, um . . ."

"Didn't expect me to say yes? My brother called me. He gave me some intel into what was going on. I half expected this, knowing you. And then there was the reg lookup. I didn't buy your story, for the record."

Stan didn't know whether to yell at Jake or thank him. Or take offense at Jessie's last comment. She decided to let it go and accept the help. "Regardless, thank you."

"Yeah. Don't mention it."

"And what about—"

"The publicist? Yeah. I'll look her up, too. Might as well completely abuse my power."

Cheered for the first time since Thursday that she might actually get somewhere, Stan hurried into the hotel and straight to the ballroom for dinner. When she pushed open the secret door she found a full kitchen with a frenzied vibe despite the soothing classical music playing through the built-in speakers. Whatever vision Sheldon had dreamt up about them all working together preparing an entire menu full of meals and smooching each other along the way had gone right into the grave with Pierre. Not to mention Joaquin's desire to welcome Sheldon back with a relaxing dinner. Instead of a zen kitchen right out of *Foodie* magazine, their workspace had deteriorated into a messy, burnt-smelling battle zone, with the stench of overcooked fish hanging in the air.

Sheldon was nowhere in sight, nor was Tyler. Stan could only imagine the activity in the realm of Sheldon Allyn Enterprises. Here, however, was a different problem. Leo and Joaquin were pressed against the counter, watching wide eyed as Maria and Marcin faced off. Marcin looked completely insane, eyes bulging, hair wild, brandishing a grilling fork.

"You made me burn my bass!" he yelled.

Maria jammed her hands onto her ample hips as she prepared to fire back, but Stan could tell the fork unsettled her.

Stan dropped her bag and cleared her throat. "What's going on?"

All eyes except Marcin's turned toward her. Marcin kept his angry gaze square on Maria with an intensity that gave Stan the chills. "Marcin's lost his mind, clearly," Maria said. Her defiant tone belied her fear, but her eyes stayed on the fork.

Leo winced. So did Stan. Probably not wise to say that to someone with a mental illness. Joaquin remained frozen in place. His eyes cut to Stan helplessly. *Do something!* they seemed to beg.

Marcin barked out a laugh and feinted a jab with the fork in Maria's direction. She jumped and screeched. Marcin muttered something about fat and stupid, threw the fork on the ground, and flounced out of the kitchen. Stan heard his feet pounding through the ballroom.

They were all silent for a moment, looking at each other. Then Leo mumbled an apology and followed his boyfriend. Stan bent to pick up the fork. Joaquin snatched a cast iron pan with blackened fish off the stove and turned the heat off, breathing a sigh of relief. Maria glared at them.

"He's crazy, you know," she said to no one in particular.

"Everyone's under pressure right now, Maria," Stan said, tossing the fork in the sink. "I'm sure he'll come around and apologize. If he needs to apologize," she added with a pointed look.

Maria's hands went back to her hips. "Of course he needs to apologize. He barged in here like a child let loose in my Italian cookie shop and went into a *fish frenzy*. Shouting about grilling sea bass, with no regard for the delicate flavors of my carbonara that he'd damage in the process!"

Stan didn't really care whose fault it was. She wasn't about to sign up to broker a truce, either. Maybe Marcin *was* off his rocker. Maybe Maria was, too. She didn't care anymore. She just wanted to get through this weekend alive and unscathed, then go home and never see any of them again. "That's too bad," she said simply, stooping to pick up her bag.

Joaquin poked at the sea bass. "If anyone likes blackened sea bass, we can have that over salad," he said, forever the optimist.

"I think I've lost my appetite," Stan said, and excused herself. This day had gone on for way too long already. She'd go order room service and try to get some sleep before her big adventure in New York City tomorrow.

Chapter 36

But the universe had other ideas. When Stan went upstairs, Sheldon paced the floor in front of her door.

"Can we talk?" he said by way of hello.

No! She wanted to shout, but didn't. "Of course. Want to come in?" Stan opened the door to the suite. "Have a seat."

Sheldon sat at the kitchen table and smoothed his hair into place. "We have a problem."

"That's been apparent since Thursday afternoon, Sheldon."

"No, I mean a serious problem. Stan, I know I can trust you—right?"

Because Pierre being dead wasn't a serious problem? "Sure."

"Thank goodness." He slumped into a chair. "Because I'm not sure whom I can trust right now. Or ever again."

Stan's patience for the drama was wearing thin. "Get to the point, Sheldon. It's late and I'm tired."

"You're right. I'm very sorry." He sat up straight and breathed in some of his normal mojo. "Someone's setting me up for this murder," he said.

"Why do you think that? Because the police questioned you?" Stan went to the fridge and took out two bottles of water. "What do you expect, Sheldon? He was killed at your house. A house no one else allegedly knew about."

"Precisely! That's exactly why. And I believe that's what Detective Owens thinks, too. It's why he didn't want to talk here. He just doesn't know whom."

Stan paced the room. "These are your people. Do you think it's someone in this group? Why do you think that? Does he have evidence? Do you?"

"No. But I feel it." Sheldon clasped his hands to his heart. "There is a cancer in my world. Isn't it obvious? If someone wanted to kill Pierre, why would they do it at my house? A house no one knew about? Why wouldn't they have done it elsewhere? And how did the press know about Vaughn before it had even become clear she was missing?"

Stan remembered Tyler saying Sheldon was suspicious of Therese for leaking the information. Did he think she could have actually murdered Pierre, too, and staged a setup? Come to think of it, she wasn't really sure what Therese did. She'd been introduced as the "anything you need girl," but Stan hadn't seen her do much this weekend.

Sheldon dropped his hands to his knees and leaned forward. "Kyle didn't have his Providence apartment anymore."

Stan said nothing. She didn't let on that she'd gotten that information already.

"So why would the allegedly bloody weapon be in that Dumpster? Someone planted it there."

Same thought she'd had. "Wouldn't that mean they were setting up Kyle, not you?" Stan asked, sitting at the table, trying to be casual. If Kyle didn't live in the apartment, and even if he did, what would the positive be for dumping the knife there if he'd done it himself?

"I don't know," Sheldon admitted. "It doesn't make sense. But I can't shake this feeling."

"Did Owens confirm that was the murder weapon?"

"The good detectives did not comment on that," Sheldon said.

"Do you know what happened to Vaughn? Did they ask you about her?"

"Of course they did. They have no evidence of any foul play, other than her car at the Los Angeles airport, but I don't believe it. I think someone got to her with bad information. Of course, her absence makes my guilt look more pronounced. I summon chefs, they die or vanish. It's *diabolical.*"

"That's a lot of work, Sheldon," Stan said. "Never mind the original murder, but tracking down this woman's flight, sending someone to apprehend her or talk her into vanishing."

Sheldon didn't seem fazed by the amount of work. "I'm telling you, Stan. There is something going on here that's very suspect."

"So why are you telling me? You've known all these folks way longer than you've known me."

Sheldon smiled, but it was tinged with something that may have been sadness. "That's precisely why I'm telling you. I have no idea who it is or what the motivation could possibly be. But I know something is wrong. Perhaps if we're both keeping our eyes out, we may get to the bottom of it."

Stan didn't like the sound of that. Sheldon clearly didn't trust any of his other people. "Tell me about Melanie Diamond."

"What about her? She's a conniving woman who capitalized on a situation that was spiraling out of control. Other than that, I don't know her."

"Who told you Pierre was using her?"

"Why do you want to know that?"

"Why don't you want to tell me?"

They stared at each other—a standoff, until Stan simply didn't feel like doing it anymore. "Whatever. You expect me to help you, but you're not forthcoming at all. So I can't." She rose, about to head upstairs and leave him at the table.

"Wait, Stan." Sheldon sighed. "You're right. I'm just so torn up about this whole thing."

Stan waited.

"It was Vaughn Dawes."

"Vaughn Dawes." As Alice would say about the rabbit hole, curiouser and curiouser. She definitely felt like Alice this weekend. "I thought she and Pierre were tight."

Sheldon shrugged. "Loyalties are fickle, oftentimes. They hadn't dated in a long time, but they did remain friends. I'm not sure why she told me, frankly."

This whole thing was beginning to sound more than fishy. "What motivation would she have to do that?" she pressed. "Were they fighting? When did she tell Tyler?"

"My dear. I have no insight into people's motivations for most things. She told Tyler within the last month. While Pierre and I were having our . . . silent battle. I'm simply telling you what I know. So will you help me?"

She paced the room, twirling a lock of hair around her finger to help her think. "I'll keep my eyes open, Sheldon, but I'm not as convinced as you are that someone's trying to hurt you. I mean, they're all a little nuts, but from what I've seen, everyone is still taking Monday seriously and trying to figure out how we're going to make it work."

Sheldon's eyes widened. "Monday. My God, you're right. I'm letting all of this distract me from why we're really here. I'm neglecting my purpose. I must go make sure everyone comes through for this dinner." He stood and squared his shoulders. "I will use my own bakers from the shop if I have to. And the mansion chefs will help. I'll talk to my contacts." He nodded. "With my oversight, we will prevail."

Stan grabbed the opening. "Why didn't we just grab your bakers from the beginning, Sheldon? I mean, I know they would have to be pretty fabulous to work for you in the first place. It seems easier than finding some-one from California. How many bakers do you have, anyway?"

Sheldon smiled, but it looked more like a lion baring its teeth. "Oh, my dear. You simply don't understand. Next to Pierre, Vaughn is *exquisite*. I do most of my own baking, you know. And closely supervise the young apprentices I have on staff. I will just have to be more diligent if they come in than I would've been if Vaughn was here. Of course, I'm hoping she will still turn up. Now if you'll excuse me, you're absolutely right. I have to put my attention on what I want, not everything that's wrong. And I want Monday to go off without a hitch, with some of the best food known to man! I know I can count on you to perfect your cat dishes."

And with that, he swept out of the room and down the hall, leaving Stan wondering what had just happened.

Chapter 37

Stan slept like the dead and woke before her alarm. She had to leave no later than seven thirty to get to Providence to catch her train. She showered, dressed in a pair of cropped jeans, a T-shirt, and comfy Keds, and tied her hair in a loose ponytail at the nape of her neck. She threw a sweatshirt and a couple protein bars into her oversized bag and propped her sunglasses on top of her head.

Nutty slept on, unaware of her plans. She stroked his back, a little worried at leaving him here with these wackos while she went to New York. She wanted to bring him with her, smuggle him in his carrier or something, but Maria would probably chase her out the door offering him prime rib. She had some weird Nutty fetish. Understandable in the sense that he was a pretty cool cat, but odd just the same. He opened one eye and looked at her.

"Will you be okay while I go out? It's going to be a late night."

Nutty gazed at her with his sweet brown eyes. He looked totally unconcerned. Stan feared he was being

lulled into submission by the king's treatment he was
receiving here. He'd probably expect the same at home.

"Don't be opening the door to strangers. Stay tucked
away in here, okay? Don't cave if they offer you food,"
she said.

Nutty purred and regarded her skeptically.

"I know. It sounds nuts. But if you have any will-
power, you'll be fine." Stan kissed his head, rose, and
left him to nap. Downstairs, she brewed some coffee.
Therese, surprisingly, appeared in the kitchen just as
she was filling her travel mug.

"Hey. Coffee's all set," Stan said cheerfully.

Therese eyed her. "Where're you going?"

"Out for a bit," Stan said. "Hey, anything new on
Vaughn?"

"No," Therese said. "She's such a *loser*. Totally got me
in trouble. Hope she's, like, happy."

Happy. Hopefully she wasn't dead. But that didn't
seem worth pointing out to this little twit. "Have a great
day," Stan said, and pulled the door open, almost bump-
ing into Joaquin. "Oh! You scared me."

"I'm so sorry! I wanted to bring you girls a coffee
cake." He brandished a yummy-looking creation topped
with fruit.

"Wow," Stan said, eyeing it.

"Unfortunately, I'm bringing bad news with it."

Stan froze. Therese did, too. They both looked at
each other, for once sharing a kindred thought: *No dead
people. Please.*

Joaquin took a breath. "Marcin had to be taken to
the hospital early this morning. For some of his . . .
ongoing issues."

"He went to the psychiatric hospital?" Stan asked.

"He went to the emergency room. From there, he'll

likely be taken for an evaluation, yes. Leo will let us know."

"So he had a breakdown," Stan said.

Joaquin sighed. "It sounds like it, yes."

"That stinks," Stan said, thinking of his outburst the previous night. "But if he was a danger to himself or others, it's for the best."

Joaquin nodded sadly. "We're shaping up for a limited menu Monday. Here. Have some cake."

Stan looked at it wistfully. "I have to go."

"Let's cut you a piece before you go," Joaquin said, leading her back into the kitchen. "Wherever it is, it'll be worth it to be late if you have cake."

Ten minutes later Stan left with her second piece of coffee cake wrapped in a napkin. *What the heck. I'll need strength for this day.*

She made it to the train station in forty-nine minutes, bought her ticket, then only had to wait five minutes until the ALL ABOARD sign clicked into place next to her train, the high-speed Acela. The regional was too slow on normal days. Today, it would've been painful.

She made her way to the platform, climbed onto the train, and found one of the double-row seats empty. She sank gratefully onto the bench, propped her feet up, leaned her head back, and closed her eyes. It felt so good to be out of the hotel and away from that motley crew. Her only anxiety was Nutty.

She pulled her phone out and checked her neglected e-mails. Treat orders had been pouring in since she'd left Thursday morning, and from the cheerful reply e-mails from Brenna, it looked like she had everything under control. Jake's little sister had quickly become indispensable to Stan's business over the past year. She did everything from baking to creating new flavors to organizing deliveries and ordering supplies. Stan relied on her for pretty much everything. And, she was helping dog and cat sit this weekend. She owed her a phone call. Brenna had tried to call her yesterday and things had been too crazy for her to respond.

She dialed her number now. It rang once before Bren picked up. "Hey!" she exclaimed. "How's it going over there?"

Clearly Jake hadn't told her anything. Good. Better she didn't worry. And she tended to not be part of Char's gossip circles. "Hey yourself. Things are going fine," Stan lied. "What are you up to? Drowning yet? I saw all the orders. My goodness, we're busy!"

"I know, isn't it great? Here you go, Scruffy. Sorry, just giving the pups some samples. Say hi to Mummy, guys! They're not talking much. Too busy eating," Brenna said. "I'm doing some chicken pot pie per Amara's request. And that new client? The one from the place in Madison? She ordered five dozen of your wild berry pupcakes. She loved your flyers."

"Five dozen? Wow. And that's a new flavor on the menu." As her demand had risen, Brenna had set her up with a graphic designer friend who had helped with an official logo, branding, and information sheets on all her products. They'd been immensely helpful in getting the word out about her offerings. "That's great. You're up early—I hope you're not feeling too overworked." She really should get home, instead of running around New York chasing down crazy chefs. There was too much to do and Brenna also worked at the pub almost every night, in addition to keeping the orders timely. "I'm sorry, Bren."

Brenna laughed. "Are you kidding? This is great.

We're having a ton of fun. We all miss you, of course," she added. "So what are you cooking up down there?"

Just some adultery and murder. And a few cat-noli. "A fish plate and vanilla blueberry cat-noli. Strawberry cake. All test dishes. How's Jake?"

"He's busy. He misses you." Stan could hear Brenna's grin over the phone. "It's cute, actually."

"Yeah?" The words sent a nice warm feeling through her body. He'd told her himself that he missed her, but it was nice to hear from someone else who had observed it. He really missed her. It was sweet.

"Yeah. So is he officially moving into your house, or what? I'm kinda thinking I need my own place, and I'm happy to take over his apartment." Brenna had been living in Jake's guest room for the last two years after moving off-campus to finish her degree.

Stunned, Stan's mouth dropped open. She didn't quite know how to answer that question. Jake stayed at her house more often than not, unless there was something big going on at the pub for which he needed to be right upstairs, but they hadn't actually talked about making it official. Which Stan knew was largely her fault—she'd been the slow-moving half of their relationship. But she had to admit, it sounded pretty darn good to have him there all the time.

"I don't know, we haven't talked about it," she said.

"Well, you should," Brenna said. "And I'm saying that for selfish and unselfish reasons. I think he totally wants to but doesn't want to push you. I'm sorry, I don't mean to stick my nose in your business. But I love you two together. And I would love my own place."

"I love us together, too," Stan said, staring out her window. Brenna was right. It was time to man up and get this relationship moving in the right direction. "We'll talk about it when I get home."

"Good. Then I can start having my new boyfriend over without feeling like my parents are chaperoning."

"New boyfriend? I've only been gone three days!"

Brenna laughed. "He was around before then. I didn't say anything because, you know, sometimes things don't work out, right? But it looks like he's here to stay, so it would make my life easier, too."

"What's his name?"

"Scott."

"Where'd you meet him? What's he do?"

"What are you, another big sister? I'll fill you in when you get home. I promise."

"Well, good. I'll work on it. I promise, too," Stan said. *Right after I find this missing chef and perhaps help solve a murder case. And get a cat investor on board so Sheldon can have his show. Unless he's arrested for said murder first.*

"Stan?" Brenna had asked her something and she hadn't even heard.

"Sorry. What?"

"I said what do you want me to tell the Madison lady? Friday?"

"Sure, if it's not too much for you to work on while I'm gone."

"Not too much at all. Getting back to work now. Don't worry about me and have a great time!"

Stan thanked her and hung up, watching the landscape fly by. Day three, and her homesickness hadn't abated. Brenna had raised a good point about her living arrangements. Left to Stan, she and Jake wouldn't have had that conversation for a long time. Life was complicated. Who knew she'd move to a teeny, tiny town and fall in love with a hot pub owner who actually seemed to love her back? And now that Brenna had raised the question, she realized she'd been waiting for her own answer for a long time.

Chapter 38

By the time the train pulled into the New Haven station, Stan had a game plan sketched out. First, they were going to Pierre's bakery to see what they could find out there. Then they would tackle Melanie Diamond. The train slid to a stop and the doors *whooshed* open. There weren't many passengers on this Sunday morning. She watched the people waiting for the train head to the nearest open door. She was just about to text Jessie when she saw her boarding the car a couple ahead. Go back two, she texted.

A minute later the door to Stan's car slid open and Jake's sister appeared. She looked nothing like a cop when she was off duty. She'd twisted her thick red hair into a clip. She wore no makeup on her perfect skin— didn't need to—and her jeans and T-shirt made her look like every other young suburban woman. If you looked closely at the shirt's logo, though, it said "Connecticut State Police." She'd left it untucked, probably to hide her gun. If Stan knew Jessie, she wouldn't go out without it, even off duty to a different state. Especially not when Stan had arranged the trip and it was related to a murder.

Stan waved, and Jessie headed for her. She sat facing her, placing her backpack next to her.

"Hey," Stan said. "Thanks for coming, again."

Jessie waved her off. "My brother says hello."

"I'll call him on our way back," she said. "I take it you told him where we were going?"

"I did. I stopped by his place. I had no one else to watch Lily."

Stan laughed. "You think he'll pay Brenna to swap roles?"

"Actually, he's fabulous with kids," Jessie said with a smile. "He loves them."

He did adore his niece; anyone could tell. Stan had just never thought of him as *loving kids*. Did that mean he would want them someday? She wasn't sure how she felt about kids herself. She'd never been quite sure what to do with them.

Jessie stared at her. "What?"

"Nothing," Stan said, fixing her smile back in place. She pushed the thought out of her head. Way too early to worry about that. "So here's what I thought we should do. Tell me if you would do it differently." She filled Jessie in on her plan to visit Pierre's bakery first and get the lay of the land, then—hopefully—pry more information out of Melanie, the secret agent publicist.

Jessie listened, those laser-sharp eyes fixed on Stan the entire time. Stan always wanted to squirm under that serious gaze. It was so piercing and intense, like she could see right into her brain and read her thoughts. And know if she was being less than honest.

"Here's her address," Jessie said, pulling a piece of paper out of her pocket and handing it to Stan.

"You *rock*." Stan looked at it. West Forty-second Street. Fancy address.

"What are you hoping to find out on this trip?" Jessie

asked finally. "Are you really interested in the dead guy, or are you looking for the guy and/or the gal who's hopefully still alive?"

"I don't think I'll find Kyle in New York," Stan said. "But maybe I'll find some insight into what Pierre was up to. Something that might have gotten him killed. That would at least get Kyle off the hook, which is the next best thing to finding him."

Jessie went silent again. "How well did you know this guy? The dead one."

This was when Stan hated the scrutinizing cop look. "Not very."

"Like how not very? Did you see him at parties and air kiss? Did you talk to him once a year? Did you guys Face Time?"

"No."

"No what?"

"No, none of the above." Stan sighed. "I never met him."

"You never met him," Jessie repeated. "Then why are you so concerned with finding out who killed him?"

"It has more to do with Kyle's disappearance than Pierre."

Jessie's eyes narrowed. "In what way?"

"I promised my sister I'd try to help her find Kyle."

Jessie smiled. "I've known you for, what? More than a year? Never heard you talk about her."

"Yeah, we're not close."

"But the Newport PD pulled her in last night to see if she knew anything about McLeod."

"You knew that?"

Jessie shrugged. "I called them. I hate being caught off guard. I told them I had a family member involved in this case, and was looking for info, cop to cop. I got a guy in a good mood, and he gave me a decent update."

"Was it Owens?"

"Yep."

Stan smiled. "He must've felt bad about the PI thing."

"The what?"

"Never mind. So what'd he tell you?"

"That McLeod vanished the night of the murder. That he's married to a nutcase from Florida, living with the hotel manager here, and was supposed to meet your sister around the time he vanished. They're strongly leaning toward him as a suspect, Stan. And now with this other woman missing, they're not taking any chances. They want this guy."

"I get it. Caitlyn thinks he's in trouble."

"Well, if they were supposed to meet and he blew her off, it's natural she'd want to think that," Jessie said.

"Did he mention finding Pierre's luggage anywhere? Or anything on him?"

Jessie shook her head. "They haven't found anything."

Stan thought about that. "Did the Newport cops call Sheldon's sister who owns the house?"

"Owens did. She and her husband were out of the country this week, so they were ruled out as potential killers."

"I tried calling her," Stan said. "She never called me back."

"You did? Why?"

Stan shrugged. "To see if she'd talked to anyone."

"So much for leaving police work to the police," Jessie said. "Where does she live?"

"Burke, Virginia. You going to try her?"

"Tell me about your sister and this relationship,"

Jessie said, changing the subject. "They're both married. Obviously not to each other."

Stan sighed. "Please don't judge her. I'm sure it's hard for someone like you to hear that and stay quiet."

"Someone like me?" Jessie barked out a laugh. "What does that mean?"

"You're a cop. You do the right things." Stan leaned back and focused out the window, watching Connecticut flash by, a high-speed montage of woods and urban areas, the picture changing every few seconds.

"Yeah," Jessie said in an oddly flat voice. "I do the right things." She leaned back and closed her eyes, signaling the end of the conversation.

Stan reached into her purse for a protein bar. Her hand brushed the folder from the retreat she'd stuck in there two days ago. What the heck, since Jessie wasn't talking. She flipped through the pages on the left. Sheldon's agenda for the weekend, which had never happened. Glossy flyer of The Chanler, photos of the backyard. In the left pocket, the investor bios. Stan flipped through them. She had never heard of most of them, but one of them could be involved in Pierre's death. She skimmed facts, looking for anything relevant. Nothing jumped out at her.

Until page six.

She stared at the picture of her mother, her stomach plummeting like she was on a particularly steep roller coaster. Her mother. She should've known. No wonder Sheldon wanted her participation so badly. Because he wanted her mother's money. And this was another way for her mother to interfere in her life.

"What's wrong?" Jessie had opened her eyes and seen her face.

Wordlessly, Stan shook her head. "Nothing."

Jessie stared her down. "I'm a cop. I mostly know when I'm being lied to."

Stan tried a smile. She failed. "Jake was right, that's all. Sheldon doesn't care about me. He wanted my mother as an investor."

Jessie processed that. "First, my brother is usually right. But that doesn't mean Sheldon didn't want you. He probably wanted both of you," she said, always practical. "You're the baker, she's the financier. Can't blame the guy for wanting the whole package."

"No," Stan said, tucking the folder back in her purse. "But he picked the wrong girl to play games with."

Chapter 39

When they erupted onto Thirty-fourth Street with the rest of the crowd at Penn Station, Jessie finally spoke. "Cab?"

Stan nodded. "It's a couple miles from here. In SoHo." She stepped into the street and hailed a cab. They settled into the backseat and the driver took off at New York speed, throwing them against the seat back. Jessie wrinkled her nose as she surveyed the interior of the cab, keeping her hands firmly in her lap. "I'm not really a New York girl."

"No?" Stan smiled out the window at the crowds of people streaming by, the brake lights pulsing in the hot summer afternoon. "I love it here."

"You look like you would."

Compliment or insult? Stan couldn't tell. "Work took me here a lot. I love the energy of the city. It's . . . invigorating."

"Do you miss your old job?" Jessie asked.

Stan glanced at her, but Jessie still focused on the views outside her window. Jessie wasn't usually a conversationalist, at least not with her, but she'd take it. "I used to think I did. But I don't. I love my freedom. I love what I'm doing now. I love where I'm doing it. I really love not having to pretend to be someone else every day. And having to bow to everyone else's demands on my schedule. I can come to New York any time I want. I don't need a corporate job to get me here."

Jessie nodded. "Sounds about right to me."

The cab driver slammed on his brakes and muttered something in another language at the car in front of them. Jessie turned slightly green as she grabbed on to the seat back for balance. "I don't know how people do this every day."

Stan laughed. "They don't. Hardly anyone who lives here takes a cab unless the weather is crap. Trust me, I don't miss the cabs. I'd rather take the subway."

The cab pulled to the curb and switched off the meter. "Thirteen bucks."

"You're kidding," Jessie said. "We barely went anywhere!"

Stan handed him cash and pushed Jessie out of the car. "You're not in Frog Ledge anymore, Dorothy. Let's go."

On the sidewalk, they surveyed the storefronts as their cab driver pulled a heart-stopping move and shoehorned himself back into the traffic. Stan glanced at her phone to confirm the address. "This is it." She nodded at the storefront of La Chocolate Bakery, the name emblazoned both on a rectangular sign and on the cherry red awning. Through the window Stan could see a pastry case jam-packed with delightful-looking creations of all shapes and colors. And coffee. "Let's go."

She pushed the door open and walked in, Jessie on her heels. A thirty-ish woman behind the counter gave them a wobbly smile. She had long dark hair pulled into two loose braids tossed over each shoulder and a black cap perched on the top of her head. A diamond stud glinted from the side of her nose. Her red, puffy eyes—she'd clearly been crying—were lined with blue liner. "Hello. Wel-welcome to La Chocolate Bakery." Her eyes welled with tears but she forced them back. "What can I get you today?"

Stan stepped up to the counter and held out a hand. "My name is Stan Connor. This is Jessie Pasquale. We wanted to talk to you about Pierre LaPorte."

The woman's eyes widened and filled with tears, but she extended her own hand and shook Stan's limply. "What . . . what about him? He's . . . dead." The last word dissolved into a sniffle and she reached for a tissue.

"I know. I'm so sorry. I'm a pastry chef also. I was at the same weekend event as Pierre."

She gasped. "Oh my goodness. You were there. What happened? We—none of us can believe it. We weren't even sure if we should open this weekend but didn't know what else to do. And then . . . we figured it's what Pierre would want, you know? To share his . . . last batch of pastries." She hiccuped through a sob. "So what's going to happen now?"

"I don't know," Stan said gently. "The police are trying to find out who killed him. And I wanted to come and see his shop. What's your name?"

"I'm Greta. I've been with Pierre now for almost two years."

Interesting choice of words, Stan thought. Not *I've been working for Pierre,* but *I've been* with *Pierre.* She didn't look like any of the women Stan had seen online when Googling Pierre. And she seemed very young.

Greta hurried out from behind the counter and flipped the CLOSED sign in the window. "I've never done that before, during the day." She laughed nervously as she untied her red apron with the shop name

emblazoned on the front. Under it, she wore a T-shirt
with a plunging V-neck, a pair of black leggings, and red
ankle boots. "I guess it's okay. No one's around to tell
me not to." The thought seemed to make her incredibly sad. "Just a couple of the bakery staff out back,
working on the cake orders for the week. Do you want
coffee?"

"I'd love a cup," Stan said gratefully, turning to Jessie,
who hadn't said a word yet.

Jessie nodded and stepped forward. "Sure, thanks."

Greta looked like she might ask something else but
didn't want to expend the effort. She went back behind
the counter to fix the coffee.

Stan walked around the bakery, checking out Pierre's
world. Recessed lights inside the pastry case gave the
treats a unique glow. Cupcakes, small, elegant cakes,
flaky pastries, fruity pastries, chocolatey delights were
all arranged with a meticulous level of care. Greta's
handiwork, probably. Her last tribute to the chef. The
walls were lined with shots of food from every stage of
the baking process. Overflowing bags of sugar, dough
in mixing bowls, a just-broken egg perfectly captured
as it dripped from its shell into a bowl. Finished products that belonged in magazine pages. Other shots
captured the people doing the cooking. Pierre was in
most of them either solo or with other chefs, always in
some form of deep creative concentration.

Stan stopped to look at the photos one by one. The
most prominent featured Pierre and Sheldon, arms
around each other in front of a cake that had to be
almost as tall as they were. Sheldon looked a lot
younger and even more flamboyant, if possible. In
another photo, Pierre and three other chefs were hard
at work on trays of what appeared to be chocolate
mousse. The other chefs, all male, were a tad blurry,

clearly in the background, but there was something familiar about one of them who was half in and half out of the frame, squeezing cream out of a pastry bag onto a cake. Stan stepped closer to get a better view.

"Here you go." Greta stood behind her with a cup of coffee, watching her curiously.

Stan whirled. "Thanks." She accepted the cup, nodding to the wall. "Great pictures."

"Yeah. Pierre was big on documenting his life. Which meant his work, because that was his life." With a nervous laugh, she went behind the counter again and returned with a small pitcher of cream and a bowl of sugar.

"Do you know all the people in these photos?" Stan asked.

Greta shook her head. "No. These are kind of old pictures, from like five or six years ago. Pierre kept saying he'd get someone in to take new ones, but it never happened. He was so busy." She went back to the bakery case and pondered the cupcake selection.

While Greta was occupied, Stan used her phone to snap photos of a couple of the pictures on the wall to peruse later. Jessie raised an eyebrow at her. She shrugged.

Greta chose three cupcakes frosted with brightly colored creams. She arranged them on a plate and placed them on the table next to the coffees. "I almost don't want to eat any of these pastries," she said, picking at her fake fingernail. "I mean, like, I know they'll go bad eventually, but I feel like it's our last piece of him." She nodded to the cupcakes. "He . . . it was from the last batch he baked before he left for Rhode Island." Her eyes filled again.

"We're so sorry for your loss," Stan said. "I was very much looking forward to meeting Pierre."

"You didn't even know him?" That made Greta cry harder. "It's so . . . messed up! Pierre was fabulous at what he did. And so generous. A true pastry artist and incredible human being." She blew her nose again, then looked from Stan to Jessie and back. "They said he was m-murdered. Who would do such a horrible thing?"

"That's what everyone's trying to figure out," Stan said, but now she was distracted. The cupcakes taunted her. She'd eaten a lot less than expected this weekend, for sure, so one little cupcake couldn't hurt. She briefly thought of this morning's coffee cake and last night's chocolate chip creation, but pushed it away. After all, she'd never gotten to have Joaquin's fudge cake with the mocha creme filling. And it had been a long time since breakfast. She selected one that looked chocolaty, with swirls of purple, pink, and blue on top, and took a bite. Decadent cake combined with some kind of creamy deliciousness assaulted her taste buds, and her eyes widened. This had to be, hands down, the best cupcake she'd ever eaten. "Wow," she managed.

"Amazing, right?" Greta nodded. "I don't think anyone will be able to replicate those. They were a new recipe. Top secret," she added in a stage whisper.

"Secret from whom?" Stan asked.

Greta shrugged. "Anyone. Pierre was working on some really exciting recipes. Like, recipes that would've blown away the Cronut." She rolled her eyes, then noticed Jessie's blank stare. "You've never heard of the Cronut?"

"Nope," Jessie said in unison.

Stan hid a smile. She'd had a few Cronuts in her time. They were decent, but she wasn't a huge dough-nut person. Or croissant person.

Greta hiccuped a laugh. "I guess you wouldn't, if you

don't come to the city much. The chef is here in New York. People do come from all over to get them, but you wouldn't know that unless you were a doughnut person, I guess. Anyway, the guy who made the Cronut, like, struck gold. He's totally known for that now. He does other cool stuff, too, but he gets mad kudos for those things. Pierre wanted something like that. He's wanted that recognition, that One Big Thing, for as long as I've known him. Now he was on the verge of it."

Stan's ears perked up through the sugar haze. "Pierre had a recipe?"

Greta nodded slyly. "He had a couple of them. Bigger than even the cupcakes." She, Stan, and Jessie looked down at Stan's plate, where only a couple of crumbs remained. Stan licked the tip of her finger and unabashedly picked them up.

"Did anyone know about the recipes? Was he close to unveiling them?" Stan asked.

"He was close. He didn't talk about it much. I'm not even sure what type of pastry. I guessed it had something to do with chocolate. They don't call him Monsieur Chocolate for nothing. That man is a *genius* with chocolate in any form." Her eyes took on a dreamy look, and Stan noticed she'd fallen back to speaking in the present tense. "He didn't want to jinx himself by saying too much. These recipes are, like, the Holy Grail for these guys, you know? If it gets into the wrong hands your career is over. But over the past few weeks especially, he was jazzed. He told me this recipe would change the pastry landscape. I think he was going to do some test groups before a mass rollout, but it was definitely happening soon."

Stan and Jessie looked at each other. Stan knew they were thinking the same thing: Was this recipe enough to kill for? The Holy Grail of pastries sounded serious.

Did someone feel threatened? Or did someone want the fame and fortune that such a recipe might bring?

"You're sure no one knew about it?" Stan asked.

Greta thought about that. "I'm not sure *no one* knew, but not many people. I know he told Sheldon. He didn't want to, but all the other work was overwhelming and leaving him with less time to perfect his recipe. The Providence orders every week were killing him."

"Providence orders?" Stan asked.

"The orders for Sheldon's place. He was totally getting sick of it. Pierre doesn't have a huge baking staff, and he has his own business to run."

"Wait," Stan said, pushing her plate aside. "I'm not following. Are you saying he was baking Sheldon's pastries?"

Greta laughed. "You bet. Mr. Pastry was either too busy or had lost his touch, but Pierre's been filling his pastry case for the past year."

Chapter 40

Stan's delicious cupcake started to roll around in her stomach. She forced the queasy feeling down. That had been one detail Sheldon had forgotten to mention in his true confession session about his falling out with Pierre.

"Greta. Are you totally sure about that?" she asked.

Greta frowned, a gesture that pulled her perfectly shaped eyebrows together. "Of course I'm sure. We had to hire two new people to keep up with it. Pierre stopped doing it himself. He wanted to focus on his own career for a change."

Stan and Jessie exchanged a glance.

"Was he using Sheldon's recipes?" Stan asked casually.

Greta scoffed. "Pierre didn't use *recipes* for simple, everyday pastries. He just baked them. He spent time with each new baker and gave them his tricks of the trade—at different levels of course, based on their ability—and then they would start by baking some of the 'everyday' stuff. So he was having the newer people do Sheldon's pastries."

"Did they have some kind of agreement that Pierre would do this for a certain amount of time? Was it to pay Sheldon back for something?" Jessie asked.

"I'm not sure. It started last year. He told me we were going to be helping Sheldon out because of the demand and Sheldon's limited time."

Last year. Around the time of his alleged drug troubles, if Sheldon's account was accurate. Maybe this was Pierre's punishment for Sheldon's involvement. Or, Sheldon's way to get his protégé to repay the debt.

"Did he have plans to stop?" Jessie asked. "Had he said anything to Sheldon about being overwhelmed?"

"I have no idea. I didn't get involved much in the business stuff. I just like to bake. And listen to Pierre. I tried to help him when he got upset about things. It's hard being a sensitive chef, you know." She paused and, for the first time, really looked at them. "Are you guys helping solve the murder? Like, police consultants or something? Is that why you're asking all these questions?"

"I'm a cop," Jessie said. "With the Connecticut State Police."

Greta frowned. "Connecticut? I thought Pierre went to Rhode Island."

"He did. I'm not here in an official capacity."

"Oh!" Greta exclaimed. "Wow. I . . . didn't realize." She glanced nervously toward the back room. Jessie followed her gaze. They could hear voices, some music, an occasional burst of laughter.

"Who's out there?" Jessie asked.

"Just a couple of the bakers. Getting a jump start on the week's orders."

"So it's business as usual, then?" Stan asked.

Greta shrugged miserably. "Until someone tells us

otherwise, I guess. Or until Sheldon swoops in and changes everything. Or fires us all."

Interesting comment. "Why would he do that?"

"Who knows what will happen? I've heard he can be ruthless," Greta said.

Stan tucked that comment away. "Back to this prize recipe. Do you know where Pierre may have kept it? Was it written down somewhere, or saved on a computer? Or was it all in his head?"

Greta narrowed her eyes suspiciously. "Why? Just because he's dead doesn't mean you can steal it."

"Me?" Stan laughed. "Not quite. I bake for pets, not people."

"You *do*? That's so cool!" Her newfound suspicion momentarily forgotten, Greta clapped her hands. "Do you have a card? A Web site?"

"I actually don't have a Web site yet. But I'm working on it." Close enough to the truth. Brenna had been trying to talk her into setting up a Web site for the past few months. She wasn't sure why she hesitated, other than their already packed baking schedule. Add more orders and shipping into the mix and she'd probably have to hire at least one more person. "Here." She fished a card out of her bag. "That's me. My phone and e-mail are on it."

"Awesome," Greta said, sliding the card into her pocket. "I have friends who love stuff like that for their pets."

"Thanks. So, the recipe."

"Yeah. The recipe." She smiled. "Pierre's a pretty low-tech guy. He loved notebooks." She went back behind the counter and took out a small Moleskine notebook with a gray cover. "He had these everywhere. This was his fancy coffee recipe book. He doesn't usually keep full recipes, though. He always thought people wanted to steal his stuff."

"So he may have had his gold medal winner on him somewhere," Stan said, looking at Jessie.

"Like I said," Greta reminded them, "there would only be pieces of the recipe. Probably the most critical measurements. A lot of the stuff he could wing, but if it was still new to him he would keep the notes handy."

"Excuse me," Jessie said, getting up and going to the back corner of the bakery. Stan saw her slip her phone out of her pocket. Probably calling the Rhode Island cops to "offer" the information—and fish around to see if they'd found something on Pierre's body.

"So, what else can I tell you?" Greta asked. She'd started to fidget and Stan sensed they were losing her.

"Just one more question," she promised, flashing her an apologetic smile. "Do you know if he was dating anyone?"

Greta's face pinkened. "Me," she admitted, and promptly burst into tears again.

Of course. Stan should've seen that one coming. The starstruck young woman would've been a perfect candidate, at least part of the time.

"I'm so sorry, again," she said quietly.

Greta cried for another minute, then pulled it together. "I'm sorry. It's just . . . you know."

"I do." Stan glanced at Jessie, who still talked on her phone. "Do you know Vaughn Dawes?"

Greta looked blank and started to shake her head when a huge crash sounded from the back room, followed by a howling that sounded suspiciously like a dog. Or a wolf. Jessie was off the phone and next to them, gun in hand, before Stan even blinked.

"Whoa!" Greta jumped up, too, hands raised. "What are you doing?"

Jessie had already started around the counter, gun leading the way.

"What's going on back there?" Stan whispered.

Chapter 41

Before Greta could respond, the swinging door flew open and a man with a shaved head and goatee ran out. Stan didn't see the dog in front of the guy until the pooch rounded the corner and skidded to a stop, tongue lolling, at her feet. He (she?) looked like an Australian cattle dog, or at least a mix.

The tattooed guy skidded to a stop when he saw Jessie and her gun. His hands shot into the air. "Is this a stickup? I don't think we have much cash. Greta, give them the cash!"

"Oh, for . . . just go bake something, Kent," Greta said, grabbing the dog's collar. "We're not getting robbed. They're here to talk about Pierre. They've been here for an hour. Where have you been?"

"Oh." His hands dropped and fisted onto his hips. "Well, his dog needs a home. Can we talk about that?" He glared at Greta. "What are you doing about it?"

"Me? Why me?"

"He was your boyfriend! This dog can't live in the kitchen. We're gonna get busted by the Department of Health. Plus he just knocked over my cake mix. Listen, you want this place to stay up and running, this isn't the way to do it." He looked at Stan and Jessie. "You cops?"

"Yes," Jessie said, without bothering to mention where. She'd already tucked her gun back in her waistband, under her shirt.

"Cool. You close to cracking the case?"

"We certainly hope so," Jessie said. "You knew Pierre well?"

"He hired me a few months ago. Cool dude. We weren't, like, friends or anything. He was a tough boss. But he knew his stuff." He leaned on the counter. "You think he got killed over pastry? Or something else?"

"That's what we're trying to find out," Jessie said.

He nodded. "Listen, I gotta go put my cake in the oven. Come on back if you want to talk to me or Alex." With one last curious glance at them, the guy headed back into the kitchen.

"Sorry 'bout that," Greta said. She glanced at the dog and sighed. "I have no idea what to do about this."

"Is this Pierre's dog?" Stan bent down and held out a hand to the pup. The dog wagged cautiously and sniffed her.

"Yeah. This is Gaston. Named after some fancy pastry chef—I forget who. He's one of the reasons I'm at the shop today." She glanced at the kitchen door where the cranky baker had retreated. "There's no one else to take him, and I can't have dogs in my building. I think he's sad. He really misses . . . Pierre." She sniffled and wiped fresh tears away. "Like I do."

The dog nuzzled his head into Stan's hand. She rubbed his ears. He was gorgeous. And his eyes did look sad. And confused. Her pit bull, Henry, a rescue from Frog Ledge Animal Control, had looked the same way the first time she'd seen him. "So he's been staying here?" Stan asked.

"Yes. And Kent is right. We could get in trouble. I just don't know what to do." She gazed at the dog sadly. "I may have to take him to the shelter."

Didn't it just figure? Stan wanted to hit her head against the pastry counter a few times. "Which shelter?"

"I don't know. There's a bunch of places around, I think. . . ." She trailed off.

"Most of those places put dogs to sleep in a few days. If not sooner. Do you think Pierre would want that?"

Jessie sent her a raised-eyebrow look, but Stan ignored her. The poor dog did not deserve that sort of ending just because his owner had gotten himself killed.

"No," Greta said uncertainly. "Pierre rescued him about five years ago from some people who weren't very nice. His name was Jaws then. They were trying to make him sound fierce and get him to do bad things. Pierre actually bought him from them so he could save him. He talks about it, like, all the time." She rolled her eyes. "I don't mean it in a bad way, you know? I mean, I like dogs, but Pierre was kind of obsessed with him."

Finally, a redeeming quality about Pierre that Stan could respect. She wondered if Pierre used to bake him treats. She bet he had.

"Plus Pierre wanted a protector. He was having a rough time back then," Greta said.

"Something happen?" Jessie asked.

"He doesn't talk about it much. Just that he had some people giving him trouble."

"He didn't say who?"

Greta shook her head.

"None of Pierre's other friends can take him?"

"I haven't asked anyone. I don't think most of them like dogs," Greta said.

"What about his family?"

"What family? He doesn't have one. Well, like parents and stuff. They died a long time ago. I don't know about other family."

Sure they did. Pierre must've really been embarrassed about his past to tell people his parents were dead. Stan sighed. She had no choice. "Do you have a leash for the dog?"

Jessie and Greta both stared at her.

"A leash," Stan repeated. "You know, you hook it on the dog's collar and walk them with it?"

"Right. A leash." Greta dashed out back to get it.

"And what are you going to do with the dog?" Jessie asked.

"I guess I'm going to call Nikki."

"Yeah, but how are you going to *get* him to Nikki?"

Stan shrugged. "We can take the Metro-North out of Grand Central back to New Haven. They allow dogs. Then I'll have to figure out how to get him somewhere until I can track her down." She pondered that. Jessie would never go for it—Jake had told Stan many times that while Jessie didn't dislike dogs, she had no desire to live with any. She could ask Jake, but he was already helping Brenna watch Stan's crew this weekend.

"You don't even know anything about this dog," Jessie said, just as Greta rushed back out waving a red leash triumphantly. It had the name of the pastry shop on it.

"Here you go. What are you going to do with him?"

"I'm going to take him to a friend who runs a rescue," Stan said. "At least he won't be in danger there, and she'll find him a good home."

"You will?" Greta's face lit up, then as understanding washed over her, her expression went from elated to distraught. "But . . . I'll miss him!" She threw her arms around the dog and buried her face in his fur.

"I'm sure you will, but if you can't keep him in a real apartment, that's not fair to him," Stan said.

Greta sniffled. "I know."

"What do you know about him? Is he good with other dogs? Cats? Kids? Does he prefer men to women?"

Confusion drew Greta's perfectly shaped eyebrows together. "I have no idea. I never did a personality test on him. He's always been well behaved. Pierre took him to school. He's got a little degree and everything."

Canine Good Citizen, probably. That was a plus. Maybe Nikki wouldn't kill her. Still, she was going to wait until the dog was in her possession before calling her. Nikki would never turn down an animal in need, but best to leave her no choice.

Stan could feel Jessie's eyes drilling a hole into the side of her head. *Great,* she'd be thinking. *Now we have to go traipsing around questioning this other woman dragging a dog with us.* Well, Jessie would have to deal with it.

"Are you going to tell me where he goes?" Greta asked. "I feel like I need to know."

"Sure. Where should I call—"

A loud rap on the door behind Stan startled her, and she turned to see two men looming in the doorway. They were large, scowling, and looked like they were about to bust the door down if it didn't open for them immediately.

Chapter 42

"Shoot," Greta muttered.

"Who are they?" Stan asked.

"Whoever they are, they don't look like they're here for red velvet cupcakes," Jessie said.

Greta shot her a look. "Pierre would *never* make red velvet cupcakes. He thought they were disgusting."

One of the men rapped on the door again and rattled the handle. Greta went to open it.

"You sure that's a good idea?" Jessie asked.

"I don't have a choice," Greta said. She unlocked the door with a shaking hand. The men shoved past her and locked the door behind them. Stan could see Jessie's hand reach casually toward her waistband, where she'd just returned her gun. The dog started to growl, low and menacing. Stan tightened her grip on the leash and tried to pull the dog behind her. He didn't budge. Either he'd seen these guys before and was not a fan, or he sensed danger. Stan didn't like either scenario.

"You hear from him?" The larger of the two asked Greta, ignoring Stan and Jessie. Fat and muscle combined to easily make him a match for a brick wall blocking the exit. His face appeared to reside in a permanent tough-guy scowl, with jowls that reminded Stan of a Great Dane and a gap between his front teeth that didn't help his credibility. The other guy exuded more brains—and more lethality. Stan watched him assess her and Greta and move on within seconds, but his gaze behind dark glasses lingered on Jessie. Hands down he'd made her as a cop, especially if he had the experience Stan guessed he did. She felt a pinprick of fear. These were the situations where things could go drastically wrong. Especially if Jessie decided to play hero. Guilt immediately hit her. She should never have dragged them into this situation.

Greta faced off with the one who had spoken, hands on hips again. She looked like a character on the side of a peanut butter jar with her braids and chocolate-stained apron. "Hear from him? Are you kidding? He's dead! And I wouldn't be surprised if you killed him!"

A fleeting look of surprise passed over the silent guy's face, and his gaze momentarily shifted away from Jessie. Stan caught her eye and shook her head slightly, hoping Jessie understood the message: *Don't try anything stupid. You're not a cop here!*

The other guy laughed, a nasty sound that reminded Stan of Voldemort from *Harry Potter*. "Nice try," he said. "I've heard that one before. Tell him we're not going away until he ponies up the cash, and if he don't pony it up in the next two days he's gonna be doing it with no legs."

Greta shook her tiny fist at the guy. "I'm telling you, he's dead, you moron!"

The dog, taking his cues from Greta, started to bark furiously at the intruders, despite Stan's choke hold on his leash. She'd pressed them both up against the wall, hoping to stay out of the thugs' line of vision. This whole scenario was reminiscent of a train wreck from which Stan couldn't look away. The kitchen door flew open and Kent stuck his head out. "What's going on out here? Can you please make the dog shut—"

The silent thug, who was apparently a lot more nimble than his friend, was around the counter with his gun stuck in Kent's face before Stan registered that he'd even moved. "Who else is back there?" he demanded, his voice a low, menacing growl that gave Stan chills.

Kent's whole face turned white and he grabbed the doorframe. "Just me and Alex."

Silent Thug shoved him through the door and out of sight. Stan could see Jessie out of the corner of her eye, weighing her options, deciding to move.

Then everything happened at once.

Jessie's gun appeared in her hand. But before she could do anything, Greta, apparently at wit's end, launched herself at Jowls, screaming obscenities at him, punching and clawing at his face. He grabbed her by the neck, trying to hold her off him as she kicked and flailed. Stan heard Jessie's muffled curse, then remembered she had her own secret weapon at her side. She let go of Gaston's leash, mentally encouraging the pup to do the right thing. He did—he launched himself at Jowls, sinking his teeth into his calf. Jowls yelped in pain and dropped Greta, trying to shake off the dog. Greta stomped on his instep and used her elbow on his neck when he bent over and screamed. Jessie, probably relieved she didn't have to shoot him, had him down on the floor with her knee in his back and arms bent behind him probably before he registered what was happening.

At the same time, crashes, bangs, and what sounded like an entire display of cookware had crashed to the ground out back. Stan heard shouts, but thankfully no gunshots, then the bleat of some kind of alarm. She whipped out her phone and dialed 911 and gave the bakery's address.

Jessie drilled her knee harder into Jowls's back. "Don't move or I'll shoot you," she warned him. "This is why I should never go out without my cuffs," she said to no one in particular.

Chapter 43

Stan grabbed Gaston and pulled him under the table to safety, still expecting the other guy to come back out of the kitchen and shoot them all. But the cops showed up first, about two minutes later. Four of them. Two immediately went into the kitchen, guns drawn. Stan heard the cops yelling something and braced herself for more mayhem. Jessie still had Jowls restrained on the floor. The other two cops took one look at Jessie with her gun drawn and immediately drew their own guns.

"Put the gun down," one cop advised her.

"I'm a cop. Did you tell them I'm a cop?" she asked Stan, putting the gun on the floor and raising her hands in the air.

"I forgot," Stan said.

Jessie rolled her eyes. The cop who'd spoken picked up her gun. The other, trying to suppress a grin, went over to Jowls.

"Where are you a cop?" the first cop asked.

"Connecticut State Police. Troop P. My badge is in my pocket. I'm going to take it out." Jessie reached for it and handed it to the cop. He studied it and returned it to her.

The swinging door opened and two other cops came in with Kent and Alex in front of them. "All clear out back. He took off. Scalia," one of them added.

Stan froze. Scalia. Maria's family name.

"Go after him. We're clear here," the first cop said. The second pair left.

"You can get off him now, Trooper," the second cop said, still smiling. "Thanks much." Jessie got up and dusted her hands off.

"Marco. Got your butt kicked by three chicks? You must be losing your touch," he said, pulling out his own cuffs and placing them on Jowls's wrists. Jowls groaned and tried to spit at him.

Greta lost it again. "You can't come in here and spit on my floor!" she shrieked. "After you killed Pierre!"

The cops immediately went back into fight mode. "Someone's been injured?"

"Not today," Jessie rushed to reassure them.

The other guy hauled Jowls to his feet. "I . . . can't . . . talk!" he rasped. "She elbowed me in the throat!"

The cop shrugged. "I'm sure you deserved it, Marco," he said, walking him out to the car.

The first cop surveyed them and introduced himself as Officer Walden. After he took their names and contact information, he asked, "So what happened here?"

Jessie, always the most succinct given her line of work, gave them the overview. The cop listened, nodding every now and then. "That's Marco 'Fat Bladder' Santiago you took down," he said when she was done. "He works for Anthony Scalia, of the not-so-famed New York Scalias. Good to see he stayed true to himself and left his friend here to rot. He did set the alarm off, though, when he took off out back."

"He destroyed an entire day's work, too," Kent said.

Greta turned on him. "He killed Pierre!"

"Ma'am. If someone was killed and you have evidence—"

"Pierre LaPorte. The owner."

The cop's eyes widened. "Pierre's dead?"

Greta nodded miserably.

"When?"

"Stan," Jessie said. "Maybe you could fill them in? About how Pierre was killed and the other chef is missing, so we thought we'd come see if she had any ties to New York?"

Thank goodness Jessie had set up the parameters. Stan still felt like a bumbling idiot in front of cops. And she always feared she'd say the wrong thing and get herself arrested for something bizarre. She gave them the Cliffs Notes version about Pierre's death, Kyle's disappearance, the request for Vaughn Dawes to come out and save the dessert for the big meal. She left out her sister's involvement, Pierre's secret recipe, the numerous love triangles, and Sheldon's feud with Pierre. Less was more.

"So you don't know if Marco or Anthony had anything to do with it," Walden said. "And he was killed in Rhode Island."

"Correct," Stan said.

"Ma'am," he said to Greta, "do you know why Scalia and his goon were here?"

The elephant in the room. Greta shifted uncomfortably. "I don't know. They've come by a few times. I think Pierre owed them money."

"You think?"

"He didn't tell me things like that," she said, barely audibly.

"I'd suggest you close up shop for the day just in case Anthony has a bone to pick before we get him," Walden said. "And take anything valuable with you. The rest of you"—he nodded to Stan, Jessie, and the bakers—"are also free to go. Trooper Pasquale, thanks for your help today."

Jessie nodded. "Glad to do it."

Stan grabbed Gaston's leash and they left the bakery. "Good dog!" Stan praised Gaston. "What a good boy, biting that jerk!"

Jessie shook her head, biting back a smile. "What now?" she asked, nodding at their new companion. "I'm presuming we can't take a cab, with our new passenger."

"I bet we can." Stan did her cab hailing thing again. The first cab stopped. She opened the back door. "Sir, can we bring the dog? He's a rescue pup and he's scared to walk. We're trying to get him home."

The cabbie observed her, then the dog, then waved at her to get in.

"Thank you so much," she said, winking at Jessie. "Six-oh-two West Forty-second Street, please."

Gaston sat between them, head on his paws. Stan fished around in her bag. She'd cleaned everything out before leaving, but she usually kept a tiny bag of "emergency" treats in the zippered pouch. Feeling around, her fingers closed over the Ziploc bag.

"Aha! I knew I had some." She pulled them out triumphantly and fed him one. He immediately perked up and devoured it. She gave him the last two. "You did such a good job in there. I'll get you more when we get back," she promised. He flopped down again, and she could swear he sighed.

The cabbie got them to their destination with a minimum of nail biting on Jessie's part. They climbed out and stood in front of the building. If Melanie lived here, then Gem Communications was a thriving enterprise. Either that or she came from money. This was one of the buildings Stan, in her days of corporate fogbrain, had dreamed of living in. The sleek structure was clearly one that attracted a certain class of people, a building that boasted indoor parking and probably an Olympic-sized swimming pool. The only downfall, in her mind, was its proximity to Times Square. Although the building itself would be quiet, you'd constantly step out the front door into mayhem.

"Okay, you're going to have to pretend you're legit police," Stan said. "Otherwise we'll never get in."

Jessie gave her a look. "I am legit police."

"Not in New York," Stan said.

"The NYPD cops back there thought so," Jessie said.

They entered the building. A doorman greeted them. "May I help you?"

Stan nudged Jessie. Jessie flashed her badge, fast enough that the man couldn't possibly get a good look at it. "I'm here to see Melanie Diamond regarding one of her clients," she said.

He regarded them long enough that Stan started to worry, but then he directed them to the fifteenth floor, and Miss Melanie could be found in apartment 1015B. He even offered Gaston a treat and invited him to play in the community puppy park, which Stan declined. Gaston took the treat, but once they were out of the doorman's sight, he dropped it. Stan stifled a giggle. He was definitely accustomed to a certain standard of food.

"Weird place," Jessie muttered as they walked to the elevator. "I can't imagine living here. Like, ever."

"I get it. You're not a city girl." Stan smiled and punched the button. "This is actually an amazing place, if you can afford it."

"How much does something like this cost?" Jessie wanted to know.

Stan shrugged. "I haven't priced New York apartments lately, but I would guess for a one-bedroom here, you're looking at four thousand plus."

Jessie's jaw dropped. "A *month?*"

"Sure." Stan stepped onto the elevator and tugged Gaston to follow her. He hesitated, then jumped over the gap in the floor to join her.

"My mortgage is twelve hundred dollars. For a *house*. With three bedrooms." Jessie punched the button for floor fifteen.

"And you have to drive an hour to go shopping. To each his own." The doors *whooshed* open and Stan led the dog out into a white hallway with a black-tiled floor. Melanie's door was three down on the left. Stan knocked.

Silence inside. The doorman hadn't mentioned that she wasn't home, unless she'd slipped out when he wasn't looking. Stan swallowed her frustration and tried the bell this time. A minute later, she heard a lock flip from inside. The door swung open, and a gun emerged, pointing straight into her face.

Chapter 44

Stan's hands went up automatically and she froze, a million crazy thoughts racing through her mind and crashing together. The friendly doorman had apparently made them as "fake" cops.

She was dimly aware of Jessie beside her, reaching for her gun for the second—third?—time today. "Are you crazy? I'm a cop," she yelled.

Gaston let out a plaintive howl. Behind the gun, the face of a woman emerged. Probably Stan's age, a few inches shorter, with brown hair styled in a sleek bob. She had a Madonna mole under one nostril and brown eyes as hard as flint. She looked like she'd just stepped out of a James Bond movie, with her white dress and chunky jewelry.

"You're not an NYPD cop. We have cameras in here, you know. And NYPD cops don't bring their friends and their puppies with them to question people. So who are you and why shouldn't I shoot you?" she said. She didn't sound nervous or scared. Rather, that she could take enjoyment from pulling the trigger.

"Put the gun down," Jessie said. "I'm a Connecticut state trooper."

"Honey, you're in New York. Not Connecticut," Melanie said. She looked like she was about to lean against the door and pull out a cigarette, but her gun remained unflinchingly trained on Stan. "You need directions home?"

Stan finally found her voice and cut in before Jessie could say anything else or one of Melanie's neighbors came out their door. "I'm Stan Connor. I'm a chef working with Sheldon Allyn, just like Pierre LaPorte. Someone murdered him this weekend and I'm trying to figure out who."

At Pierre's name, Melanie blinked. Her eyes shifted to Jessie, who still had her hand poised over her gun. "You knew Pierre?"

"I hadn't met him. He was . . . dead when I arrived at the house."

Melanie spent another minute observing them both, then she lowered the gun. "So what do you want from me? And how did you find my apartment?"

"I found you," Jessie said.

She and Melanie faced off for another few seconds, then Stan said, "Can we come in?"

Melanie looked at the dog and wrinkled her nose. "I'm not really a dog person. Is he going to pee on my carpet?"

"No," Stan said. "He's Pierre's dog. He's well behaved."

Melanie didn't look convinced. "I know she has a gun. Do you have any weapons?"

"No weapons." *Just some pet food treats.*

Melanie still hesitated.

"We won't take up a lot of your time," Stan said.

Another beat, then she swung the door wide. "Kevin—my doorman—knows you're not NYPD. I told him to let you up, but if he doesn't hear from me in fifteen minutes to send help. So that's how long you have."

Stan and Jessie exchanged looks as they stepped inside. What would drive a public relations person to carry a gun and be so paranoid? Unless she'd had a bad experience that had nothing to do with them.

Melanie, clearly not wanting to turn her back, stood to the side and kept her eye on them. Jessie did the same thing as she walked in. Figuring she'd let them assess whether or not they needed to shoot each other, Stan led Gaston in. Melanie didn't tell them to sit down, so Stan remained standing and checked the place out. Her assessment outside had been right. The apartment's open floor plan gave it an extravagant feel, with gleaming hardwood floors in the living and dining space and a wet bar in a corner of the room. Floor-to-ceiling windows made you feel like you were always a part of the city, even while inside. The views were to die for.

Like her name suggested, Melanie Diamond's living space glittered with gold-plated mirrors, elegant glass coffee tables with expensive-looking trinkets strategically placed, and sleek, minimalist furniture. To the left, a modern, spacious kitchen with a small bar in the middle. And a woman, her hands wrapped around a cup of coffee, sat at it. She wore her blond hair pulled back in a headband and red lipstick that left a kiss on the rim of her white coffee cup. Stan could only see her from the side, but she looked incredibly familiar.

Jessie saw her at the same moment Stan did. Her hand went to her gun again. "Who's that?" she said.

"That's a friend of mine. She doesn't have a gun. On her," Melanie added, just to be clear.

Stan felt like she'd dropped into a Stephanie Plum novel. She took a few steps further into the apartment.

Gaston strained at the leash. Before Stan could get a better grip, he took off into the kitchen and launched himself at the other woman. The woman's eyes widened, then she bent down and hugged him. "Hey, Gaston!"

She knew the dog? Stan moved closer to get a better look at her. She still couldn't see her whole face.

"Do you always answer the door with a gun?" Jessie asked Melanie.

Melanie turned those hard eyes on her. "Ever since people started showing up at my door with them. Gotta keep up with the Joneses."

"Someone came here with a gun?"

"A couple of someones, actually. And I think your friend Sheldon Allyn had something to do with it."

"Sheldon? Why would Sheldon—" Stan stopped. Kind of a silly question, given the rants Sheldon had indulged in the past couple of days. "Do you know who it was?" she asked instead.

"A couple of goons. This mob thing is really passé. Someone should tell them."

"What did they want?"

"To threaten me," Melanie said. "About my lowlife clients and the things they're having me do for them." She rolled her eyes. "It's tedious, really. They weren't very good at their job, but I never appreciate having a gun put in my face when I open my door."

"Same here," Stan said.

"Well, that couldn't be helped."

"What did these guys look like?"

Melanie made a face. "Like Scalia's guys. They all kind of look the same."

Scalia again. Was Maria's family just looking to mess with Pierre because of Maria's goal to be Sheldon's favorite? Or did this have to do with Pierre's drug habit?

"Have you done anything about the threats?" Jessie asked.

"I've reported them to the police." She shrugged. "Unless they catch them in the act, not much they can do."

The other woman finished petting Gaston and sat up, turning more fully toward Stan so she was able to catch a glimpse of her face.

Stan felt the shock of recognition at the pouty lips from her recent Google search, devoid of lipstick but still unmistakeable. "You're . . . you're Vaughn Dawes," she said, moving into the kitchen.

Vaughn smiled. She didn't have the flinty eyes Melanie had, but she did have an air of *Don't mess with me* about her. "Busted," she said. "But you can't tell anyone, or we'll have to kill you."

Stan looked nervously over her shoulder. Melanie smiled, still holding her gun. Stan had a sneaking suspicion they weren't kidding.

"Clock's ticking," Melanie said, tapping a diamond-encrusted watch. "Why are you trying to solve Pierre's murder? Don't they have police in Rhode Island?"

"They do," Jessie said. "They even managed to snag a detective or two. But my colleague misspoke," she said, with a *stay shut* look at Stan. "We're not actively working on the Pierre LaPorte homicide. I have no jurisdiction there. But we are looking for someone else at that cooking event who vanished after the murder. That search led us here."

Vaughn pouted a little. "What, you weren't looking for me?"

"That too," Stan said.

Melanie motioned them all into the living room. Once Stan and Jessie sat, Gaston at Stan's feet, Melanie chose a chair opposite them and laid her gun on the coffee table within easy reach. Stan breathed a quiet sigh of relief. This trip had turned out to be a lot more life-threatening than she'd suspected during the planning phase, between Fat Bladder and this crazy chick.

"Vaughn, come in here," Melanie said.

With a sigh, Vaughn obeyed. Unlike Melanie, she'd dressed down in leggings and a beaded tunic. She took the chair opposite Melanie and sipped her coffee.

"So you're looking for Kyle McLeod," Melanie said. "I've been watching the news."

Please don't let her be sleeping with him, too, Stan thought.

"We are," Jessie said.

"Isn't that the police's job?"

Jessie shrugged. "They're not finding him fast enough and we worried that he was in trouble. But then again, we worried that *you* were in trouble," she said, looking at Vaughan.

"You'll pardon me asking," Stan said, "but why haven't you let anyone know you're safe? Is this really a PR stunt to make Sheldon look bad?"

Melanie and Vaughn looked at each other and burst out laughing. "Is that what he said? He's too much." Melanie shook her head almost fondly.

"Then what's the story?"

"I'm not sure why I have to tell you that," Vaughn said. "I don't even know you."

"True. Did you know Pierre?"

"Sadly, yes," Vaughn said.

"Why sadly?"

"Because he really was a jerk."

"Didn't you date him?" Stan asked. "Your pictures are all over the Internet."

Vaughn shrugged. "Everyone makes mistakes."

"And you were his public relations person?" Stan asked Melanie.

"For a short time, yes."

"So is it true that Sheldon and Pierre were not getting along and Pierre hired you because he was jumping ship and needed his own brand?"

"To a degree," Melanie said. "I'm not sure he was ever going to jump off Sheldon's ship. But he did want to branch out."

"How'd he find you?"

Melanie smiled again. "My reputation precedes me."

"I introduced them," Vaughn said. "Which I immediately felt badly about."

Stan turned to Vaughn. "Didn't you tip off Sheldon that Pierre was using Melanie?"

"I told Sheldon in passing. I didn't realize it was such a crazy subject for him. But I thought he could work with Melanie if he needed to. His person is pretty new."

"Why was Pierre such a jerk?" Stan asked. She was starting to wonder if Vaughn had been in New York the whole time, not LA. Maybe she had killed him.

"He's not a nice person," she said. "Mainly I wanted him to stop stalking me."

Great. Add stalker *to Pierre's list of attributes.* "Were you in LA Thursday?" Stan asked casually.

Vaughn looked amused. "You think I did it? It's not that crazy," she said. "I could see it happening eventually. But it didn't happen yet. I didn't even know he was dead when I agreed to come."

Melanie sent her a warning glance. "Pierre had some issues. He was in competition all the time, even when there was nothing to compete for. He and Sheldon were having problems. Said that Sheldon used Pierre's expertise, which had now surpassed his own." Melanie shrugged. "I don't know what was true and what was false. I just tried to get him in the headlines for positive things. Then he tried to get Vaughn to go into business with him, but it was mostly for her money. He pulled the we-used-to-be-a-couple card."

"All the more reason not to do it," Jessie said.

"Exactly," Melanie said with an approving nod. "But Pierre wouldn't let it go. He kept harassing her. You would think he knew how it felt, after he had a similar experience. I was close to terminating him as a client when I found out."

Stan's blood thrummed. "What do you mean, a similar experience?"

Melanie hesitated.

Vaughn answered instead. "Pierre had his own stalker a few years ago," she said. "Someone who would bother him on and off. Do creepy things like leave baked goods made out of something rotten near his apartment door. Phone calls. Usual stalker stuff."

She said it in such a blasé tone that Stan wondered if all famous chefs had stalkers. Yet another reason to stay under the radar.

"And he never figured out who it was?"

Vaughn shook her head. "Eventually, it died off. But it creeped him out for a while. I'd never seen him rattled by anything, but this rattled him. It's actually why he decided to get Jaws here." She smiled. "I wanted to name him Monty. Gaston is so predictable for a chef."

"Did he ever report it?"

"No. It never got that bad that he felt justified. Most of the time he blew it off as some random crazy."

"Did Pierre still bother you?" Stan asked.

Vaughn shrugged. "Not so much lately."

Stan looked at Melanie. "So why didn't you terminate him?"

"I didn't terminate him because he stopped bothering

her, like she just said. He got involved with a new business associate and focused on squeezing money out of him. And he finally thought he had a recipe that would make him famous. Assured me that I'd be revealing a fabulous milestone for him in the near future."

That prize recipe again. "Frederick Peterfreund. The motorcycle chef?" Stan asked. "Is that whom he was squeezing money from?"

"Yep."

"Was he getting it?"

Melanie laughed. "Frederick is ambitious, not stupid."

"You think there was some issue between Frederick and Pierre about this recipe?" Jessie asked.

"He didn't need Pierre's secret recipe, trust me. I work for Frederick, too. He has an impeccable reputation and a unique twist to his work," Melanie said. "He's extremely well known."

Stan turned back to Vaughn. "Did Sheldon call you to go to Rhode Island?"

"He did."

"Personally?"

"Yes. I figured he'd finally gotten sick of Pierre and wanted some new blood in the fold." She made a face. "I didn't realize how crazy he was, too."

"He didn't tell you Pierre was dead?"

Vaughn shook her head slowly. "Nope."

Great detail to leave out. "Why are you in New York instead of Rhode Island?"

"Because someone else called me right before I got on the plane and told me . . . what happened. What was going on. Said I should avoid the whole thing like the plague."

"Who?" Stan asked.

Vaughn hesitated. "I don't really want to say. If it gets

back to Sheldon, I'm sure there'll be consequences, but this person was trying to help me."

"If you tell us, it might help us," Jessie said. "We're certainly not going to tell Sheldon anything, but the police could pull your phone records."

Vaughn sighed. "There's simply no privacy anymore," she told Gaston, who wagged in agreement. "It was Joaquin Leroy."

"Joaquin?" Stan asked, surprised.

"I know, he's usually crazy loyal to Sheldon. But he's fond of me. We've worked on some projects together long distance over this past year, so even though we've never met in person, he knows me. He tries to salvage what's left of my sanity and figured this wouldn't be good for me."

Stan thought about that. Joaquin had certainly done a good job of convincing her he was worried about Vaughn's whereabouts. Was he that worried about her safety, or was there another reason he didn't want her involved?

Melanie checked her watch. "What else, ladies? I have plans."

"Were you putting together a campaign to discredit Sheldon?" Stan asked.

Melanie chuckled. "Please don't insult my intelligence that way. I have serious clients, not clients who belong in the *National Enquirer*."

Good enough. "One more thing. Who worked with you on the statement? Who gave you the information that Pierre died and that Vaughn was missing?" Stan asked.

"Pierre's brother," Melanie said. "He called me early Saturday and asked me to prepare a statement. Said he'd seen my name on something relating to Pierre and asked for help. Said he worried that something strange was going on, given the two missing people."

"Pierre has a brother?"

Melanie shrugged. "Guess he had a whole family he didn't like to acknowledge."

And he'd told Greta his family was dead. She turned to Vaughn. "What are you going to do?"

Vaughn shrugged. "Lie low, I guess, until this is solved."

Stan frowned. "Are you afraid for your life?"

"I don't know what to be, honestly," Vaughn said. "I just know that every time I get mixed up with Sheldon or Pierre, my life totally unravels. And this time I don't want to watch it happen."

Chapter 45

They made it onto the nine o'clock Metro-North train seconds before the doors *whooshed* closed behind them. Stan sank gratefully into the first seat she saw. Gaston jumped up onto the seat beside her. Jessie dropped into the one facing them. Luckily their car was empty. Stan certainly didn't feel like dealing with other people right now. And Jessie often felt that way. They were silent for a few minutes. Then they both looked at each other.

"Yikes," Stan said at the exact same moment Jessie said, "Wow."

Stan smiled. "Welcome to the world of gourmet food, I guess?"

Jessie shook her head. "It's beyond me who would want to live like that. No offense," she added.

"None taken." Stan didn't point out that many people wouldn't want to live in Jessie's world, one full of guns and danger and criminals. "So Pierre had a brother. I wonder how long it's been since he's seen this long-lost family."

"Interesting," Jessie said. "And I wonder if the people

showing up at Melanie's door are the people who showed up at the bakery. Maybe they're trying to get whatever Pierre owed them from every known associate. That's how those thugs work."

"If they're the same people, they're related to one of the other chefs. There could be a threat thing going on."

Jessie sighed. "I should've guessed." They fell silent, lost in their own thoughts.

"Listen. About Gaston here," Jessie said. The dog's ears perked up at his name.

"Yeah. He's cute, right? I feel bad for him." Stan rubbed the dog's nose. He gazed adoringly at her, apparently content despite this new adventure. "I have to call Nikki." She pulled her phone out.

Her friend answered right before it went to voice mail, sounding harried. "Hey."

"Hey, Nik. Sorry to bother you. I need help."

"What's wrong? Canine, feline, or corpse?"

That almost got Stan to smile. "No corpse. Canine. I had to rescue a dog tonight. We're on the train back from New York."

"New York? I thought you were in Rhode Island. Hold on." The sound of barking grew louder, then silenced. "Sorry. So what happened?"

"I had to go to New York today. Jessie came with me. The dead chef's dog was living in his bakery and the Health Department was about to shut it down. His name is Gaston. He's neutered, about five years old, an Australian shepherd or a mix."

"God, I hate people." Nikki blew out a frustrated breath. Stan could see her raking her hands through her short hair, causing it to stand up in spikes. "So you took him. Nice job, Connor. I taught you well. You need a place to put him?"

"Yes."

"What about your house?"

"Are you kidding? If I keep taking in animals I'm going to have to build an addition. Remember when I had one cat? And tomorrow's that stupid dinner at the mansion."

"Okay. I'll come get him."

"You will? You're the best, Nik."

"You can keep him tonight?"

"I'll smuggle him into the hotel. Shouldn't be a problem. I already have a cat in there."

She thanked Nikki and hung up.

Jessie wore an amused smile and shook her head. "You need to get back to Rhode Island tonight, though."

"I do."

"And Amtrak doesn't allow dogs."

"No. Guess I'll have to rent a car to get back."

"At this hour?"

Stan glanced at her phone. Jessie had a good point. "Shoot."

Jessie's look said *Maybe you should have thought of that before you took the dog on the train,* but mercifully her mouth didn't. "Hang on." She pulled her own phone out of her pocket and pressed some buttons. "Hey," she said when the other party answered. "Sorry to wake you up. Yeah, I'm fine. I just . . . had to help Stan with something. You feel like taking a drive? Good. Meet me at the station in New Haven in two hours and I'll tell you the rest." She ended the call.

Stan frowned. "Who was that?"

"Marty."

Stan grinned. Jessie and Marty Thompson, who

owned a local moving company, had become an item this past spring. Jessie didn't talk much about her personal life. Stan sensed she hadn't had much of one outside her daughter in a long time. This was good news. "How's that going?"

"Fine," Jessie said, but Stan could see the blush traveling up her neck.

"I would say better than fine. He's doing your bidding at two in the morning."

"Yeah, well, he's a night owl. So here's the deal. Marty's going to meet me at the train station. You can take my car to Rhode Island with the dog. I'll come get it tomorrow."

"Are you sure? That's a lot to ask. On top of what you just did."

"Of course I'm sure. I called Marty, didn't I?"

Stan grinned. "Yes. Yes, you did. You going to tell anyone Vaughn's okay?"

"I have a civic duty to let the police know." She paused. "That doesn't mean they should make it public. I'll tell them she feels threatened. They'll keep it under wraps."

"What a crazy story. I don't know whom to believe."

"Sounds like they all have their flaws," Jessie said. "Like the rest of us."

"Yeah." Stan dropped her head back and closed her eyes. "Speaking of flaws, I haven't heard from my sister. I hope she's okay. After the whole police debacle and all."

Jessie turned her head to look out the window on the other side of the train. Stan couldn't see her face when she spoke. "I understand how she feels."

"Hmmm?" Stan tried hard to stay awake, only half listening.

"I said I know how she feels. It stinks."

Stan opened her eyes and glanced at Jessie sideways, suddenly aware there had been a shift in Jessie's tone. It wasn't über-cop right now. It was . . . a regular woman. One who sounded sad.

"What do you mean?" Stan asked.

Jessie was silent for a while, then turned back to face Stan. "I was in your sister's situation a few years ago. Minus the murder suspect part."

Stan tried to keep her mouth from dropping open. "You . . . What situation?"

"I was married, and seeing a married man," Jessie said simply. "I totally knew better, and I did it anyway, and then everything blew up. As it should, right? I mean, no one should ever expect to get away with that."

A Twilight Zone-like feeling had settled over their train car. Stan thought maybe she'd fallen asleep and couldn't wake up. This was not like Jessie. Jake's sister was all business, all the time. It was one of the most admirable, if not annoying, qualities about her. And since she didn't let anyone really get to know her, it was one of the only things Stan had to admire.

Until now.

"What happened?" she asked, trying not to break the mood.

"Lily was almost two. I'd had a really hard time after she was born. I lived down by the shore and worked on a local police force. I came back on dispatch after my leave and worked nights so I didn't have to leave Lily during the day. But I was bored. I love being a cop, and I wasn't doing what I loved. Every time a call came in I wanted to run out and deal with it and I couldn't. So when I was home with her in the mornings, I was drinking. A lot. It was . . . not good."

Riveted, Stan stayed silent, afraid if she interrupted her Jessie would never finish the story. But she remembered when she'd first gotten to Frog Ledge and Jessie wouldn't even set foot in Jake's bar. Here was the story behind it.

"I met Tim when he was assigned to a task force working with some of our cops. They were investigating a child prostitution ring. I weaseled my way into some of the work. My boss knew I missed it and let me work some overtime with the force. I loved it. I immersed myself in it. And I started spending a lot of time with Tim." She shook her head. "One thing led to another, as it always does. And then I didn't know how to stop it. Hell, I didn't want to stop it, honestly. He was exciting and smart and a good cop and we had so much in common. My ex is a financial advisor." She wrinkled her nose. "Guess your sister and I have something in common."

No wonder Jessie hadn't been enthused about her from the start, seeing as she came from the same boring industry.

Jessie finally cracked a smile. "No, I didn't hold that against you," she said, reading her mind.

Stan burst out laughing. "You're totally lying."

"Well, maybe a little." Jessie sobered. "But seriously. I didn't belong with a person like that. He's not a bad guy, just not my speed."

"And you think Jake's going to be in the same boat with someone like me." Stan's gaze dropped to her lap. She hadn't realized how much she didn't want to hear Jessie's real opinion of her. Jake and his sister definitely had their differences and issues, but she knew he respected what she thought.

But she wasn't prepared for Jessie's reaction. "Are you freakin' kidding me?" Good thing there was no one else in their car to hear her shriek.

"What?"

"I said, are you freakin' kidding me? You're nothing like my ex."

"I don't know him, so I can't comment. But I lived in that world."

"Yeah, but you lived in it differently," Jessie said. "Doing media relations is not the same thing as advising people on decisions that could financially make or break them. The ego involved in that job . . ." She shook her head. "Anyway, not what I was saying. I actually think you're good for my brother."

"You do?"

"Why do you sound so surprised?"

"Come on, Jessie. Half the time I don't know if you even like me."

Jessie narrowed her eyes. "You think I'd be schlepping around New York City at this hour with you, chasing down crazy cooking people who belong in a canceled reality show, if I didn't like you?"

Stan shrugged, feeling her face redden. "I figured Jake put you up to it."

"You're a dope." Jessie put her feet up on the bench and crossed her arms in front of her.

But now that she had her talking, Stan wanted to know. "You heard about my sister. Is that why you wanted to help?"

Jessie nodded slowly, still facing front. "I wanted to help because I understand the situation she's in. It could easily have happened to me. But I also wanted to help you. And no, not just for my brother. You've kinda grown on me."

Stan smiled a little at that. "Same here," she said. A beat, then she asked, "What happened to Tim?"

Jessie shook her head and glanced out the train

window to watch the darkness rushing by. "He finished his assignment and left. Last I heard he went back to Georgia or somewhere down south." She shrugged, and Stan swore her eyes were wet. "Those kinds of things? They never work out."

Chapter 46

They spent the rest of the ride alternating naps until the conductor called out for those disembarking in New Haven. Stan led Gaston off the train behind Jessie. They walked through the station and out the front door. Marty stood in front of his car, leaning on the hood.

"Hey, beautiful," he said to Jessie, leaning over to kiss her. Jessie looked uncomfortable at the outward show of affection. Marty didn't look like it bothered him. "Hi, Stan," he said, leaning over to shake her hand. "Been a while."

Stan thought Marty was adorable. Part of his appeal, in her opinion, was his regular guy-ness—he liked sports, he liked to take care of his lawn, he fished in the summer and rode snowmobiles in the winter. He worked hard and liked to relax and drink average beer on the weekend and take vacations twice a year. A really good balance for someone like Jessie, not to mention Lily. "It has. How are you, Marty? I'm so sorry to have you up in the middle of the night. Thank you so much for doing this."

He waved her off. "Anytime. And anything for the love of my life and her friends."

"Seriously, Thompson?" Jessie said.

Marty grinned. "I love making her squirm," he said to Stan. "And here's the lucky fella," he said, bending down to Gaston. "Hi, boy." He held out his hand and let the dog sniff before he patted his head. "Cutie. So, Stan, you sure you're awake enough to make this drive?"

"Yeah, I'll be fine. We slept on the train," Stan said. "Jessie can fill you in on all the excitement in New York."

"It's the city that never sleeps," Marty said.

"This was much more than the typical New York excitement," Stan said.

"My life never used to be exciting until Stan moved to town," Jessie said to Marty.

"Hey, there's something to be said for excitement," Marty said. "Nothing wrong with that. Jess, where's your car?"

"It's in the outside lot. I'll walk Stan over. You can meet me at the gate."

"Will do. Drive safe, Stan."

Stan hugged Marty good-bye and she and Jessie walked the block to the parking area, Gaston trotting along happily beside them, tongue hanging. "You sure you're not too tired?" Jessie asked again. "My brother will kill me if you get in an accident."

"I'm fine. I'll get a coffee. Although not much is open at this hour, is it?" Stan thought about it. She should detour through Frog Ledge. Maybe she could call Izzy to brew her some fabulous coffee. Or she could pop in on the pub's last call. But that was way out of her way. And if she went home, she'd never go back. And she couldn't do that, with Nutty still in Newport. If she stayed on 95, she could make it back in under two hours. *One more day and you can go home.* "I'll find a Dunkin' Donuts somewhere," she said with a grimace.

Jessie, who was not a coffee person and clearly couldn't adequately compare Dunkin' Donuts and Izzy's organic, bold brew, shrugged as if it made no difference. "I'm sure you'll find something." She beeped the alarm, and a Volkswagen Tiguan up ahead flashed its lights. "Here's the keys." She handed Stan her key ring containing her car key, a mini Maglite, and a couple of other keys. Nothing like Stan's, with so many keys and useless key chains that it added three pounds to her purse. "Should be plenty of gas. Don't worry about the dog," she said, reading Stan's mind. "I have a kid. He's not going to get it any dirtier than she does."

"Thanks so much, Jessie." On impulse, Stan hugged her. She didn't know which of them was more surprised.

"Not a problem," Jessie said. "Call me when you get back. And don't crash."

"You'll be asleep."

"Call anyway."

Stan saluted her. "Will do."

"I expect we'll hear more about those goons from the bakery," Jessie said. "The cops might want to follow up."

Stan shrugged. "I'm used to cops following up these days. Come on, I'll drive you out of the gate."

She delivered Jessie to Marty and followed them to the highway. Having traveled this route a number of times, she knew her coffee prospects were poor, so she buzzed the windows down and the sunroof open— thank goodness Jessie saw the value of a sunroof—and cranked the radio. Surprisingly, the no-frills Jessie had also sprung for satellite radio. Stan found the eighties station and sang along with her favorite hair bands.

She easily jetted past Marty, lifting her hand in a wave through the sunroof. Once they hit cruising altitude, Gaston hanging over the console, eyes on Stan, she turned the radio down and forced her tired mind to process the day. She had to laugh—it had been straight out of the movie *Adventures in Babysitting* from her childhood.

All had ended well tonight, but Stan felt like she still wasn't any closer to the truth. She'd learned a lot of random things. In the category of Side Two of a Three-Sided Story, she had Melanie saying Sheldon's claims about her campaign were outrageous. In the category of Pierre's Dirty Little Secrets, he was involved with some bad people, he'd stalked his ex, and his girlfriend seemed younger than Brenna. But perhaps most interesting was the Vaughn Dawes angle. Why had Joaquin warned her not to come? Did he fear for her life? Did he think she would regret being involved? Did he dislike her? Did he think she was conspiring against Sheldon? She wished she could ask him, but Vaughn had sworn her to secrecy.

Any of these chefs could've killed Pierre. Kyle, for reasons unknown, but given his absentee status, it was believable. Marcin, because he was mentally ill and may have blamed Pierre for his screwed-up life. Leo, because he blamed Pierre for Marcin's screwed-up life. Maria, because she wanted to be Pierre's pet. Sheldon, because of so many things. The motorcycle-riding chef could be a suspect, too. And anyone who wanted Pierre's top-secret recipe notes.

Sheesh. Her head started to hurt, so she focused on her music and sang along to Pat Benatar, Laura Branigan, and Bon Jovi. She drove into the hotel parking lot at nearly two A.M., surprised she'd stayed awake the entire time. "We'll go in the back," she decided, and drove around to the other door. She parked and grabbed Gaston's leash.

"Okay, dude, here's the deal," she said to the dog, who turned attentive ears toward her. "I'm going to sneak you inside, and you need to be super quiet. No barking, you hear? And there's a cat, so you better like cats. No chasing him, okay?"

Gaston blinked at her. Stan took that as assent and grabbed her bag. She let him out of the backseat, keeping a close grip on his leash, and led him through the back entrance. Luckily, she didn't bump into any hotel staff before she got in the elevator and pressed the button for her floor with a sigh of relief. She slid the key into the lock and quietly turned it, listening as she pushed it open. No sounds. She closed and locked the door behind her. She headed for the stairs without encountering Therese or Maria. With another relieved sigh, she slipped into her room and locked the door behind her.

"Nutty," she called softly, looking around, keeping Gaston on a short leash. She really hoped he had no issue with cats.

But Nutty wasn't on his window bed, on her bed, the second bed, or snuggled in the cat bed on the floor. "Nutty?" She checked in the bathroom and under the beds. No Nutty. He could've sensed the dog coming and hidden really well.

But it didn't *feel* like he was here. Where could he have gone? She knew she'd shut the door securely behind her. Unless Maria had taken him into her room? Or brought him downstairs to feed him? She put Gaston in the bathroom just in case Nutty was still in the room and bolted downstairs. Trying to be as quiet as possible, she flicked on lights and checked rooms, calling him. Therese wasn't in the living room, so she checked there, too. Nothing. Desperate and on the verge of tears, she fled to Maria's room and pounded on the door, not caring if she woke her up. If Maria had stolen her cat, she'd have a lot more to worry about than lost sleep.

It took a few poundings before Maria flung the door open. Her Jersey hair was wild and sticking out, and she held a short red bathrobe closed. She glared at Stan out of half-focused eyes. "Have you lost your mind?" she demanded. "Do you know what time—"

"Where's Nutty?" Stan pushed past her into the room, feeling around for the light switch. Her fingers grasped it and she flipped it on, bathing the room in light.

"What do you think you're doing?" Maria grabbed her arm, but Stan didn't fight her. Instead, she stared in amazement at Sheldon, who had just jumped out of Maria's bed.

Sheldon stared back at her with the same amount of amazement. "What on earth . . . Stan? What are you doing up at this hour? What's wrong?"

Other than you in Maria's bed in the middle of the night? That put a whole new spin on things. "Nutty's missing from my room." She spun back to Maria. "I know you've taken him out before to give him food. I don't care if you did, I just want to know where he is now."

"I didn't take Nutty out of your room." Maria dropped her arm. "Are you sure he's not in there?"

"Positive. He's just gone." She choked back tears.

"That can't be possible," Sheldon said.

Stan glared at him. "Well, it is. I went out earlier and the room was shut. I came back and he's gone."

"When did you come back? It's nearly three in the morning," Sheldon said, sounding a lot like her dad used to sound.

Stan shot him a look and didn't answer him. "Where's my cat?"

"Honey, honestly, I have no idea," Maria said. She'd gone from annoyed to worried. "I can help you look."

"I just looked everywhere." Stan felt the tears she'd been holding back fill her eyes. "Nutty's my first baby. Nothing can happen to him."

Maria gave Sheldon a look. "I'm going downstairs with Stan. You should probably go. Stan, you won't mention to the others . . ." She tilted her head toward Sheldon. "I don't want them to think I have an unfair advantage over anything."

"I don't really care whom you're sleeping with. I want to find Nutty. Now."

But Sheldon didn't seem like he was ready to go anywhere. "Now, we should all just calm down," he said.

Stan whirled on him and jabbed a finger into his chest. "Calm down? I'll calm down when you find my cat. This entire weekend has been a disaster, to say the least. I've put up with it, gone with the flow, even tried to help. Now someone either let my cat out or stole him. I swear, if I don't get him back . . ." She hiccuped through a sob.

Maria came over and hugged her. "It will be okay, honey. We'll find him. If it's the last thing I do, I'll find him. He's a gorgeous cat. My favorite roomie for the weekend, I'll tell you," she said with a glare at Sheldon. "Let's leave my door open in case he's out and about. He might come in looking for food. Sheldon, get out." She pointed to the door. "Stan doesn't want to see your face right now."

Chapter 47

"Actually, hold on," Stan said. "I do have something I need to ask Sheldon. A couple of things." She met his eyes with a steely glare. "Maria, can you give us a second?"

"Of course," Maria said. She looked hurt, but to her credit she didn't make a stink. "I'll start looking for the baby. I'll get some food out."

"Thank you," Stan said.

"No worries, hon." Maria left the room but didn't shut the door behind her, probably hoping to hear.

Sheldon watched her go, then turned to Stan. He looked apprehensive. "What did you want to ask me?"

"Tell me about your bakery."

"My bakery?" He smiled, puffing his chest out a bit, his nervousness clearly alleviated. "You know about my bakery. You've been there. It's fabulous."

"Who's on your staff?"

"You'll meet them tomorrow. Well, later today," he amended, checking his watch.

"Who are they, Sheldon? Do you really have people? Or are you doing it?"

"I'm doing quite a bit of it, but as you know, I would

never have time to do it all. Especially with two stores and the potential for a third."

"Tell the truth. You don't do it, and you don't have people. People of that caliber, anyway. You got Pierre to do it for you. And you're claiming his work as your own."

Sheldon's face absolutely drained of color. "What . . . what on earth are you talking about?"

"Don't 'what on earth' me," Stan snapped. "You know exactly what I'm talking about. It's one of the reasons Pierre was angry at you. Admit it."

"I'll admit no such thing," Sheldon said indignantly. "Pierre and I were colleagues. As such, we helped each other out—"

"I heard all about it from his girlfriend at his bakery," Stan said. "About how fulfilling your demands as well as his was getting to be too much for him. It was why he wanted more from you, or wanted to terminate his business with you."

Sheldon marched past her and slammed Maria's bedroom door. "Fine. Pierre's been sending me pastry. So what? We had an agreement. And if anything, that should tell you that I didn't kill him, if that's what you're still after. I needed him." He looked disgusted to admit it. "All these years and I've never leaned on anyone, but when I opened the second shop in Boston, I wasn't able to keep up. And good help is hard to come by."

"So how did you get him to do it?"

"I promised him we'd do a bakery together in Los Angeles. I just didn't promise him when." Sheldon shrugged. "He became impatient. I tried to explain I didn't have the capital, but he refused to listen."

"How are you funding all these places?" Stan asked.

Sheldon sighed wearily. "My dear, I'm in debt up to

my eyeballs, and then some. That's why this dinner tomorrow—today—is so important."

"Sheldon." Stan paced the room. "Take me off your list. I don't need you to fund a pet patisserie in Frog Ledge."

"Nonsense. You are going to be a household name in just a few short years. The first pet pastry chef to be known around the world! And I discovered you." He clasped his hands and got that dreamy, Mr. Pastry look again. "I want to be part of that."

And part of the payout, Stan thought. Well, she had news for Sheldon. After this dinner, she was out. Done. Back to Frog Ledge as a simple, two-woman show. If she needed an investor, she'd ask Jake. That was a partnership she could count on—a low-maintenance one at that.

"This is troubling," she said. "It's bad enough you've been lying about it and taking credit for Pierre's work, but to keep it quiet under the circumstances is too much, Sheldon."

"Don't you dare judge me. You have no idea."

"Oh, I do. I'm going to wager a bet that this whole story about Melanie Diamond and her campaign to destroy you has been greatly exaggerated as well. Hasn't it?" She stared daggers at him until he shifted uncomfortably.

"Maybe slightly, but only because I haven't experienced it yet. That's not to say she isn't capable—"

"Save it," Stan snapped. "You sent goons to her door."

Sheldon paled. "I didn't send them. Honestly. I was very angry with her for humoring Pierre. I told Maria about it. Maria does not like to see me upset. It takes away from my creativity, my focus, she says. So unbeknownst to me, she called some, er, family members. They paid Ms. Diamond a visit."

"Are they the same goons who showed up at Pierre's bakery and wanted to break his legs?"

Sheldon didn't seem to know the answer to that.

"Forget it," Stan said. "I don't even care about Melanie or the goons. But I'll tell you what I do care about. I care about you begging my mother for money. Or using me to get to that money."

Now he went from pale to ghost. "Stan. If that's what you think—"

"Why shouldn't I think that? That's what happened, isn't it?"

"No. *No.* She's a no-brainer, Stan. She's very support-ive of arts and culture. She's obviously attuned to the desires of the wealthy. She has money to invest. What else would she rather invest in than something involv-ing her own daughter?"

Sheldon should have been happy she wasn't a violent person by nature. "I can't believe you did that without asking me. It's disgusting. Where'd you get the so-called cat investor? Is she even for real?"

"Yes!" Sheldon's panicked face told Stan he hadn't really thought this through very well. "Of course the cat is for real. And the investor. Mrs. Pamela Mulcahey. She and her husband have basically built the children's wing of the hospital. She wants a different project to back, and she loves her cat. Very much believes in the same principles you do. That is absolutely for real. Don't you understand?" Sheldon stepped forward and grasped her arms. "This is a beautiful opportunity for you both. Just beautiful. Your mother is so delighted to be part of your world. You have no idea."

Stan narrowed her eyes at him. "You'll say anything

to keep me from walking away, because you might lose her."

He dropped her arms and turned away, but not before she saw hurt pass across his face. "No," he said. "That's not true. But I can't change your mind, of course, so you'll have to do what you wish."

She stared at him in utter disgust. "I'll cook the stupid meal. But I'll do it for myself, because I'm not a quitter. And then, we're done. Do you understand? *Done.* And if I don't find my cat, I'll sue you." With that, she walked out of Maria's room and slammed the door so hard it echoed throughout the entire suite.

Chapter 48

Maria had probably heard the entire thing, given her white face and pursed lips. Stan didn't care. As long as she helped her search. And search they did, the entire suite, but found no trace of Nutty. Nothing. He didn't come out for food; he wasn't hiding under furniture. He simply wasn't anywhere. At some point, Sheldon slipped out. Maria, to her credit, went with Stan to search the hall and even other floors, in case Nutty had gotten out and onto an elevator or into the stairwell. Stan alerted security, who promised to keep an eye out. They returned to the suite at five A.M. Therese was nowhere in sight either. Stan doubted she'd stolen the cat, though—she'd barely given Nutty a second glance this whole time.

Stan cried herself to a restless sleep. She jolted awake less than two hours later, hoping it had all been a bad dream. But reality settled onto her like the morning dew. It wasn't a bad dream. She'd left Nutty alone in a hotel full of lunatics, and now he was gone.

She'd slept with her bedroom door bolted and the desk chair shoved under the knob. She didn't trust any of them. Gaston had curled up next to her. She'd welcomed the company and cried into his fur. He was a sweet dog. Stan was glad that she'd been able to save him. At least going to New York hadn't been a completely horrible experience.

Her head pounded so bad she thought she had a migraine. That would not do at all. She needed her wits about her to face this day. First, Stan called the front desk and asked for Lucy. When she got her voice mail, she left a message about what had happened and begged for any help she could give. Next she called Jake.

As soon as she heard his voice, fuzzy with sleep, she lost it again. She didn't think she'd cried this hard when her father died.

"Stan? What's happening? Are you all right?" He snapped to a more awake state. "I'm coming to get you. This is stupid. I'll leave now."

"I can't . . . I can't leave tonight. I have to come back to the hotel after this godforsaken dinner."

"What do you mean?"

"Nutty's m-missing."

"What? How?"

"I got home late. Well, early. You know that, though—I'm sure Jessie told you about our adventure. And he wasn't in my room when I got home."

"That crazy lady have him? The one who keeps feeding him?"

"No. I went straight to her room. He's definitely not there. She helped me look for most of the night."

Jake didn't sound convinced. "That doesn't mean anything. You think she stole him and took him somewhere?"

"I don't know. I have no idea what to think. You were right, Jake. This weekend was a horrible idea. And now Nutty's gone. He must be so scared." Just the thought of her fur baby lost in the hotel, or even worse, outside, terrified her.

"I didn't think it was a bad idea, babe. I think that Allyn character is bad news. There's a difference. Look. I'll see if Jessie can be ready early. We'll come up and search for Nutty while you do your dinner thing."

As usual, he had a solution.

"*Yes.* Thank you. I have to go look some more before the *Foodie* reporter comes."

"Okay. Don't worry—we'll find him."

"I hope so," Stan said. "He's the reason Pawsitively Organic exists. It wouldn't even be worth it without him. And there's something else."

"I'm afraid to ask."

"My mother is one of the investors Sheldon invited."

Silence. Stan figured Jake would throw Sheldon into the ocean when he arrived. "What a slimy piece of—"

"Jake? I told him I'm done with him. The only way there'll be a shop in Frog Ledge is if it's our shop."

"You—okay. Okay, good. Cool. We'll figure out the shop." He sounded more surprised than anything. She knew the feeling. She'd surprised herself.

She hung up and miserably pulled the covers back over her head. She wanted to curl in a ball and cry, then go look for her baby again. But she had to get out of bed and put on a show today for a bunch of people who expected poise, grace, and delicious food. Not to mention a cat who would likely be picky as all get-out. Whatever. She had no stake in the game anymore. If the whole dinner crashed and burned, it wasn't her problem.

Chapter 49

Stan dragged herself into the shower and let the hot water wake her up. After she dried off and dressed, she went downstairs with Gaston. Maria was in the kitchen pouring coffee. When she saw Stan, she sent her a pitying look and handed her a steaming mug. Then she noticed the dog.

"Who is this?" She held a hand out to Gaston. He approached cautiously, tail wagging, and sniffed, then licked her hand. "When did he come in?"

"Last night. His name's Gaston. He needs a home. It's a long story." She didn't want to get into the whole Pierre's dog thing.

"He's gorgeous. How are you feeling?"

"Like crap." Stan took the mug and sipped. "I'm going to take Gaston out, then look around the hotel for Nutty again."

"You are?" Maria asked, checking her watch.

"Yeah. I am. Why?"

"No reason. Sheldon'll want us downstairs shortly, I imagine. And the photographer will be here soon."

"Sheldon can get started without me." Stan swallowed more coffee, then set her mug down. "Ready, G?"

Gaston wagged. She led him out the door, downstairs, and outside to do his business. While she waited for him, she thought about seeing her mother today, and Char's advice. She wondered if Patricia'd heard about Caitlyn's plight yet.

Gaston finished, sat, looked at her, and wagged. "Done? Good job." She gave him one of Nutty's treats, then led him inside. She stopped at the front desk and asked for Lucy.

"Let me see if she's in," the clerk said, and picked up a phone. A minute later Lucy came out from a room behind the counter.

"Stan? What can I do for you today?"

"I just wondered if you'd heard my message. About Nutty."

Lucy frowned. "I haven't been to my office yet. What's wrong?"

"He's missing."

"*Missing*? What do you mean, missing?"

She repeated the sad story for the third time that morning.

"That's impossible. I'm going to get some folks to help you."

"I already told security."

"That's okay. I'll get them to make it a priority."

"We have to leave soon. To go to the mansion."

"Then they'll look while you're gone. Robert, can you call Miguel and tell him I need six, maybe eight people for a special project?" she asked the man behind the desk. "Leave me a picture," she said to Stan. "Who's the pup?"

"Long story."

Lucy smiled. "Why do I get the sense most things with you are a long story?" She squeezed Stan's arm. "We'll find him."

"Thank you."

"Hey, Stan?"

Stan turned.

"Any word on Kyle?"

Stan shook her head. "Nothing."

Stan brought Gaston to the kitchen with her. No way would she leave another animal alone in her suite. She probably should ask Lucy to keep him for the day. Sheldon had already started his briefing when she entered. The only chef there besides her was Maria. They were the last two standing. Tyler, Therese, and Joaquin stood silently by.

Sheldon looked so bright eyed and bushy tailed that Stan couldn't help but wonder if he'd had some chemical help. He hadn't looked that good a few hours ago when she was revealing all his dirty little secrets. But the prospect of a photo spread in the top food magazine must've been a good incentive to pull himself together.

"The Chanler staff has retrieved everything on our original menu list, as well as some alternate items," he said, studiously avoiding Stan's eyes. "Marcin, unfortunately, can't be there, but Leo will meet us at The Chanler. I have a couple of bakers arriving shortly to help with the desserts. Which I'll be largely deciding on and preparing." He continued to avoid looking at Stan with this comment. "The photographer is due here by ten. We'll take photos of prep work here—staged, of course, to look like our practice sessions this weekend, and then she'll photograph everything when we get there. So let's get this kitchen rocking and rolling! We want to put our best *food* forward, don't we, before we head over for the main course?" He laughed gaily at his own plays on words. No one else did. He continued, unfazed.

"The reporter will arrive at The Chanler around two. He or she will likely be more interested in how we've overcome Pierre's death. So let's be ready. We are not going to comment except to say how much he is missed. We'll leave here promptly at one. There will be a cocktail event from three to six. Dinner will be served at six thirty. That's all for now."

He motioned to Joaquin to follow him. The two began walking out of the kitchen, passing Stan and Gaston. Neither of them had noticed the dog yet. Gaston, however, noticed them. He assessed them, then started to growl, a low, foreboding sound accompanied by bared teeth.

"Whoa. Heel," Stan said, pulling on his leash. She had no idea if the dog knew "heel," but so far he'd been well behaved.

Gaston continued to growl.

Sheldon and Joaquin stopped and stared. "Where did you get the puppy?" Joaquin exclaimed. "And why is he angry at us?"

Stan didn't bother to answer, just tightened her hold on the leash.

"Try not to let him bite me, my dear," Sheldon said, only half-kidding, as he slipped past the dog. "And make sure he's gone when the photographer gets here. That will be a red flag for the Health Department."

Joaquin followed. Gaston's snarls increased. Maria watched curiously.

Once they were past, Stan exhaled.

"What was that about?" Maria asked.

Stan shrugged.

Tyler, who'd missed the whole thing, came up with Therese. "Hey, Stan. Hey, pup." He patted Gaston's head. Stan held her breath.

Gaston wagged his tail.

Maria raised her eyebrows.

Stan left Maria fussing with tomatoes in the kitchen and walked out. Sheldon and Joaquin huddled in the corner of the function room. She kept a firm hold on Gaston's leash as she led him back to the lobby, discouraging him from noticing them. "That wasn't good," she scolded as they walked to the elevator bank. Gaston wagged again. It couldn't be a guy thing, because Pierre had, obviously, been a guy. Gaston hadn't growled at the guys working at the bakery, or at Tyler. He had, however, growled at the bad guys who came in the bakery looking for Pierre. So who was the bad guy here? Sheldon? Joaquin? Or did one of them look like someone Gaston didn't like?

Stan shivered and pressed the button as her cell phone rang. She recognized the distinctive voice before the caller identified herself.

"This is Melanie Diamond."

Stan frowned. She'd left Melanie her number but hadn't expected her to use it. "What can I do for you?"

"I just got a phone call from Agatha Landsdowne. Pierre's mother. She asked why I'd put out a media statement on behalf of their family when I hadn't spoken to anyone in the family. Apparently his family consists only of his parents. No siblings, no grandparents, one cousin who lives abroad."

Stan moved into the empty bar area to take the call in private. "But I thought . . ."

"So did I. Apparently his 'brother' doesn't exist. And wherever Mr. and Mrs. Backwoods are, they don't follow the news outlets that first broadcasted this story. A friend heard a fleeting mention on CNN and called them."

"Really," she said, warning bells going off in her head. "That's interesting."

"That's one way to put it," Melanie said. "I'll still answer my door with my gun. Just thought you might want to know." She hung up.

Stan remained seated at the bar, phone in hand. Who had contacted Melanie and posed as Pierre's long-lost brother, claiming to know about the other missing chef and calling for an investigation on Sheldon?

The timing was interesting, because Sheldon's group had been the catalyst of all the news. Sheldon had identified the body. Joaquin had tracked down the records with Pierre's emergency contact information, which prompted the police reach-out. Tyler had worked on all the PR, and he and Therese were the first to know about Vaughn, because she hadn't gotten off the plane. Word hadn't circulated more broadly until later in the day Saturday that she could be missing.

She thought of Frederick, the mysterious motorcycle-riding chef. But even if he'd known Vaughn was missing, what would he have to gain by posing as Pierre's family member? It didn't sound like Sheldon's existence fazed him. He had his own niche, his own following, and his own success, by all accounts. So with Pierre gone, it didn't make sense for him to care. Which meant that whoever had orchestrated the statement had a bone to pick with Sheldon. Could it be Kyle after all, calling the shots from some clandestine location?

But Kyle wasn't here to know about Vaughn. Unless someone had kept him informed.

Had Joaquin been in touch with him, too?

Suddenly Gaston, who'd been sitting quietly at her feet, jumped up at some noise, or smell—Stan wasn't sure what. He caught her off guard. Before Stan could tighten her hold on his leash he jerked it out of her hand and took off, back through the lobby toward the kitchen.

Stan raced down the hall after him, her heart in her throat. What if he bit someone? "Gaston!"

He was fast. She only saw the tail end of his leash, disappearing around the door into their private function room. Someone had left the door ajar. She heard growling from inside. And then a voice.

"Seriously, Jaws, you bite me and we're gonna have a problem," Joaquin's singsong voice said. "So you better go on your way."

She froze, hand on the door. *Jaws?* That was the name the dog had been rescued with, according to Greta. Which had been a number of years ago. Way before Joaquin said he'd met Pierre.

She pushed the door open and stuck her head in. Joaquin stood alone in the function room. He and the dog squared off. He looked startled when he saw her. Stan grabbed the leash off the floor. "Gaston! Bad dog. Sorry about that," she said.

"No trouble," Joaquin said. "I'm not afraid of dogs. He doesn't appear to like me, though."

"I'm curious," Stan said. "What did you call him?"

"Call him?" Joaquin looked blank, then laughed. "Just now? Oh, I called him Jaws. Because he was snarling so much he reminded me of the shark. Ready to take my hand off."

"Yeah, I'm not sure what's come over him," she said. "He's been mellow so far."

Joaquin winked. "I guess I just have that effect," he said. He walked away, leaving Stan staring after him.

Chapter 50

The photographer arrived promptly at ten and introduced herself as Alice Wolcott. Alice, a thirty-something who wore a photographer's vest with lenses in every pocket, did not appear starstruck at all to meet Sheldon. Which won her points in Stan's book.

"Here's what I want to do," she said once she'd met Maria and Stan. Maria had already dressed for the big day in a glittery dress that barely covered anything. Stan hadn't bothered yet. She still wore yoga pants, a T-shirt, and no makeup. She grabbed a white chef's coat from a hook on the wall and hoped it would suffice. "I want lots of pictures of food. Veggies. Bright colors. Sharp knives. Pans and sizzling oil. Herbs. You hear me, right?"

Maria nodded. "I have some things set up. You tell me if they work." She motioned for Alice to follow her.

"Is there a cat here?" Alice asked. "I'm supposed to take pictures of two cats." She pulled out her notebook and flipped a page. "A coon cat and a Siamese."

Stan swallowed. "The Siamese will arrive later at the mansion. The coon is my cat. He's . . . missing."

"Missing?" Alice repeated.

Stan nodded, eyes filling again.

"Maybe the dog instead?" Maria suggested.

"No." Stan shook her head. She'd left Gaston with Lucy Keyes, who'd promised to keep him under lock and key. "He's got nothing to do with the dinner."

"What's your specialty?" Alice asked Stan.

Murder. "Pet treats. Hence the cats." She squared her shoulders. "Can we just take some shots? I need to keep looking for Nutty."

"Of course. Let's get you set up." Alice surveyed the options. "Here, do you use mixing bowls?"

Stan nodded. Alice handed her a bowl and a spoon and positioned her in a chef-with-attitude pose. "There. Love it. Hang out for a minute." She swapped lenses and snapped away. "A few more. Now tilt this way."

Stan kept her smile in place until her face felt like it might break. Maria watched, clearly annoyed. Alice didn't seem to care. Finally she gave Stan the nod. "Great. Thanks. Oh, hey. Do you have photos of your cat? I can try to use one. I feel bad leaving him out."

Stan brightened. "I do." She took out her phone and found her camera roll. As she scrolled, she remembered the photos from Pierre's bakery. She had to look at those today. After finding a couple good photos of Nutty that made her cry again, she e-mailed them to Alice and went upstairs.

She locked herself in her room and threw on the one dress she'd brought for the weekend, which was now wrinkled from sitting in her suitcase the entire time. She stuffed her heels—she'd gone with Marc Jacobs for this occasion—into her bag and slipped on her flip-flops. She had to check in with Lucy. But first, she took out her phone and pulled up the pictures from the bakery. She found the one with a bunch of people in the background and zoomed way in, moving the photo around with her finger to try to see the faces.

The person she'd thought looked familiar appeared as a blurry half person. But the features . . . She studied it for a minute, then zoomed out and looked again. Then zoomed back in.

He held a pastry bag, squeezing frosting onto something. She zoomed again. Then she realized what had caught her eye.

His nails were blue.

Stan's heart flipped slowly in her chest. Blue nails. Granted, pastry chefs were an eclectic bunch. She'd seen that firsthand. Joaquin couldn't be the only one who painted his nails. This person looked a lot slimmer and had a much larger nose, and a small goatee. But something about the face, the smile.

Get a grip, Stan. This picture is five or more years old.

Five or more years ago when Joaquin wasn't supposed to know Pierre. Yet he'd called the dog Jaws. His old name from five years ago. Coincidence? Stan hated coincidence. But why would Joaquin lie about knowing Pierre then?

She closed out of the photos and opened her browser. She typed in "La Chocolate Bakery" and found a phone number. *Please answer. Please answer.*

Greta did, after three rings. "Good morning. La Chocolate Bakery," she said, her voice subdued.

"Greta? It's Stan Connor. We met yesterday."

"Oh, yeah!" Greta's voice brightened. "How's Gaston?"

"He's good. Listen, I need a favor. That picture on the wall, with a bunch of people in it with Pierre? You know the one? He's decorating something in the main shot?"

"I think so," Greta said. "What about it?"

"Can you get me the names of the people in the photo?"

Silence. "I guess," she said. "Why do you need that?"

"It's really important, Greta. Please? You can text me." Stan repeated the number in case Greta'd lost her card.

"Okay. It might take me a bit. I really don't know who knows them."

"That's okay. Just try to hurry. Thanks."

Someone knocked on her bedroom door, a pleasant, quick rap. Stan sat up, dread pooling in her stomach. With shaking hands she disconnected and threw her phone into her bag.

"Yeah?" she called, working to make her voice normal.

"Stan? We're getting ready to load into the car," Joaquin called. "Are you almost ready?"

"Just finishing getting dressed," she called back. "Be right out!"

"Lovely! I'll wait for you."

"You go ahead," she said. "I promise I'll be right there."

"Not a chance. Too many missing people," he singsonged. "I want to escort you myself. I know you're worried about the kitty, but I promised Sheldon I'd help hurry you along."

She grabbed her bag. Holding her breath, she yanked the door open. Therese waited, her foot tapping in a five-inch stiletto heel.

"Are you, like, ready?" she demanded.

Stan let out her breath in a *whoosh*. "More than ready. Let's go."

Chapter 51

The limo driver held the door for them. Maria, Tyler, and Sheldon were already seated. Sheldon apparently wasn't bringing his pink Caddy to this shindig. Alice, tucked into the far end of the car, snapped a picture. Silver balls of light danced in front of Stan's eyes.

"Gorgeous dress," she said, as Stan climbed in.

"Thanks." She sat next to Maria. Therese and Joaquin followed. Joaquin sat on Stan's other side. He wore funky platform shoes today with his plaid vest and tight pants. And he seemed happy as always. Stan studied him critically. He looked nothing like the person in that photo. She was reaching.

"Any luck with the cat?" Alice asked.

Stan shook her head. "Sadly, no. But I have friends coming to look, and the hotel staff is looking, too."

"Where's the pup?" Joaquin asked.

"I found someone to watch him," Stan said.

Joaquin smiled. "I hope he likes them."

"Is that your only cat?" Alice asked.

"No. I have another cat and two dogs." Stan pulled out her phone and showed Alice pictures of Scruffy, Henry, and Benedict, as well as Duncan, whom she considered hers by extension. Scruffy, especially, was very photogenic, just like Nutty.

"Cute furries! Can I see?" Joaquin asked. He leaned over to look. When Stan held the phone closer to him, he reached for it. "I left my glasses," he said by way of apology, then scrolled the pictures himself.

She watched him as he studied each one before swiping to the next. He went through the animal pictures, appropriately *oohing* and *aahing*. With each swipe, Stan's stomach dropped further. Any minute, he would see the photos from Pierre's bakery.

Then, Joaquin swiped to it. His eyes lingered on it for a minute, then brightened. "Look at that! Vintage Pierre." He raised the phone for a closer look. "Wherever did you get that? And OHMYGOD. Is that Felix Paulson?"

Stan stared at him. "I have no idea."

"Of course it is! He was quite the up-and-comer a few years back. Tragedy, what happened." He leaned closer and stage whispered, "He killed himself."

A text message alert sounded. Joaquin paused, then handed the phone to Stan. She took it and checked the readout. A New York number. The message read:

It's Greta. I asked Sheldon about the people in the pic. Couldn't think of anyone else who would know.

It's Bill Gregory, Armando Rosenburg, Felix Paulson, and Stefan Loomis. Left to right.

She'd asked Sheldon? That could be bad. Stan pulled the picture up and matched names to faces. The person with the blue nails, according to Greta, was Felix Paulson.

Joaquin was right. She searched her exhausted brain.

Why did that name sound vaguely familiar? Not from yesterday. Melanie and Vaughn hadn't mentioned . . .

Vaughn. Char. The restaurant. Yes, that was it! Char said the chef from Vaughn's restaurant in LA was named Felix Paulson. That couldn't be a coincidence. And the timing would've been about right, if the picture in Pierre's bakery was about five years old.

And now, according to Joaquin, he was dead.

Chapter 52

The limo driver pulled up to The Chanler's front entrance. The restaurant was closed to the public for the day, but it still bustled with activity as staff polished and primped and set things up for the event. A man in a tuxedo waited at the front door for them. He introduced himself as Andrew and led them to the kitchen. Stan found herself in the middle of Sheldon and Joaquin for the walk. Sheldon had his arm through hers, as if he feared she might take off at any moment and let him down. Or for another reason? Now she'd become paranoid.

She had to slip away to the ladies' room and call Detective Owens. She wanted to run some of this by him, see if he could check out Joaquin. And Felix Paulson.

"Here is your work space," Andrew announced with a sweeping hand gesture. Stan gaped at the sight. The kitchen could fit the entire first floor of her house. Enough ovens were in place for all of them to have different food going at once. An overwhelming amount of food had been set out. Produce of all shapes and colors, fresh fish and cuts of meat, oils and wines and chocolates, fruit—she barely knew where to start. Three men were already chopping and sautéeing with a vengeance. The Chanler kitchen staff, probably. They raised their hands in acknowledgment.

"Would you like to see where the party will be held?" Andrew asked.

"I'm dying to!" Sheldon exclaimed.

He led them outside to the backyard, where an elegant wedding-style tent stood at the ready. A bar on the patio had been stocked full with colorful bottles. Its awning extended over the small cocktail tables. A marble fountain in the middle of the lawn, which looked like a small pool, spewed sparkling water to great heights. Staff set up the rest of the tables with elegant, lacy tablecloths, napkins, and candles. Beyond the party, the ocean shimmered below the Cliff Walk.

"Gorgeous," Sheldon declared. "Exactly what we imagined it would be."

"Excellent." Andrew looked pleased. "The guests will be brought in the front entrance and escorted back here, where they will have cocktails and passed hors d'oeuvres, which we have supplied. The wine is local, as you requested. There's a side door over there"—he pointed behind the tent to the left—"so unwieldy trays and servers won't be blighting the patio doors."

"And for the cat?" Sheldon inquired.

The man smiled. "Yes, sir. Right this way." Stan followed him to one of the tables inside the tent. Next to the chair was a booster seat with a pink cushioned cat carrier built onto the top, complete with a tray for food dishes.

"Delightful." Sheldon clapped his hands. "This will be a night to remember. Don't you think, Stan?"

Stan looked around. Despite the beauty of the

scene—the gardens, the mansion, the backdrop of the sea—a sense of foreboding hung over the day like an ominous fog that wouldn't lift. She nodded, fighting off the feeling of dread.

"I think you're right," she said.

Chapter 53

Sheldon shepherded them back to the kitchen. "I trust you'll be getting busy," he said, his gaze lingering on Stan.

"Absolutely. What a fabulous place to cook!" Maria exclaimed, "I'm so excited." She made a beeline for the food. Alice followed, snapping pictures.

"Tell me how I can help," Joaquin said. "Stan? I enjoyed working on the cat-noli with you the other day. I'd love to help you whip that up." He dropped his small backpack next to the fridge and tucked it against the wall.

"Sure," Stan said. She gathered ingredients, her mind shifting and organizing the few facts she had to prepare for her call to Detective Owens. She watched him as he added ingredients to the bowl, humming to himself. The dog thing bothered her. A lot. Plus Joaquin had called Vaughn Dawes and warned her not to come this weekend. Maybe the picture had nothing to do with anything. But even if Joaquin knew Pierre and his dog from years ago, why kill him today? And what about

Kyle? Then there was still the whole mystery about the house.

Stan measured out the ingredients to mix the cream for the cat-noli.

"This should do it. Can you work your magic with the food processor while I run to the ladies' room? I've been dying to go since we got here," she said with an exasperated laugh. "Too much coffee."

"But of course," Joaquin said. "I'll make sure it's extra fluffy."

Stan left the kitchen. She had no idea where the bathroom was. After wandering into one hall that had a rope blocking it halfway down and another with so many doors she felt like she was on a Disney ride, she saw a staffer down the hall. "Bathroom?" she asked.

"Go back that way and take a right. You'll see it on your right, second door."

Stan hurried to it, making sure no one was behind her. She ducked into the bathroom and found herself in an elegant waiting room with couches and mirrors galore. Best of all, a lock, which she promptly deployed. Around the corner through another door were the toilets, with marble floors and walls and thick wooden doors that closed and locked. Complete privacy. She checked to make sure no one else was in the bathroom, locked herself in a stall, and took out her phone with shaking hands. She scrolled through her contacts for Detective Owens's number and dialed.

Voice mail. She groaned in frustration. "Detective Owens. Stan Connor. I wondered if you could check out Joaquin Leroy. He may have known Pierre and this crew a lot longer than he claims. Don't call me. Just come. We're at The Chanler. I have another name, too. Felix Paulson. Not sure if it's anything."

She hung up and tried Jessie. No answer. She shot off a text and prayed Jessie would see it. Check out Joaquin Leroy and Felix Paulson. She waited an agonizing amount of time for the reception to take her message where it needed to go. When it finally dinged as Sent, she deleted the message and pocketed the phone, then prepared herself to return to the kitchen and act like nothing was wrong.

Chapter 54

Stan had her hand on the kitchen door when someone grabbed her arm. Gasping, she turned, ready to claw and kick her way free. Then she realized it was Leo.

"Leo!" She threw her arms around him. "So glad to see you!"

Leo hugged her back but looked at her curiously. "Me too, me too. Is everything all right?"

"Fine. How's Marcin?"

Leo shook his head. "Sick, I'm afraid."

"I'm so sorry."

"It can't be helped, my dear. I've been in denial, I'm afraid. Now it's time to own up to my life." He smiled, but he looked exhausted. "Let's get this nightmarish event over with, shall we?"

Stan nodded. "Amen to that."

They walked into the kitchen together. "Look who I found," she called cheerily.

Sheldon, Maria, and Joaquin turned and clapped.

"New blood," Alice said approvingly, snapping a

photo of Stan and Leo. "Let's get you in some of these shots!"

She led him away. Stan surveyed the kitchen. Sheldon's other bakers had arrived, so there were six additional chefs, plus Joaquin. They'd started all the ovens. Pots boiled on stoves, vegetables sautéed in cast iron pans, oil cheerfully spattered out of hot skillets.

"Perfect timing!" Sheldon declared. "The reporter just arrived, and Tyler is working with him. Therese is assisting. I think we're in delightful shape. Don't you, Stan?"

"Yeah. Great," Stan said.

"Yes." Sheldon rubbed his hands together, not even registering her lack of enthusiasm. It was like he'd forgotten about their whole conversation. Such a strange man.

She went back to her station. One of the mansion chefs-on-loan hovered, watching Joaquin whip something in a bowl. He handed her a bowl of gorgeous, perfectly whipped cream.

"That looks amazing," she said.

He bowed slightly. "Happy to serve."

"He's a genius," the other chef said. "You're all geniuses. I can't wait to see this meal."

Joaquin placed his whipping spoon on the counter. "I'm going to see what Leo needs." He smiled at her. She smiled back. His gaze seemed to last longer than usual. Stan pushed the thought away. *We just have to get through this afternoon. Detective Owens will come. It will be fine.*

Sheldon stuck his head in the kitchen right at three to let them know the investors were arriving and they needed to get out and mingle. Stan laid a tray of treats just out of the oven on the counter to cool and untied her apron. She couldn't wait to get outside. Between the photographer's incessant shooting and Joaquin's stifling presence, she couldn't breathe. She kept hoping Owens would walk through the door, but he didn't. She didn't dare check her phone in front of them, and if she ran to the bathroom every five minutes that would look suspicious, too.

With everything going on in her head, she hadn't rehearsed what to say to her mother when she arrived, wearing her investor hat. She couldn't decide between *Hey, where've you been?*, *Hi, how are you?*, or *How could you agree to do this?*

Probably option two, given everything else going on. She stepped out into the blinding sunlight. At least it was another beautiful day. More beautiful to think Detective Owens would show up any minute and solve this case, she'd find Nutty, and she could go home to Jake.

She lowered her sunglasses over her eyes and surveyed the small crowd gathering. She didn't see her mother yet, but a woman with a pink suit and matching hat held a cat carrier. The Siamese. She waited to feel anxious, but it didn't come. Maybe because she'd already told Sheldon to stuff it. She watched Joaquin, over by the bar. He spoke in low tones with Sheldon. From the way they were gesturing, they were discussing table setup. Joaquin's eyes strayed to Stan, as if he felt her watching him. He waved.

Stan waved back, swallowing the fear curdling in her throat. She resisted the urge to check her phone, but after she went out to meet the cat, she was definitely heading into the bathroom to get a status update. Owens had been on them the entire weekend; now all of a sudden he'd vanished into thin air, too. It figured.

She made her way over to the cat woman. Pamela Mulcahey, Sheldon had said. She introduced herself.

Mrs. Mulcahey looked her up and down. "You're going to feed my Charles?" she asked haughtily.

"I certainly am," Stan said.

"Well, I hope he enjoys it. Right, my boy?" She held up the carrier. Stan peered inside. Charles was a Siamese snowshoe. He looked as haughty as his owner, sitting on a purple pillow, coolly regarding Stan. She put her finger to the cage. He didn't even deem to sniff.

"Make yourself comfortable," Stan said. "I can't wait to see how Charles feels about his dinner." She turned and hurried away, searching for everyone's position. Sheldon worked the crowd with Joaquin by his side. Tyler trailed after a man with a notebook. Leo and Maria spoke with a couple who looked very familiar. A minute later she realized why, when the woman turned and shaded her eyes from the sun. Her mother and Tony Falco, the unpopular mayor of Frog Ledge. She quickly turned away. She didn't have time to talk.

But before she got inside to call Owens again, she saw a familiar face slip out of the patio doors with a couple of the arriving guests. The detective had dressed in a suit to blend in, but he was still recognizable. He met Stan's eyes across the lawn. She wanted to weep with relief. He shook his head slightly, as if to deter her from coming over.

Shoot. She had to get to him. But she didn't want to alert everyone else. She stayed where she was, still scanning the crowd. She saw Sheldon talking with her mother. He studiously avoided her eyes. But Joaquin wasn't anywhere near him. Stan's heart skipped. He'd probably gone back inside to fool around with more food, she reasoned. Or maybe he'd sat and she couldn't see him.

Or he'd caught sight of Owens? He had to be suspicious, after she'd questioned his identification of Jaws.

Frustrated, she pulled her phone out, thinking of sending Owens a text across the lawn, when she saw a text message teaser light up her screen. Jessie.

Candace Kramer talked to Sheldon's assistant, Joaquin, this week. He called about the property taxes on the rentals. He wanted to confirm addresses. I called Owens. STAY AWAY.

Chapter 55

Stan glanced up, trying to look casual despite her pounding heart and the cold sweat dripping down her neck. Owens's back was to her. She still couldn't spot Joaquin. If he had a clue they were on to him, he'd vanish into thin air and this whole mess would never get solved.

That couldn't happen.

He must've gone back inside. Maybe he planned to head out the front entrance. She started toward the door, moving through the thick of the party. More people had arrived and the yard was full. All across the lush lawn people sipped cocktails and servers in black tie passed hot hors d'oeuvres.

And then Stan saw a shock of red hair, in the middle of the crowd near the fountain. If the woman with the big hat hadn't bent over to pick something up, she would've missed it. Joaquin had somehow managed to blend in, but now he moved fluidly through the crowd toward the back of the yard. As Stan watched, frozen, he glanced over his shoulder.

He met her eyes for a split second, then turned and moved faster.

She started toward him. The crowd spanned the length of the yard, so it was slow going. Joaquin was going to slip down the back stairs from The Chanler's grounds onto the Cliff Walk, and from there he could get anywhere. He could turn the corner and disappear into the crowds on Memorial Boulevard, or he could vanish down the Cliff Walk and up one of the other staircases onto another adjacent street.

He picked up his pace, breaking free of the crowd, not looking back, just focused on getting out. This yard was huge, and he had a good head start. And a lot of people cover.

Stan texted Owens with shaking hands:

Joaquin's on the run out the back way to the Cliff Walk

I'm following, going to keep him in sight

Get backup!

She kicked off her shoes and took off at a run through the yard. A woman with a tray of tiny meatballs in single-serving plates froze when she saw Stan coming. Stan tried to avoid her but clipped the tray on her way by. The meatballs—closely followed by the server—hit the grass. Sauce splattered onto Stan's dress. She kept running. Joaquin had vanished down the small outdoor stairwell when she'd taken her eyes off him in the meatball confusion. She followed, figuring he'd opt for the main road.

But when she got to the stairs, she saw a high, orange construction gate blocking the Cliff Walk entrance. Sheldon must've paid extra to stop as many gawkers as he could. He couldn't block off every entrance, but he could limit the traffic from the main one.

She turned right and began running down the Cliff Walk, almost barreling into a woman and her little girl walking. The woman stared at her, then her eyes traveled to the orange gate with minor alarm apparent at being trapped.

"Did you see a guy run by? Bright red hair, big shoes?" Stan asked.

The woman looked uncertain, then nodded and pointed behind her. "That way."

"If you see him again, call nine-one-one," she said, then kept going. She couldn't run even if she wanted to, between the people and the narrow path. The pavement burned her bare feet, and rocks and who-knew-what-else sliced into her skin. She didn't care. She focused on one thing only—catching up with Joaquin.

Behind her, she could hear shouts, but she didn't stop to look. She prayed Owens was coming. She skidded around tourists clogging the path, lingering over the ocean views, feeling like she was traveling through molasses. Why were so many people still out in this heat? Sweat had plastered her dress to her body. The sauce splattered on her dress probably looked like blood. Her hair had turned into a mess of frizz, and she shoved it out of her eyes as she searched for Joaquin's shock of red hair. Would he still have his platforms on trying to run on this narrow pathway, or had he ditched his shoes like she had?

She stepped on something sharp and cursed, stopping to rub her foot. Blood smeared on her hand. Great.

Then from just around the next bend, a scream.

Chapter 56

Stan broke into a run again, but it was more like a hop. She ignored the pain in her foot, dodging people who stopped and stared. In her disheveled state she must've been quite a sight. Rounding the bend, she saw a woman sprawled in the path in front of her. Stan stopped and bent down. "Are you okay?"

The woman nodded, pushing herself up. "Some guy in a crazy outfit shoved me down. He looked . . . disturbed."

"Stan!"

She turned at the voice shouting her name. Owens raced toward her.

"He on the move?"

Stan nodded. "It's only a half mile to Narragansett Ave., the next big mile marker. But he could go up one of the smaller exits."

Owens squinted ahead into the sunlight. "Try to keep anyone from continuing down the path in this direction," Owens said to the woman. "I have more police coming. Stan, stay here." He started moving again, also awkward in his suit and dress shoes.

"No way," Stan muttered, and took off after him.

They didn't have much farther to go. Around the next bend in the path, they found Joaquin. He'd slowed on the dirt shoulder of the path, close to the edge of the rocks, breathing heavily. He wasn't the most in-shape person Stan had seen, and this was a distance to run if you weren't used to it. Especially in platform shoes. He teetered dangerously close to the edge of the cliff, bushes and trees his only barricade against the ocean below. Not all points of the Cliff Walk were high, but this piece dropped straight down onto the rocks.

Owens stopped, his hand shooting out to curtail Stan's forward movement. "Joaquin," he said. "Stop. It's over."

Joaquin fisted his hands in his red hair. Despair and panic had turned his soft, chubby features into a grotesque mask. "Stay away from me!" He took a step back. Just behind him, the dirt and greenery gave way to thin air and deep, blue sea. "I don't know why you couldn't have just let Golden Boy Kyle take the fall. It was supposed to be Sheldon. It *would* have been Sheldon, if everyone had stayed out of it! But Kyle would've been fine, too. He was one of *them*."

Owens's hand rested on the butt of his gun. "What do you mean, one of them?" he asked.

Stan held her breath, hoping Joaquin would succumb to the conversation. It might get him away from the edge. But he said nothing.

"Joaquin, it's okay," Owens tried again. "Come away from the edge of the cliff. Let's talk it out."

"Talk. Ha!" Joaquin glanced over his shoulder and took another uncertain step. "I don't want to talk."

"What do you mean, it was supposed to be Sheldon?" Stan asked, taking a step forward and avoiding Owens's eyes. She didn't want him to stop her.

"Because he knew about Pierre! He knew and he didn't do *anything*!"

"Knew what about him? What did Pierre do?"

Below them, the ocean crashed against the rocks. The sound of children further down the path, blissfully unaware, reached her ears, a startling contrast to the scene unfolding in front of her.

"What did he do? He stole my career," Joaquin said simply, and Stan saw a glimpse of a sad little boy, probably a misfit, who'd finally found his path in life only to find out it had been blocked off by a natural disaster. "He stole my prize recipe and used it to woo Sheldon. I'd been working on it for years. Vaughn helped me. We were going to unveil it together at her restaurant in LA."

Stan could feel Owens's eyes moving back and forth between them. For the moment, he said nothing. "I don't understand. I thought you've only known Sheldon and his chefs for a year."

He laughed, a brittle sound that made her skin crawl. "As Joaquin Leroy, yes. But before that, I was a chef, too. I worked with Pierre. And Sheldon. But you know that. You saw our picture. Tell me, what gave it away? The picture or the dog? Stupid dog. I blew my own cover. Jaws never liked me." He shook his head in disgust. "Felix Paulson. That was me. I killed him off, you know. Got some plastic surgery, started over. But they had to be punished." He focused on Stan again. "Do you know they never even realized who I was? Not even Pierre. I had to tell him before I killed him."

From somewhere out of Stan's sight, she heard shouts. The other police, running up the path. She could see Owens assessing when to make a move and sent him a mental message to wait. "So he stole your recipe and took your chance away?" she asked, keeping her gaze focused on Joaquin.

"Yes!" Joaquin cried, taking a step toward her. His foot wavered on those silly shoes and the uneven terrain. "Finally someone understands. And Sheldon took him on, and he became his star pupil. Later, his star chef. And I failed at everything I touched after that." He looked so sad, so defeated. Stan wanted to reach out, pull him away from the edge of the cliff.

Then everything happened at once, in slow motion.

A contingency of Newport police rounded the corner, guns drawn. Owens's eyes flickered to them and he cursed.

"Stand down," Owens commanded.

But Joaquin saw them coming, too. Startled, he took a step back, eyes wide and fixed on all those guns facing him. His foot caught a rock, or a branch. Stan wasn't sure which. But he lost his footing, and with those silly shoes he couldn't regain it. Stan watched, horrified, as he stumbled backward. He tried to right himself, hands flailing wildly as he grabbed for purchase but only found air.

He almost caught himself.

Then he fell from view.

Chapter 57

Owens rushed forward and peered over the drop. Stan could tell by the defeated slump of his shoulders that Joaquin hadn't managed to grab hold of something and hang there waiting for help to arrive. Another cop reached for his radio and called for an ambulance. The others all moved into preserve-the-scene mode. Stan wondered vaguely if they'd need to call the coast guard to retrieve his body.

Genske, who'd rushed in with the group of police, took Stan's arm. "Are you okay? Was anyone else hurt?" she asked.

Stan shook her head.

"What happened to your feet?" Genske asked.

They both looked down. One foot was bloody. The toenail polish had scraped off several toes. She was pretty sure she'd ripped off a layer of skin.

"Stan!"

Stan turned. Jessie ran up the path at full speed. "What happened? Did they catch him?"

Stan shook her head. "He fell."

"Fell?" Jessie's eyes traveled to the cliff's edge. She grimaced. "Ouch. Suicide? Or did he really fall?"

"Fell," Stan said miserably. "He was talking but . . . he lost his balance."

"Are you okay?"

Stan thought about that. Physically she was fine, feet aside. Mentally, she felt like a truck had run over her. She stared helplessly at Jessie, not sure how to answer.

"Hey, you have bare feet," Jessie said.

"Don't remind me."

"Here." Jessie pulled her sneakers off. "I have socks on. Take these."

Stan didn't even argue with her. Grateful, she pulled the shoes on. "What happened?" she asked Jessie. "You talked to Candace?"

Jessie nodded grimly and pulled her out of the way as the police swarmed the area. "Yes. Joaquin called her last week, before she left for her trip. He said he was working on tax stuff with Sheldon, getting a head start, whatever. He wanted to make sure he had all the personal property addresses right."

"So he asked her to cross-reference them," Stan said. "Pretended to make sure she didn't get put on the hook for any taxes. He knew from Sheldon that was her big issue."

"Bingo," Jessie said. "And that included Sheldon's apartment, and Kyle's old apartment Sheldon had rented in Candace's name because he didn't want anyone else who worked for him to know."

"Which would explain why the pizza cutter was in that Dumpster," Owens said. "That never made sense to me."

"Joaquin thought it was Sheldon's Dumpster," Stan said. "He said something about how Sheldon was supposed to take the fall, but Kyle would've been okay, too." She felt sad for Joaquin. Which was absurd—he'd killed a man over a recipe—but he'd seemed so lost. If

Joaquin—Felix—had put his energy into forgiveness and creating something even better, he could've had an amazing life. Instead resentment and jealousy had eventually killed him.

"How'd you land on him?" Jessie asked.

"He called Pierre's dog by his old name," Stan said. "I thought it was odd because he'd only claimed to have known these guys for a year. I figured it was coincidence. But then there was this picture in the bakery," she explained to Owens. "It wasn't clear, but the guy in the photo was familiar. Joaquin saw it, too, and named the guy as Felix Paulson, said he'd committed suicide. But I recognized the name—it was tied to Vaughn Dawes." She shook her head. It was all so complicated, and her head hurt. "It looked like he'd gotten major plastic surgery, if he could hide in plain sight with these guys. Or maybe they really are that clueless and wrapped up in themselves."

They were all silent for a moment. Then Owens turned to Stan.

"Why don't you go on back. You look like you've had it. Will you be around for a while?"

"Until I find my missing cat," Stan said.

Jessie slung an arm around her shoulder. "Let's go. Jake's waiting. And we tracked down Kyle," she said as they started walking.

"You did?"

"Yep." But instead of looking pleased with herself, Jessie looked like she didn't like what she had to tell her. "Apparently he'd gone off the grid. With a woman."

"No." Stan covered her face with both hands. "My sister is going to lose it. How did he manage that?"

Jessie shrugged. "He called some girl he had on the side. Apparently he needed comforting because of the dead guy." She rolled her eyes. "They took off to

Nantucket for the weekend. Claimed they left their phones behind and had no contact with anyone to see or hear what was going on." Her tone suggested she didn't quite believe it.

"In Lucy Keyes' truck." Stan shook her head. "I don't want to be the one to tell Caitlyn."

"Don't worry," Jessie said. "Owens said she left word with the police to call her with an update when they found him. I'm sure she knows by now."

Chapter 58

Stan limped back to The Chanler with Jessie. The police had closed off the Cliff Walk in both directions while they spoke with witnesses, gathered what evidence they could, and began the process of recovering Joaquin's body.

Jake paced the lawn near the gate. She'd never been so happy to see him in her life as she hurried through the gate. She caught the relief, elation, and something else—love?—that passed over his face as he opened his arms to her. She closed her eyes and breathed in the familiar scent of him. He felt safe and warm. Like home.

Neither of them spoke for a long moment, then he said softly near her ear, "You're killing me. You know that, right?"

A laugh bubbled up in her throat and she stepped back to look at him. "At least I keep your life exciting."

"Something like that." He looked her up and down. "Are you okay?"

"Yeah."

"Your shoes don't match."

They both observed Jessie's sneakers. Stan shrugged. "Could be worse," she said.

"What about him?"

She shook her head. The stress of the day finally hit her, and tears bubbled up again. She swallowed them. "Where's Sheldon?" she asked instead, not wanting to lose it yet. "Is he okay?"

"He's over there," Jake said, jerking his head toward a small circle behind them. Stan caught a glimpse of Sheldon, a puddle of despair in the middle, Maria holding him up. "He's not taking the day's events well."

Stan felt a little badly for him. Nobody deserved to have their assistant revealed as a murdering psychopath. But before she could go over to see him, her mother appeared at her side, dragging Tony behind her.

"Kristan. Tony and I have been frantic ever since we heard you took off like a maniac after that awful boy."

"You certainly gave everyone a fright," Tony said, leaning over to kiss Stan's cheek.

"Did you get hurt?" Patricia's gaze fell to Jessie's sneakers, dreadfully mismatched to Stan's dress, and lingered.

"I'm fine, Mom." They looked at each other, a million things passing through that one look. "We have a few things to catch up on."

Her mother nodded. "We do."

"How's Caitlyn?" Stan asked, but her cell phone started ringing. She glanced at the readout. Lucy Keyes. "Hang on, Mom." Squeezing Jake's hand, she stepped away and answered.

"Can you come back to the hotel?" Lucy asked.

Stan's heart sank. "What's wrong?"

"Nothing. Nutty wants to see you."

"Nutty? He does?" She probably shrieked but didn't care. "You found him?"

"We did. He was in Sheldon's suite."

Sheldon's suite. And Joaquin's. Stan thought back to yesterday when she'd left for New York. Joaquin and Therese had been in her suite. Joaquin could've been suspicious about what she knew even then. Maybe he'd taken Nutty as leverage. Regardless, she was about to get her cat back. "I'll be right over," she said.

She hung up and went over to Jake. "Lucy found Nutty. Can we go get him?"

"She did? Thank God." He hugged her again. "I was so worried. We started looking and then Jessie got that call and we rushed over here."

Stan didn't know whether to laugh or cry again at his reaction. He was amazing. And all hers.

"Then can we go home?"

"I thought you'd never ask," Jake said.

But as they turned to go, Patricia Connor tapped Stan on the shoulder. "Honey? Can you wait a minute? I have something to talk to you about." She looked at Jake. Something passed between them.

Stan looked from one to the other. "What's going on?"

"Your mom has something to ask you," he said, squeezing Stan's hand.

Now she was suspicious. What could Jake and her mother possibly be conspiring about?

"I've decided," her mother said, "not to invest with Sheldon. But I do want to invest in a worthwhile, up-and-coming business." She paused, clearly wanting some kind of encouragement to continue.

"Okay," Stan said, not sure why her mother felt that now was the right time for this conversation. The adrenaline rush had started to wear off and she felt exhausted and sad and just wanted to see her cat. "What did you want to do?"

"I want to work with Jake and help you start up your store." Patricia beamed at her. "Since it looks like I'll be in Frog Ledge more often now, I thought I should invest in something close to home. You see, Tony's asked me to marry him."

Chapter 59

One week later

The flash made Nutty squirm. Stan held him tight on her lap. "One more, I promise," said Tyler Hoffman from behind the camera.

Next to him, Cyril Pierce watched with approval. "I think we have plenty to choose from."

Tyler nodded and put the camera away. Nutty jumped off Stan's lap and rubbed against Tyler's legs. Tyler scratched his head absently as he put his gear away. "I'll see you back at the paper," Tyler said to Cyril, then headed out Stan's front door, leaving Stan with Cyril and his open steno pad.

"I think it's great you have Tyler working for you," Stan said. Tyler's family ran the Happy Cow Dairy Farm down the street. When Tyler's father had been killed last year, it had been rough on his oldest son. But the teenager had bounced back and found a home working with Cyril expressing his hidden talent as a photographer.

"I think it's great I can finally have staff," Cyril said with a small smile. "And stories like yours are definitely keeping me on track."

Stan rose and returned her chair to the table. She moved to the coffeepot and busied herself loading Izzy's coffee into the machine. Cyril's enthusiasm was dampened only by the fact that his latest big story involved more tragedy.

A cacophony of barking jarred her out of her thoughts. The front door opened and she heard the sound of nails scrabbling over hardwood, then four dogs bounded into the room. Nutty, who'd been quelling his indignation with a freshly baked treat on the counter, glanced up disdainfully as the canines raced in, sliding and skidding and falling all over each other. Benedict, Stan's orange cat, bolted out of the room and raced for the stairs.

"Hi, guys!" Stan dropped to her knees and hugged as many of the pooches as she could fit. Scruffy, her schnoodle, licked her nose. Duncan, Jake's dog, did his usual jumping routine. Gaston, Pierre's orphaned pooch who had charmed Jake into claiming him before Nikki could drive over to get him, followed suit. Henry, the pit bull, sat politely waiting for Stan.

"Is the photo shoot over?" Jake appeared in the doorway, a cardboard box in hand.

"Hope so. Nutty's done, anyway," Stan said.

Cyril snapped his notebook closed. "I think the interview is done, too. Stan, I'll follow up if I have any questions. Thanks for this exclusive. It's going to be huge for my ratings." He nodded at Jake as he passed him. "Welcome home."

Surprise passed over Jake's face. "Thanks, man." He watched the quirky newsman leave. "Did you tell him I was moving in?"

Stan shook her head. "He's a journalist. He knows everything. Or at least as much as Char tells him." She rose and went to him.

He dropped the box and hugged her tight. "How was the interview? Rough?"

She shrugged, her face still buried in his neck. "He already had all the information that's been coming out. He just wanted my firsthand experience."

Joaquin—Felix Paulson—had planned his revenge for a long time. After a brief period of stalking Pierre, he'd gotten smarter, dropped off the radar, and changed his looks and his name. Then he showed up in their lives as the helpful, starry-eyed apprentice. After his death, the police found Pierre's luggage in Joaquin's apartment, as well as his missing red Moleskine notebook with the nearly indecipherable ingredients to Pierre's legendary new recipe.

Stan found the whole thing incredibly sad.

Sheldon, who'd been devastated the day of the doomed investor dinner, had bounced back quickly after his investors disappeared with their checkbooks, not wanting to fund a scandal. But The Food Channel had called him anyway. Nothing said ratings like a chef involved in murder, mystery, and madness. Stan heard he'd inked a two-year deal for a cool three million bucks. She had no idea if he still planned to back bakeries, but she'd sent him a note that hers was no longer up for grabs. He hadn't responded.

"Hey." Jake pulled back and tilted her chin up. "I know it's hard. But it's all over. Okay?"

He waited until she nodded, then stooped to pick up his box. "I'll put this upstairs, then we have to go meet your mother."

Her mother was heading to Main Street in half an hour so they could powwow on the storefront that would be home to Stan's new pet patisserie. She should feel ecstatic, she knew. She was free from Sheldon. But instead, she felt sixteen again, at her mother's mercy.

"Jake, I'm not sure how I feel about this," Stan said. "I don't think I want my mother having a say over my business."

"That's why I'm the sixty-percent investor, and she's the forty." Jake winked. "Don't worry, babe. I've got your back." He disappeared upstairs.

Stan watched him go, her heart full. Of course he had her back. She shouldn't have doubted it for a second.

Scruffy stood up on Stan's leg and barked at her, an adorable *woo woo* that melted Stan's heart every time. She scooped up the little dog and kissed her head. Nutty flicked his tail disdainfully. The other dogs chimed in barking, wanting their fair share of attention. Upstairs, Jake would be coaxing Benedict out of his hiding place as he moved in. To their house.

Smiling, she headed upstairs to change. It would be important to dress appropriately for her first business meeting with her mother.

RECIPES

Pumpkin Twists

½ cup water
1 tablespoon canola oil
1 egg
½ cup natural canned pumpkin
1½ cups whole wheat flour*
1⅓ cups unbleached flour*
½ cup cornmeal
dash of cinnamon

Note: Gluten-free flour can be used as a substitute.

—Preheat oven to 300 degrees.

—In large bowl, combine water, oil, egg, and pumpkin. Mix well and then add in dry ingredients (flours, cornmeal, cinnamon).

—On a lightly floured surface, roll out dough to ¼-inch thickness. With a knife or pizza cutter, cut out strips 4 inches long and ½ inch wide.

—Twist strips and place on a greased baking sheet.

—Bake for 30 minutes, turn oven off and let cool inside oven for 20 to 30 minutes.

—Cool and store in a sealed container. Treats may also be dehydrated to extend shelf life.

Grain-Free Veggie Tails

    8 oz. frozen peas and carrots
    ½ cup low-sodium chicken stock
    1 cup potato flour
    1 teaspoon vegetable oil

    —Preheat oven to 350 degrees.
    —Defrost frozen vegetables in microwave and then
mince in food processor (or mash with fork).
    —Combine all ingredients in bowl and mix well. Add
small amount of water if mixture is too dry.
    —Put mixture into a pastry bag with a star-shaped
pastry tip. (Use a variety of sizes and shapes of the pastry
tips to suit your preference!)
    —On a greased baking sheet, squeeze mixture out of
pastry bag into 5-inch sections.
    —Bake 20 to 25 minutes.
    —Cool and store in sealed container. Treats may be
dehydrated to extend shelf life.

Apple Cinnamon Drop Cookies

    3 cups wheat flour (or gluten-free flour)
    1 whole apple
    1 egg
    1½ tablespoons vegetable oil
    4 dashes cinnamon
    1 cup water

    —Preheat oven to 350 degrees.
    —Slice apple into small bite-size pieces.
    —Mix all ingredients in stand mixer (or by hand).

—Scoop dough with cookie scoop and place on cookie sheet.

—Bake for 20 to 25 minutes.

Option #2:

Cut into apple-shaped cookies with a cookie cutter and coat with melted peanut butter chips and/or melted yogurt chips.

Treats may be dehydrated (approx. 8 hours) to extend shelf life.

Peanut Butter Crunch Bones

1½ cups whole wheat flour*
1½ cups white flour*
1 cup natural crunchy peanut butter
½ cup vegetable oil
1¼ cups water
1 tablespoon honey

*Note: Gluten-free flour can be used as a substitute.

—Mix all ingredients in stand mixer and knead for 2 minutes. Ensure dough is pliable and not fracturing.

—Roll out dough to ¼-inch thickness and cut into desired bone size.

—Convection bake at 350 for 18 to 20 minutes.

Note from the Author

While The Chanler Mansion and the Cliff Walk are real places in Newport, Rhode Island, I changed certain details for the purpose of the story. All discrepancies are mine.

Acknowledgments

I am beyond thankful for all the people who have helped this series continue, especially my editor, John Scognamiglio, and my agent, John Talbot. Sherry Harris, editor and my fellow Wicked Cozy Author, your talents at making my books better never cease to amaze me.

I wouldn't have as much joy in my work if I wasn't sharing this ride with Sherry and the rest of the Wickeds (and their alter egos), Jessie Crockett/Jessica Estevao, Julie Hennrikus/Julianne Holmes, Edith Maxwell/Maddie Day, and Barbara Ross. You guys are my lifeboat.

With every book, I choose a few special rescue organizations to mention in honor of my rescue dogs and cats. This time, I'm proud to mention these amazing animal angels:

Lisa Starker Shackett and Mary's Kitty Korner, Inc., in Granby, Connecticut, online at maryskittykorner.org.

Joni Nelson, Fred, and the Feral Cat Warriors of Boston's Forgotten Felines, Roslindale, Massachusetts, true warriors for the cats.

Angels Among Us Animal Rescue in Brighton, Tennessee, online at angelsamongusanimalrescue.org.

Vanessa at the Big Biscuit in Franklin, Massachusetts—thanks for your awesome recipes!

As always, thanks to Cynthia and Doug Fleck for being two of my biggest fans.

A thank you that will never be big enough to Kim Fleck, wearing two hats: First as Brand Fearless for her social media prowess and photography skills, and more importantly as herself for her never-ending support, patience, and love. I truly have no idea where I'd be without you. You make it all possible and worthwhile. Love you.

And to the readers—there are no words. Thank you for loving books, and for reading mine.